M000032347

Katy Regnery's

a m o d e r n f a i r y t a l e

Collection

The Vixen and the Vet
(Beauty & the Beast)

Never Let You Go
(Hansel & Gretel)

Ginger's Heart
(Little Red Riding Hood)

Dark Sexy Knight
(Camelot)

Don't Speak
(The Little Mermaid)
Coming 2017

Swan Song
(The Ugly Duckling)
Coming 2017

The *Vixen* and the Vet

a modern fairytale

Katy Regnery

Dear Laurie,
Thank you for sharing your cinematic vision with us!
all B my Katy xo

Cover by Marianne Nowicki

Please visit my website at www.katyregnery.com

First Edition: June 2014
Katy Regnery
The Vixen & the Vet : a novel / by Katy Regnery – 1st ed.
ISBN: 978-0-9912045-4-0

With grateful thanks to all of the men and women who protect
and serve The United States of America, and to Operation Mend,
who serve the returning wounded among them.

And for my father, who insisted that my brother and I
stand up at parades whenever veterans walked by.

CHAPTER 1

"Savannah Calhoun Carmichael, are you even listenin' to me?"

Savannah's sister Scarlet sat in the porch swing on the veranda of their parent's Victorian house giving her older sister an exasperated look. With her lips pursed, they were a perfect match to the bright red geraniums that hung cheerfully over her head. Savannah may have gotten more of the brains, but Scarlet had certainly gotten more of the beauty.

"Yes," Savannah sighed, adjusting her perch on the porch railing and glancing at the thick, glossy bridal magazine that Scarlet anchored in both hands. She dutifully repeated the information that Scarlet had just shared with her. "'The twelve most important milestones in any relationship: one, the first time you sit in comfortable silence; two, the first time you realize you enjoy his company more than anyone else's, three …'"

Scarlet raised her eyebrows in challenge, and Savannah chuckled. "Okay. I admit it. You lost me at three."

"Savannah, you're impossible. This is important information. Doesn't it bother you that your little sister's walking down the aisle before you?"

Savannah, who was an ancient twenty-six to her sister's adorable twenty-two, cocked her head to the side, searching Scarlet's face for meanness, but found only worry. Scarlet had never really understood Savannah's decision to leave Danvers, Virginia, and move to New York City, to become a reporter. The one time Scarlet had visited, she spent the entire weekend ensconced in the relative safety of her hotel room, despite Savannah's efforts to get her out and about.

"Marriage has never really been on my radar, Scarlet. That's your territory."

"Don't you want to be one of those career women who has it all? Exciting job, hot husband waiting in bed for you at night?"

Savannah rolled her eyes. Reporting the news wasn't exactly a nine-to-five gig, not that Scarlet had ever understood that. After graduating from high school, Katie Scarlet Carmichael had upped her hours at Fleurish Flower Shop from part-time to full-time and plastered a can-do smile on her face when Trent Hamilton returned home from the University of West Virginia every weekend. Sure enough, through four years of college temptation, nothing turned Trent's head as much as Scarlet, and by the time he graduated, her patience had paid off; he proposed the very same day. And now here was Scarlet, a year later, thumbing through bridal magazines in preparation for her July wedding. Savannah didn't generally envy her sister— they'd chosen extremely different paths for their lives—but sometimes she envied Scarlet's single-mindedness. All she'd ever wanted was to become Mrs. Trent Hamilton, loving wife, mother, and pillar of the community, and, *voilà!*, that's exactly what she was getting.

Savannah softened her expression. "I guess I wouldn't mind the hot man part."

"Husband," said Scarlet. "*Husband*. Flesh and blood. Not just the characters on your HBO shows. Now, listen up. 'Number three, the first time you look like hell and he couldn't care less.'"

"What man on the face of the earth doesn't care when you look like hell?" Certainly not the couple of guys Savannah had dated in New York. She winced as Patrick's face flitted through her mind. Damn Patrick Monroe anyway. He had sure done a number on her.

"One who's head over heels in love with you. 'Number four' ... oh," murmured Scarlet with a sigh. "'The first time you talk until dawn.' That's a good one."

8

Yeah, thought Savannah. That's a good one unless everything he's telling you until dawn is lies and you don't realize it because you're blinded by lust—she refused to admit to the *other* "l" word—and you believe everything he says because how could he be lying and still worship your body like he's been schooled in the erotic arts?

"'Number five, the first time you bring him home to meet the family.'"

Savannah looked at the fresh white paint of the porch clapboard siding and the cheerful sky-blue paint of the ceiling. The bright red geraniums that her mother had placed at intervals swung lightly in the late afternoon May breeze. At the bottom of the porch steps a brick walkway divided a well-kept patch of grass and ended at an azalea-flanked white picket gate that opened onto the sidewalk of a tree-lined street. It was the quintessential all-American home, and yet she'd never had the guts to bring Patrick home to meet her parents. He'd grown up on the Upper West Side, attending private schools and summering in Nantucket. Danvers, Virginia, wouldn't have been sophisticated enough for his tastes, and she couldn't have borne the amusement in his eyes when he surveyed the home she loved. She'd decided not to risk it.

"'Number six …'" Savannah looked up at her sister and watched her fan herself as her cheeks flushed a pretty pink. "Oh my. 'The first time you're naked together and you don't feel a shred of insecurity.' Well, my stars …"

Savannah grinned. "Please tell me that you and Trent have done the deed in broad daylight."

"That's my private business." Scarlet's flush increased. "H-have you? Done that?"

"Had sex in broad daylight? Of course."

"With that Patrick?"

Scarlet had not been a fan of Patrick's when they'd had dinner together during her disastrous visit to New York. She told Savannah she felt he was politely laughing at her, and honestly, Scarlet was right. Later, when he and Savannah were alone, he'd called her sister's accent "powerful" and added that it was "lucky she's cute so she can get away with it." When he asked why Savannah didn't speak with the same accent, she explained she'd worked hard to lose it during her four years at NYU. By the time she'd taken the job at the *Sentinel*, it was all but gone except for when she drank too much.

"I didn't like him, Vanna. I know you did, so I'm sorry it didn't work out, but I just know there's someone better out there for you. Someone right."

"It's okay. He turned out to be a rat."

Scarlet nodded. "You can say that again."

"It was my own fault for not seeing what you saw over one dinner. What's number seven?"

"Oh!"

Scarlet turned her attention back to the magazine while Savannah leaned forward to pick up her glass of iced tea. The glass was sweaty with cool droplets that dripped into the space between her breasts as she sipped.

"'Number seven, the first time you realize that you don't want anyone else but him.'"

Well, Savannah had certainly reached that point with Patrick, unable to see anyone but him, all other men paling in comparison to his tony pedigree, patrician looks, and far-reaching contacts. Too bad Patrick had never subscribed to the same devotion. Finding out he'd been dating someone else while they were sleeping together had just been salt in the wound after she discovered that he'd single-handedly destroyed her professional credibility, reputation, and career.

"Next," demanded Savannah.

"I love this one. 'The first time you see a future with him.'" Scarlet sighed. "First grade. Playground. Trent pushed me on the swings even though the other little boys were makin' fun of him."

Savannah loved her sister, but she couldn't imagine plotting out her future with someone who'd pushed her on the swings in first grade. She'd never understood how Scarlet could be so content to be born, grow up, get married, and die in one small town when there was a whole wide world out there just waiting.

"How about number nine?"

Scarlet's dreamy expression turned to a grin. "'The first time you take a trip together.'"

"That's a mixed bag."

"How do you mean?"

"Hard to look perfect when you first wake up in the morning. Not to mention, travel breeds stress."

"I though you loved travel!" exclaimed Scarlet. "My globe-trotting sister."

"Oh, I do. Alone. To chase a story. Why in the world would I want to go away with someone else?"

"Because you love them? Because Hawaii is more fun with …" Scarlet's cheeks pinked delicately, and she averted her eyes.

"I don't remember you and Trent ever goin' to Hawaii," teased Savannah.

"Honeymoon," said Scarlet in a dramatic whisper.

"Aha. So you've decided. Well, I've heard it's *very* romantic."

Scarlet's delicate blush spread to her neck as she turned redder.

Savannah laughed at her prim little sister. "Scarlet, you'd think you'd never kissed a boy, for heaven's sake. What's next?"

"'Number ten, the first big blowup fight,'" Scarlet sniffed. "Well, I just hope I never have to experience *that*." She rapped her fingers lightly on the arm of the swing, her pink lacquered nails catching the warm light of the low sun.

"Do you mean to tell me that you and Trent have never had a big fight?"

"Vanna, honey, why in the world would I want to have a spat with the man I love? The odd quarrel's one thing, but more than anything, I want to make him feel loved and comfortable and happy. Besides, he's so smart and so good to me, he's almost always right."

"And when he's not?"

"You get more bees with honey."

Savannah laughed lightly. "So you use your wiles to get your way?"

"It beats fighting."

"I'm guessing you've never had makeup sex, though, Scarlet. You're missing out."

Scarlet shrugged, expertly avoiding the implied question. "Nothing's worth bein' at odds with Trent. Nothin'."

"Fine. Have it your way. What's next?"

"'Number eleven, the first time you realize he's your home.'" Scarlet sighed. "Doesn't that sound lovely?"

For all of Savannah's world-weary cynicism, she had to admit that it *did* sound lovely. As she'd fallen in love with Patrick, she started to realize how wonderful it would be to give her heart to someone, how amazing it would be to know he had her back and was on her side, how, yes, *lovely* it would be to know that her life was safe with his: entwined, inextricably bound together.

She forced herself to remember the cruel glee in his eyes when he confessed that, yes, he had fed her bucketfuls of misinformation in an effort to subvert the true story behind the embezzlement of his father's financial firm. And Savannah—stupid Savannah, who thought she was falling in love with him—had been nothing more than a cheap mark, a cheap lay, and in the end, totally expendable.

"Sorry, kid," he'd said, with what must have passed for regret in his world. "You were fun, though. And the story was a miracle. You made a great case for my father's partners shouldering the blame."

"When it was your father all along? He cheated all those people?"

"What matters is the court of public opinion. And you've done a great job for our … cause."

"But he deceived all those people …" Her voice trailed off as she realized the further ramifications of her story. "And the *Sentinel* printed it. And it was all garbage. It was libel. Oh my

God ... my career."

"You're tough. Hell, you made it to New York City from some backwater town in Virginia, kid. You'll land on your feet."

But she hadn't landed on her feet. Once the hate mail started pouring in, she was fired. A retraction was printed, but Patrick's father's partners sued for libel, assessing over three million dollars' worth of damage.

With nowhere else to go, Savannah broke her lease, packed up her belongings, and headed home in shame under the guise of taking the summer off from work to help with her sister's wedding. Her parents and sister knew the truth, of course, but the rest of Danvers was a sleepy little town, and the reaction from most of the townsfolk had been: "How lovely that you're back, dear. And just in time for Scarlet's big do!"

"Katie Scarlet, I'm about to go diabetic from so much sweetness. Finish up and put me out of my misery. What's number twelve?"

"'Number twelve, the first time you realize that he loves you as much as you love him.'"

"What happens after twelve?" asked Savannah, half kidding.

"After twelve, you're ready for forever," said Scarlet, not kidding one bit.

Savannah smirked humorlessly as her little sister closed the mammoth magazine with a flourish.

"And now I am going to go get ready for tonight's dinner-dance at the club. Sure you won't come, Vanna? Trent could get you a date."

"With one of his frat brothers? Five years younger than me? Or, worse, with his brother, Lance? No thanks, Scarlet. But you have fun."

As her sister headed inside, Savannah let the words roll around in her head: *loves you as much as you love him*. Her heart clenched with a weakness, a longing, that she tried to ignore. She'd given love a chance, and she'd been blindsided, duped, and destroyed. Lost her home and her job and everything else that she'd worked for. She looked up as two blond-haired kids rode by on bicycles decorated for the Memorial Day parade tomorrow and tried to find the silver lining. But she couldn't. She'd worked her whole life to get out of Danvers, Virginia. And yet, here she was, right back where she started.

She was surprised to feel her cell phone vibrating in her back pocket. Once upon a time her phone had been the epicenter of her world, as she fielded calls and texts, chased down stories, and followed leads as the up-and-coming star reporter for the *New York Sentinel*. But, over the past two or three weeks, it hadn't buzzed more than a couple of times. She pulled it out of her pocket and looked at the unfamiliar area code: 602. She thought for a moment. Hmm. Phoenix. Who did she know in Phoenix?

"Savannah Carmichael, *New York Sen*— Um, this is Savannah."

"Hey, Savannah. It's Derby Jones."

Savannah drew a blank. "Mm-hm. What can I do for you, Derby?"

"For starters, you can remember me," said the woman in a cheerful, knowing voice. "We met at the West Coast Journalism Conference out in LA last fall. I was doing a story about—"

"Health care for seniors!"

"Yep! I knew you'd remember me once you remembered the story."

"I'm like that weird lady at the dog park who knows people by their dog's names. Spot's mom. Rex's dad. Senior health-care story."

Derby laughed. "I don't know if you remember, but I was stuck on that story. I couldn't figure out the angle, but you stayed up until well after midnight with me, looking over my notes, talking to me about what I wanted to say. When the sun came up, I had an angle."

"That's right." Savannah smiled. "I was glad to help. How was the article?"

"Actually, it was so good, I won a Sunshine Award from

the SPJ."

"Valley of the Sun?"

"Yep. It also won me a raise and a promotion."

"That's great, Derby. Your star's rising, I guess." She tried her best to sound enthusiastic, even though it stung a little bit.

"And yours is falling."

Ouch. "Umm ..." started Savannah, at a loss for words.

"Jeez, there I go. I'm not known for my tact."

"You don't say."

"Listen, let me get right down to it. I've been keeping tabs on you since that conference, reading your articles, following your stories. You wrote that groundbreaking piece on the New York subway system. And you deserved the award you won for the article on the preferential treatment some lawyers are given in the DA's office. Not to mention the time you rode in the back of an NYPD police car for a week and did that terrific piece about the habits of New York's Finest. You're talented, Savannah. More talented than most. I can't figure out what happened with the Monroes, but it sounds like you were taken for a ride."

Savannah swallowed the lump in her throat. "It was my fault. I should've seen—"

"We all get a bad source now and then. That was a doozy."

Savannah grimaced, wondering if Derby would ever get to the point of the call and stop making her feel about two inches tall. She started every day with a heavy heart, grieving the loss of her dream; she didn't exactly need someone to drive it home for her.

"Anyway," continued Derby, "I already knew it that weekend, but you're a heck of a reporter. Top-notch. I'm betting you'll never make the same mistake again with a source, and any paper would be lucky to have talent like yours."

"Well, that's, er, nice of you to—"

"So here's the scoop: the *Phoenix Times* is looking for someone to take over the Lifestyles section. I know it's not New York, and I know it's not the *Sentinel*. But for someone with ambition, someone looking to get back on her feet …" Derby let that thought linger, and Savannah battled her conflicting emotions.

Lifestyles?! She'd been an investigative reporter for arguably the most well-regarded newspaper in America. Lifestyles would mean reporting on cook-offs and fashion shows, charity benefits, and star sightings. Not to mention, the *Phoenix Times* was second-string at best. And it was in … Phoenix. Hot, dry, middle-of-nowhere Phoenix.

Then again, it was Phoenix. The sixth-largest city in the United States and a hub of Southwestern activity. Far enough from New York that her calamitous failure at the *Sentinel* would feel removed, yet close enough to LA and San Francisco that maybe she could segue to one of those bigger outfits after a few successful years. And no, Lifestyles wasn't exactly her dream department, but it was a way back in, wasn't it? After a few months—a year, tops—she could ask for a transfer to one of their other departments.

"Derby," she said, determination lowering her voice to a serious pitch. "What do I have to do to make it happen?"

"Our editor in chief knows who you are. He's willing to give you a swing at the job, but you have to wow him with a Lifestyles piece first."

"Oh, I have a ton of stuff I could send—"

"No, Savannah. You don't. I tried to find something, anything, that you wrote that could pass as a human interest piece. I came up dry."

Savannah nodded, gloom encroaching. Derby was right. She didn't have anything.

"But Maddox McNabb, our editor, he's all about hot scoops and he loves that you're coming from a New York background. He can be a little heavy on the edits, but I haven't had any complaints so far. He makes a good story more sensational, and at least a quarter get picked up on the national news wire."

"Wow. Great numbers. Sounds like he's got the magic

touch."

"Like I said, no complaints. Anyway, he needs a piece. Something big and heart-tugging and personal in time for the Fourth of July. That's, uh, five weeks from now. Think veterans. Think returning soldier dad home in time for the big Fourth of July barbecue. Small-town Americana stuff that makes every reader cry before breaking out in a chorus of 'America the Beautiful.' How you write it is up to you, but Maddox wants updates every Friday from now until the second. If he likes it, he'll run it on the front of Lifestyles on the Fourth, and let's just say he'd probably like to see you in Phoenix soon after."

Savannah's brain whirled, but she could feel the excitement gathering inside her. No, human interest wasn't her forte, but she could change that. She'd write the best goddamn piece of lifestyle Americana the *Phoenix Times* had ever seen.

"I'm all over it. Tell Maddox he'll have the idea and the first installment by next Friday. Six days."

"I knew you'd bite," said Derby, her voice laced with approval. "I'll e-mail you with Maddox's info. The rest is all you."

Savannah shook her head, smiling into the phone, marveling at second chances that came from unexpected places, and determined not to squander this chance. "Derby, I don't know how to thank you. Really. I don't even know what to say."

"Hey, I'm not Mother Teresa. You come work here? I figure you owe me a few more of those late-night sessions cracking stories. I sure wouldn't mind another Sunshine Award."

"You got it," Savannah said with feeling. "Anything I can ever do for you, all you have to do is shout."

"I hope you don't regret that offer," said Derby, "because I promise I'll be collecting."

Savannah chuckled and exchanged information with her guardian angel, thanking her again for reaching out and sending her thanks to Maddox for the chance. When she hung up the phone, the sun was even lower, aggressively gold on the horizon, brightening the hills beyond her small neighborhood.

She squinted, her eyes pulled to the grand, old Victorian house straight ahead, about two miles away, up on the hillside.

Asher Lee's house.

The front door of her own house opened, and Scarlet appeared dressed in an adorable cotton candy–pink sundress, modestly covered with a mint-green cardigan.

"Hey, Scarlet," Savannah said, still staring at the massive brown house in the distance. "What do we know about Asher Lee?"

"Asher Lee?" Scarlet fanned herself as she followed her sister's gaze into the distant hills like her sister. "Some folks call him "Hermit" Lee. Poor thing. Used to be a big-time football star over at Danvers High. But he got his face and hand blown off in some war, and no one's seen him for a million years. He got real strange when he came home, refusin' to go into town, hirin' Miss Potts to be his maid. No one's seen him in almost a decade. Nobody knows what he does up there, but there's the normal fiddle-faddle about the bogeyman and such. Really, it's easier just to forget he's up there. It's just so awkward and sad."

"Have you ever seen him?"

Scarlet shook her head pursing her lips and looking away from the old brown mansion. "Why are you so interested?"

Savannah turned to her sister, cocking her head to the side. "I think it's about time someone showed a little Southern hospitality to our very own wounded veteran."

"What're you up to, Vanna?"

"Nothing bad, little sister, don't trouble yourself. I just wonder if he'd like to tell his side of the story."

"Leave him be. All he wants is his privacy."

"Not if he's got a story to tell, Miss Scarlet. Not if he has a story he'd like the world to know."

CHAPTER 2

Asher Lee did not anticipate or appreciate visitors. While Danvers had not been especially welcoming upon his return home, at least the locals had seen fit to respect his privacy.

Which is why, when his ancient doorbell rang on Sunday afternoon, he started, jumping a foot in the comfortable reading chair that sat by the window on the west side of his vast office. Once upon a time the room had been called the library, and it still maintained an impressive collection of books that rivaled that of the Danvers Public Library. And in the years since Asher had returned home, he'd added to the collection, occasionally hiring out-of-state woodworkers to expand the cherry bookcases to house more and more books. Books were his refuge, his only real pleasure.

At present, he was deep into the romances of Jennifer Crusie, an author who wrote with excellent pacing and laugh-out-loud wit. He'd already read six of her books and had three more to read before he'd move on to a different author. But not romance this time—there was only so much romance he could read before his heart bled from living vicariously, knowing that life loomed long and his own chances at happily-ever-after were nonexistent. Sometimes he argued with himself—why torture yourself reading about what you can't ever, ever have?—but a few weeks would go by, and after the thrill of mysteries, the voyeurism of biographies, and the swashbuckling satisfaction of adventure, he'd find himself gravitating toward romance. Again.

He reasoned that he had no one to impress. Aside from Miss Potts, who did his cooking, cleaning, laundering, and shopping, and the occasional craftsman who worked on his monstrosity of a mansion, he saw no one. Despite the injuries he'd sustained, at thirty-four years old he was physically fit enough to live until a hundred. In short, he had a long, lonely road ahead. He could read what he wanted.

When the bell rang a second time, he stood up from his chair, his muscular body moving with surprising grace, made his way around the attractive cherry desk that served no real purpose—he wrote no letters, and his bill payments were automated on the laptop that sat lonely in its center—and headed to the library door. He cracked it just enough to hear Miss Potts's light step on the front hall marble, then hurried out into the upper gallery, moving as quietly as he could to a spot that had been rigged with decorative mirrors at clever angles to show who was at the door. There he stood, eyes on the mirror across from him, as Miss Potts opened the door.

He forgave his quick gasp.

It had been years since he'd been this close to a woman. To a young woman. To a young, very beautiful, woman. His heart kicked up as his eyes widened, and he twisted his head as close as possible to the stairs so that he could pick up the sound of her voice.

"Miss Potts!" she said, and he watched her embrace the older woman.

"Why, Savannah Carmichael! I'd know you anywhere!"

Savannah Carmichael. Savannah Carmichael. Her last name was vaguely familiar, but he definitely didn't know a Savannah Carmichael. He would have remembered her name. It was like music, like the heroine from one of the more melodramatic historical romances he sometimes read.

Her brown hair was straight and shiny, pulled back into a ponytail at the nape of her neck, and her brown eyes were serious and determined. Her lips were full and pink, and though he couldn't see the rest of her body, the V-neck of her sundress was tight across her chest, making his heart speed up again. He stared at the sacred valley of white, lightly freckled skin that led south to the swell of her breasts and started a whole different swelling on a southern part of him. Sucking in a breath, he looked away. There was no chance in hell he'd ever have the opportunity to visit that particular corner of heaven ever again. Didn't make any sense to torture himself by looking at something he couldn't have.

"Miss Potts, I knew you were here working for Ash—Mr. Lee. It's so great to see you!"

Asher was surprised by her smooth, refined voice. Miss Potts obviously knew her, but most folks in Danvers had thick accents, and hers was light at best. Had she moved away at some point and just recently returned home?

"And you, dear. I heard through the grapevine that you're home for the summer? Helping with your sister's wedding?"

"Yes. Scarlet's getting married. Can you believe it?"

"In fact, I can. Scarlet was making cow eyes at Trent Hamilton in the second grade, dear. Had to separate those two from day one. Some folks are just meant to be together. From the cradle."

Hmm, thought Asher. She had a sister, and both had been Miss Potts's students, so despite her lack of accent, she *was* a lifetime resident of Danvers.

Miss Potts still hadn't invited her in, per Asher's wishes. No one was ever to be let into the main house. Never, ever. Under no circumstances.

"It is so lovely to see you, dear, but Mr. Lee does keep me busy. Is there something I can do for you?"

She cleared her throat, and he took a quick look in the glass again.

"I don't know if you know," she began, "but I went into journalism after college. I'm taking a break from my job at the *New York Sentinel*, but I've been commissioned to write a piece for a very notable national newspaper, the *Phoenix Times*. They want a human interest piece in time for the Fourth of July, and I thought … well, I wondered if Mr. Lee, that is …"

He stared at her pretty face, watched her cheeks flush with color. Interesting. She was determined to get the interview, but uncomfortable about asking.

"Oh, my dear. I'm sorry but it's out of the question. You see, Mr. Lee doesn't talk to anyone. No one. And certainly not a reporter."

She squared her shoulders. "But he must have a story to tell. And I want to hear it. And I want to tell it. With him. *For* him."

"I'm afraid it's quite impossible, dear."

For the first time he noticed the foil-covered plate in Savannah Carmichael's hands, which she offered to Miss Potts. "I made brownies. It's Scarlet's recipe, and they're very good. I've taped my card on top. Won't you give these to him and just ask if he might consider calling me?"

Brownies. His mouth watered. He couldn't remember the last time he'd had homemade brownies. Interesting tactic for an interview. Smarter than coming with guns loaded about his service record. He would have resented her presumption that she knew him when she didn't know the first goddamned thing about him or his life.

"It won't do any good, I'm afraid."

"Do you refuse?"

Miss Potts lifted her chin a notch, and even though he could see only her back, he knew the look Savannah was presently enjoying. The no-nonsense look of a grade school teacher who'd had just enough of Savannah's shenanigans.

"I don't refuse. I will give him the brownies. But the answer will still be no. In fact, the answer will be silence. I don't want any misunderstanding between us, dear."

"There isn't any," said Savannah, and Asher clenched his jaw at the brave disappointment in her tone. "I don't expect anything. But promise you'll give them?"

"I promise." She took the brownies, and Savannah nodded once with a sheepish smile, deepening the worry on her pretty face.

"Thank you."

"Of course. You run along now. Wish your sister all the best from Miss Potts, dear."

He watched as Savannah lifted her eyes to the mirror on the landing of the double staircase. He was unable to glance away as her eyes reflected into five mirrors in a flash, and finally slammed into his. Her eyes widened, and he heard her gasp before he jerked himself back, out of view. He rested his head against the dark wood paneling of the gallery, berating himself for being such a fool. She'd seen him. Minimally she'd seen his eyes. Damn it. She knew he was home. She knew he'd been eavesdropping. Damn it again.

Without waiting to hear the rest of the good-bye pleasantries between the two women, he stalked back to his office, flinging the door open with such strength that the door smashed into the wall, echoing in the quiet of the gallery, before slamming shut with a bang.

He moved quickly to the front window, where he could look out at the circular driveway without being seen. He watched as Savannah Carmichael stopped on the edge of grass in the center of the circle and, turning around, gazed up at the house.

She was trim and lovely, in her mid-20s, with intelligent, searching eyes and a thoughtful countenance. She cocked her head to the side and narrowed those determined, chestnut-colored eyes, as if assessing whether or not what she'd seen was real or a figment of her imagination. Finally she looked right at the window where Asher stood, and even though he knew she couldn't see him through the glare of glass and the darkness of the room, he held his breath until she turned on her heel and headed back down the driveway to her waiting car.

***

The mansion had been an almost-otherworldly mix of creepy and elegant, from what little Savannah had seen from the doorway where Miss Potts stood guard. The elegant marble flooring was a striking contrast to the worn, once-garnet-colored carpet that lined the stairs, and the dark woodwork was so shiny and ornate in the front hallway she could almost close her eyes and imagine she'd walked into the 1890s, visiting the grandest house in town. It smelled clean and old, a mix of lemon oil and leather-bound books, and as Savannah wound down the hillside roads back toward town, she found herself even more intrigued by the reclusive veteran who lived a hermitlike existence at the edge of an all-American town from which the smell of barbecues and bonfires wafted up.

But the oddest thing of all were the eyes she thought she'd seen in the mirror at the top of the staircase right before she turned to go. Was that a trick of the light, or had she actually seen Asher Lee's brown eyes staring back at her for an instant? She didn't know for sure. She'd gasped and blinked, and they were gone. If they *were* his eyes, they'd arrested her completely for the short moment they'd smashed into each other, and a strange, unexpected warmth had flooded her veins as she searched the mirror for one more glimpse. There had been none.

Trick of the light, she told herself, wondering if Miss Potts was currently throwing her brownies in the dustbin.

Who was Asher Lee? As she stopped at the first of several stoplights on Main Street, she berated herself. Since when did Savannah Carmichael approach a source with brownies instead of good, old-fashioned research? Why, she hadn't even bothered to stop by the library to look into the Lee family history, and Asher Lee's in particular. He'd always existed beneath her radar—considerably older than she and immensely tragic, it was easier to file him away as a small-town oddity—but that was no excuse for taking brownies instead of asking for the interview with an angle built from professional expertise and research. She detoured sharply at the third light, turning onto Maple

Street, where she parked in front of the small brick public library. She was going to find out a few things about Asher Lee, and then return with a solid, professional angle to finagle that interview. And this time, she wouldn't take no for an answer, come hell, high water, or Matilda J. Potts.

***

Asher had just about had it with Miss Potts's good intentions. He knew how much she wanted him to be a part of the world again, but she didn't seem to understand how much her pushing infuriated him, only serving to increase his frustration that the reward for serving his country was to live out his life in a lonely prison of his own making.

Pounding out his anger on the treadmill hadn't helped, nor had doing bicep curls on his good arm until it burned. He stared at the business card in his hand for the umpteenth time, mulling over the scorching argument he'd had earlier with his maid/housekeeper/surrogate grandmother/meddler extraordinaire.

After saying nothing about Savannah Carmichael's visit, she had cleared his dinner plate and sat down across from him at the massive mahogany table that his grandfather had imported from England in 1925. From her lap she produced the foil-covered plate with the business card neatly taped to the top, set the plate on the table in front of her—just out of his reach—and met his eyes.

"I know you were watching. She caught your eyes in the mirror."

He glowered at her, and she sat back, her lips tilted up subtly.

"She's always been an ambitious thing, Savannah Carmichael. But she's good people. Her folks take the collection at Stone Hill Methodist every Sunday, and her sister's a terrible flirt with a heart of gold. They keep their lawn neat, pull their garbage cans off the curb before nightfall, and I've never heard of Frank Carmichael needing a ride home from Ernie's. The Carmichael's are solid folks. But Savannah … that girl was special."

Miss Potts carefully started loosening the edges of the plate as she rhapsodized about the perfectly perfect Carmichaels.

"Like you, she didn't feel like Danvers was enough. She wanted to see more of the world. Six years after you went into the service, she went to New York University. You ended up getting your hand blown off; she ended up getting fired from the most prestigious newspaper in the country. You both came home to lick your wounds."

Asher winced when Miss Potts, with her usual no-holds-barred directness, compared their lives so nakedly. He clenched his jaw, his eyes flicking to the plate before looking back up at her. For the past eight years, since he returned home after sustaining "calamitous" injuries, Miss Potts had been his most important friend, the only person he trusted.

"Except her life was just starting when mine ended," he said in a level voice, peppered with a good bit of anger. He'd been injured in the service of his country, but he hadn't exactly been welcomed home, and for the first five years after his return, he'd wallowed in it, drinking too much, raging at all hours of the day and night. Miss Potts had stayed quietly by his side, as loyal and kind during the dark years as she'd been when the Lee family library started to, literally, save his life.

"Only because that's how you want it."

He leaned forward, resting his elbows on the table and thrusting his left index finger up toward his face. "I *wanted* this?"

She remained expressionless. "No. I didn't say you wanted your injuries. But *you've* decided to live your life like a hermit. That was *your* choice."

He didn't need to get up and look in the ornate, gilt-edged mirror over the massive fireplace to know that *calamitous* was the accurate word for his face. His right eye drooped, and the right half of his face was a gnarled mess of scar tissue. He was missing a small chunk of his nose on the right side, and he wore his hair shaggy to conceal the scar where his right ear used to be.

But no amount of hairstyling could conceal the fact that his right arm was missing below the elbow. And his right leg, also injured in the blast, would always cause him to walk with a slight limp. Once a handsome young man, he was now a monster. A beast.

"You don't remember what happened when I first got back."

"Maybe not," she said, lifting the foil and leaning down to press her nose close to the dark chocolate frosted treats. "Mmm."

"You didn't see the faces of my fellow townsfolk," he spat out. "My friends. People I'd known all my life. Who'd known my parents and grandparents. Who'd looked out for me after my parents' accident. They couldn't *look* at me. They gasped and cringed and looked away."

All chances of rejoining society had crumbled after those first few spirit-killing weeks, and Asher had decided to turn his back on the people who had turned their backs on him.

"Mm-hm. That's what I heard." She lifted a brownie and bit into it, sighing with appreciation. "Oh myyyy ..."

"They didn't come 'round to see the old football star. They were more comfortable pretending I was dead up here in my quiet prison, so I gave them their wish. I pretended I was dead too. And that's all I ever wanted: to be left alone."

Miss Potts took another bite, then looked up at Asher. "What, dear? Did you say something?"

He pounded his hand on the table so hard the plate in front of her jumped, then clattered back down. "Don't mock me!"

Without lifting so much as an eyebrow, Miss Potts said, "Oh, I'm not. I'm enjoying one of Savannah Carmichael's excellent brownies."

He pointed his finger at her. "You're trying to provoke me."

"I wouldn't dream of it," she said, taking another bite.

"You want me to call her? Let her come on up here to see the freak? Under the guise of an interview? Maybe I should tell her to bring her camera too."

"If you like."

Asher's nostrils flared, and he curled his good hand into a fist.

"But best let's brush out that mane of hair first? Make you presentable, hm?"

"I'm not doing it," he said. "I barely look human. I'm not fit to rejoin the human race." *Not that they'd have me anyway.*

Miss Potts had had enough. She calmly put the last bite of brownie back on the plate and cut her sky-blue eyes to Asher's furious brown.

"Asher Sherman Lee! You're more human than the lot of them. And so is Savannah. She's in a bind, and you'd be saving her hide. When's the last time you got a chance to play the hero?"

He clenched his jaw at her indelicacy, but she surprised him by sliding the plate across the table to him with one good push.

"You want your life to look different, Asher? Then change it."

He scowled at her. "Oh, it's that simple, huh?"

"Just don't wait too long. She's a survivor, that one. If you won't help her? My money's on her finding someone else who will."

She stood up, dabbed at the corners of her mouth with the pad of her thumb, and left the room.

Asher seethed for the better part of an hour, the chocolaty goodness of Miss Failed Reporter's brownies nearly as distracting as the memory of her beautiful brown eyes. They'd widened in surprise as they caught his, and he couldn't help but wonder how they'd look widening in pleasure, in—

No. No, you do not get to think about women in that way. You will not torment yourself with the impossible.

Without agreeing to do her interview, he felt like a cad eating one of her brownies, but he was weak for home-baked brownies like his mother used to make, and one turned into two, turned into three. Still feeling miserable, he'd ended up on the treadmill for an hour after that. Though his limp inhibited his speed and pace, the exercise usually helped release some of the tension from the helplessness and anger.

It didn't help tonight. Tonight he wanted to break into a sprint, and it killed him that he couldn't. He wished he had a chance with a girl like Savannah Carmichael. He longed for friends and family around him, but he had neither. With every fiber of his broken being, he wanted to be whole again, but he wasn't. And he never would be. Ever again.

He lived in a house on a hill, almost totally devoid of human contact, not because that's what he *wanted*, but because that's how his life had turned out. Right? Right. And no amount of prodding from Miss Potts was going to change that.

His leg ached when he got off the treadmill and limped to his desk. He sat in the stiff chair, beads of sweat trailing down his face, his tangled hair soaked from the workout. He stared at his phone, then back at Savannah's card, his phone, her card.

Of everything Miss Potts had said tonight, what needled him most was this: *You want your life to look different, Asher? Then change it.* Did he wish his life looked different? Hell, yes. But he wasn't sure how giving an interview to Savannah Carmichael was going to change things. A woman as beautiful as Savannah would never see him as anything but a story. Still, he could help her, right? He hadn't been useful to anyone in a long, long time, yet he could help her by giving her a story, just as Miss Potts had suggested. And maybe in return she could remind him what it felt like to be among decent people again.

"Damn it." He picked up the phone and dialed the number on the card. "I hope you're happy," he muttered toward the ceiling, where Miss Potts was likely watching reruns of her favorite program, *Bewitched*, as she folded laundry and ironed.

"Hello? This is Savannah Car—"

"It's Asher Lee." He grimaced at the abrupt way he'd interrupted her, but holy hell, it'd been over a decade since he'd called a girl.

"Mr. Lee!" The warmth in her voice made his heart speed up, made him squirm, made him want to go back to church. "What a surprise!"

"You make a good brownie." Cradling the phone between his cheek and his shoulder, he slapped his forehead with his hand. *You make a good brownie? Real smooth, Asher!*

"Well, now. That's so nice. It's my sister's recipe. I'll be sure to let her know."

An awkward silence settled between them, and he realized she was waiting for him to explain the reason for his call. He cleared his throat and swallowed.

"You wanted an interview?"

"Yes! Yes, I've been commissioned to do a human interest story in time for the Fourth of July. I thought, well, a hometown hero couldn't be a better—"

She stopped speaking when he snorted, and he winced again. But "hometown hero?" That conjured images of flags and parades, not bitter, disfigured recluses.

"I have some conditions."

"Go ahead," she said, her voice professional and level. He wondered if it hid nerves.

"No photos."

"Done."

"We meet at my house."

"Done."

He took a deep breath. He didn't know what she'd say to his last condition, but if meeting with Savannah Carmichael was the first step in rejoining the human race, he'd need to see her more than once.

"We'll split the interview into multiple sessions."

"Um, of course," she said.

"Mondays, Wednesdays, and Fridays. Four o'clock. For the next four weeks."

She hesitated, and he wondered if she was considering backing out of so many afternoons with "Hermit" Lee, the mythic beast of Danvers.

"Will there be enough to talk about to fill that amount of time?" she asked. "By my calculations, that's about twelve hours."

He panicked, snapping, "Do you want the whole story of how I became the town freak, or not?"

"Mr. Lee, I—I've insulted you. It wasn't my ... I mean, I'm so sorry that—"

"You didn't insult me. Do we have a deal?"

"Yes," she said, low and certain.

His eyes fluttered closed as his shoulders relaxed, and his heart, already racing, pounded against his ribs with increased fervor. *Tomorrow.*

"Good," he said.

"Good."

"Miss Carmichael?"

"Yes, Mr. Lee?"

"I'm, um ... I've been alone for years. I'm unpolished."

"Well, then," she said, and he pictured those pretty pink lips lifting when he heard the humor in her warm voice, "you'll be in good company."

His lips twitched in an unfamiliar motion, and he realized that his mouth was attempting to smile. It had been weeks, if not months, since he had smiled from human contact, and it was so bewildering to him that the smile quickly disappeared.

"See you tomorrow," he said.

"Four o'clock," she said, before the line went dead.

Asher put the phone back into its cradle on his desk and stared at it, dumbstruck, for a full minute before slumping back in his desk chair.

Holy hell.

CHAPTER 3

The first time you sit in comfortable silence

Savannah looked at the note cards spread out on the porch coffee table, swapping two, then glanced at her watch again. Twenty past three. She didn't want to be late, and she still needed to change into something less edgy than her usual black. Yesterday she'd borrowed Scarlet's too-tight V-neck sundress to complete the country-girl-with-brownies picture, and she guessed it would be smart to do the same today. Anything for the story, right? This piece was her chance, and she wasn't going to blow it. If Asher Lee liked country girls and brownies, then a fresh-faced country girl is what she'd deliver.

She turned her attention back to the cards spread out before her. Her sojourn to the library yesterday hadn't been in vain. She'd learned an impressive amount about her subject, as attested by the note cards, which created a solid time line of Asher Lee's life.

The only son of impressively wealthy Pamela and Tucker Lee, Asher Lee had been poised for greatness from birth. He attended local schools, where he aced his studies, participated in several clubs and was the star quarterback in his junior and senior years. His parents had been killed in a chartered plane crash during his junior year of high school, and Miss Matilda J. Potts, a dear friend of his late grandmother, was named as his guardian. Even with the heavy burden of grief, his grades did not falter, and he was accepted at the University of Virginia, where he enrolled in pre-med studies. But this is where it got cloudy.

Savannah noted his acceptance at the Johns Hopkins School of Medicine, but he either rejected the admission or deferred it to serve as an enlisted Army medic. Why? Why hadn't he completed med school first? Did he want frontline medical experience? Did he have a deep yearning to serve his country? Did he have a death wish? Savannah placed a gold star on that note card, indicating an area of his life that required more explanation.

The next time Asher Lee surfaced in the media was in *The Danvers Gazette*: a notice of grievous injuries sustained in Afghanistan, almost four years after enlistment. One month shy of his twenty-fifth birthday, a land-mine style IED exploded near him as he tried to drag a fellow soldier to safety. According to the report, it severely injured the right side of his face, severed his right hand, and led to injuries in his right leg. He underwent extensive surgery in Kandahar and again in San Antonio before returning home to Danvers almost a year later.

There was a notice of his homecoming in the local paper, but then ... nothing. Not a peep. Not a word. Not a mention. For eight years. Nothing. He disappeared entirely from public view.

Why? What happened once he got home? Why hadn't he been able to acclimate to civilian life? Savannah didn't remember ever hearing much about the Lee family growing up, though she was sure her parents were at least familiar with them. And she was leaving for college right around the time that Asher Lee returned home. But she couldn't help but wonder how the captain of the football team, a U.Va. graduate, a veritable golden boy, had become a hermit? And what in the world had he been doing with himself for all these years?

She checked her watch again. Three-forty. She pushed the cards into a neat pile, put a rubber band around them, then slipped into the house.

"Scarlet?" her mother called.

"It's Savannah, Mama."

Her mother, Judy, stepped out of the kitchen, her thick middle wrapped in a floral apron and a smudge of flour on the tip of her nose. "I'm baking muffins. Want a plateful? You can't go empty-handed to visit that poor man."

Judy Carmichael's heart was solid gold, and she refused to see meanness or badness in anyone. When Savannah informed her mother she'd be interviewing Asher Lee over the next few weeks, her mother had smiled and patted Savannah's hand like she was an angel from heaven on a mission of mercy.

"Banana nut, Mama?"

"My specialty!"

In truth, every baked good known to man was her mother's "specialty," as evidenced by the framed blue ribbons covering half her kitchen wall—one for just about every year she entered baked goods in the State Fair.

"I'll take three?"

"Take four," said her mother, bustling into the kitchen. "You're skin and bones."

Savannah grinned, because that was not true, then took the stairs two at time, ready to pilfer something sweet and pastel from Scarlet's closet before her four o'clock meeting.

***

Asher paced his study, stopping again to glance at his reflection in the full-length bathroom mirror. He started from the ground up.

Black driving moccasins looked comfortable but rich. His eye traveled up his Levi's-clad legs and he had to admit, so far so good. His legs were long, the scarring hidden behind the light denim, and his waist was still as trim as it was during his football days. A pressed, light-blue oxford shirt was tucked into the jeans, which was belted with supple black leather. His uncomfortable, seldom-used prosthetic hand dangled from the right sleeve. It was an old, outdated model that was covered with a flesh-colored latex and had no real mobility. He knew that newer models acted like bionic skeletons, but Asher had gotten so used to one hand, he hadn't bothered with the trip to Walter

Reed to have a new hand fitted. Maybe someday. For now, as long as he kept his "hand" in his lap, the disfigurement was less obvious.

He held his gaze on the body that looked surprisingly normal, forcing himself not to look above the neck. Finally he nodded once, ready to face the inevitable. Maybe it wouldn't be so bad. Maybe time had worked its magic, and he wouldn't look handsome, but he wouldn't look so, so … He raised his eyes and gasped, then winced.

Time had not been kind to him, but it didn't matter. The doorbell rang. Savannah Carmichael was here, and it was too late to turn back now.

***

This time, Miss Potts didn't make Savannah stand in the doorway like a vacuum cleaner salesman. She swept open the door, smiling in welcome.

"Why, Savannah! What a pleasure to see you again so soon! And you've brought treats too."

"My mother sends her regards, Miss Potts. She made her award-winning banana nut muffins today and insisted I bring a plate to share with you … and Mr. Lee."

"Ah! How kind. And speaking of Mr. Lee …" Miss Potts flicked her glance to the stairs.

Flanking the mirror in the center of the landing, two windows cast late-afternoon light into the front hallway like spotlights, obscuring the features of the figure standing at the top of the stairs. She stared at him, her breathing relaxing as her eyes adjusted. Why, he wasn't a monster at all. Even in the strong glare, she could make out his long legs in jeans and the wide chest behind his crisp blue shirt. His face, catching the full force of the glare, was all but silhouetted from where she stood, but it didn't matter. He was tall and stood straight and strong, nothing like the hunchbacked ogre she'd been led to expect from the few snippets of gossip she'd collected from her sister.

She stepped forward, feeling her smile broaden as she said, "Mr. Lee."

Slowly, with what she perceived as a slight, but well-controlled, limp, he came down the stairs, his face and form coming into sharper focus. As her eyes adjusted, she braced herself and said a thousand prayers of thanks to the reporter who'd given a detailed report of his injuries so she could prepare herself.

Oh my God. Oh my God.

She licked her lips nervously, but as soon as she found his eyes, she made sure to hold them. Like a child told to pick a spot from a spinning carousel pony and not to let it out of sight, lest she become sick, she stared at those rich brown eyes like her life depended on it. Her gaze didn't flick to the mottled scar tissue that covered his right cheek, the drooping eye, or the burned skin on his lower cheek extending into his neck. She had read he lost his ear, and she could see his long, shaggy hair in her peripheral vision, covering the place where his ear would be. She held his eyes like a challenge, and without letting her smile weaken, she purposely lifted her left hand to him so they could shake hands skin to skin.

"Miss Carmichael," he said in that low, deep, blue-blooded voice that had so discomfited her on the phone, and reached out to take her hand.

His hand was soft and warm, and she could feel the coiled muscles under his skin as he pumped her hand gently. Of course this hand would be strong. It's the only one he had. Still, the strength and tone surprised her, and she felt her cheeks flush as his eyes searched hers.

"Thank you so much for agreeing to meet with me," she said. She'd never maintained such intense initial eye contact with a subject in her life, and though she knew it was entirely necessary, it felt too intimate for a first meeting.

"It's my pleasure. Thank you for agreeing to my terms."

His voice was smooth, but stilted, like it knew what to do but hadn't been allowed to do it for way too long.

"Of course."

"And thanks for the brownies. Though they forced me to log an extra half hour on the treadmill last night."

He still held her hand, and between the heat of his skin and the heat of his eyes, she was about to turn into mush. She dropped his glance and pulled her hand away. When she looked back up, he lifted his chin, as if bracing himself for her inspection.

She refused to inspect his face, but from what she could gather from her peripheral vision, it was as disfigured as the reports had indicated. Looking down again, she pretended to rifle through her bag, relieved to find a little notebook and pencil at the bottom, and held them up for him to see.

"Shall we begin?" she asked, capturing his eyes with precision.

His good hand swept up toward the left side of the stairs. "After you."

***

Well, well. Savannah Carmichael was a lot tougher than he expected. And more professional. And, he thought, ruefully wondering where she'd gotten her information, she was prepared: she'd offered him her left hand to shake and she'd always looked him directly in the eyes, not allowing her gaze to wander across his injuries. He followed behind her up the stairs, his entire body responding to the light sweetness of her perfume, the way her hips swayed gently in the lavender-flowered sundress she wore with a cream-colored sweater that just hit her trim waist.

"To the left or right, Mr. Lee?"

"Asher," he responded. "Left. My office is the first door on the left."

She stopped in front of his office door, as though she expected it to open magically for her. He reached over her shoulder, pushing the door open, breathing in the scent of her shampoo or perfume—whatever it was, it smelled like a goddamned miracle. His blood rushed south and he cursed softly. He didn't even know her. She could be dating someone, or engaged. He had no business thinking about her like that. Thinking about her, period.

"Are you married, Miss Carmichael?"

"Savannah," she said, taking a seat in the guest chair in front of his desk. "No. I'm not with anyone."

He ignored the leaping in his stomach from that simple admission.

"I thought we'd sit by the windows," he said, walking over to a pair of wingback chairs facing an antique stained glass window that made a rainbow of light on the hardwood floor.

He quickly moved behind the chair on the left, pulling it out for her. If he had to be interviewed, he'd at least be sure that when she looked at him, she saw his good side.

After she was settled, he took the seat beside her, letting his long legs drape languorously in front of him, crossing them at the ankles. Savannah dropped her purse to the floor and crossed her legs toward him.

"I don't want to tire you," she said gently, turning her neck to look at him.

"You won't."

"I must admit, you don't look like you'd tire easily."

And damn it, he didn't mean to take her comment sexually, but there it was: the image of her beneath him as he continued not-to-be-tired all night long. He must have blushed, because her eyes widened with surprise, and she looked away.

"I just meant that you seem fit," she said, a hint of teasing in her tone.

"I *am* fit."

It was her turn to blush and he cleared his throat, unaccustomed to company, to having a beautiful woman within reach.

"I told you I'm unpolished. I haven't spent time with anyone but Miss Potts in years. I don't want to scare you off with some stupid comment or other."

"I don't scare easily," she said, grinning.

"Do you mind if I ask you a few questions before we get started?" he asked, turning slightly to look at her, but making sure that she could see only his good side.

"Fire away." She shifted in her seat so that her adorable backside was shoved into the corner of the chair farthest from him, and her little pink ballet flat almost grazed the side of his thigh.

"Who is this article for?"

"The *Phoenix Times*."

"You write for them?"

"This is a freelance assignment," she explained, a tad defensive. He didn't blame her. She barely knew him—why should she share her recent bad luck at the *New York Sentinel*?

"A human interest piece?"

"Mmm." She glanced down.

He narrowed his eyes. "You're not crazy about doing it, though?"

Her face whipped up, and her eyes met his. It was the most unguarded moment he'd had with her yet, and the spirit in her eyes took his breath away. "I never said that."

"Your eyes did."

She flinched in annoyance, then, to his surprise and admiration, she nodded. "I was an investigative journalist in New York in a previous life. Lifestyles isn't really my thing."

"And yet reporting my story seems important to you. A home visit, brownies …"

"I need to nail this story," she admitted. "I need a heart-wrenching story about an American hero."

"How do you know my story is heart-wrenching?"

Her eyes widened, and her little pink tongue darted out to lick her lips. It was a nervous tic, but he'd be lying if he said it didn't affect him. It did. A lot. He shifted toward her in his seat slightly.

"You were the all-American golden boy. Now …"

"Now he's Asher Lee, man of leisure." Miss Potts's cheerful voice echoed through the quiet of the room, slicing through the intimacy of the moment as she set down a silver tray on the table between them.

Asher scowled but was quickly distracted by the smell of homemade muffins.

He turned to Savannah. "You made muffins this time?"

Savannah started to say something, but Miss Potts interrupted. "She did—what a clever little thing. And so lovely. You'll notice two are gone, Savannah. I couldn't help myself."

Savannah blushed again, then looked up at Asher, and something miraculous happened. For as long as he lived and breathed, he wouldn't forget it, because it was really and truly miraculous on the order of the loaves and fishes. Savannah Carmichael, one of the most beautiful girls he'd ever seen up close, looked at his face. And she smiled.

***

Miss Potts chatted with them for a while, pouring them each a cup of steaming hot coffee, as they munched on Savannah's mother's muffins, then left them alone to resume their conversation.

"A man of leisure. What does that mean?"

He shrugged, tucking into the last chunk of muffin. "Mostly I read."

"Fiction? Nonfiction? Poetry?"

"A little of everything," he said. "Don't you need to take notes?"

She glanced down at those long legs of his. *Yes*, was the answer to his question. *Yes, I should be taking notes.* But ever since she'd arrived, the visit had felt so much more social than professional, she'd been lulled into a comfortable repartee, and she didn't feel like breaking it by taking out her notebook and scribbling notes. She had all night to write down her thoughts and reflections. She could always fact-check later. Wasn't the important thing to create a relationship with her subject? Yes, of course. This first meeting was about creating a baseline comfort. She was doing everything right.

"Next time. We're just getting to know each other today." She grinned at him. "What're you reading right now?"

"*Right* now? Oh, um … a very informative book about, um, interpersonal relationships."

He blushed as he said this, and she wondered why it embarrassed him but didn't ask. His voice was deep and warm and soothing, and she could have listened to him talk about books for hours. He also told her about his childhood, which seemed idyllic, and gave her a basic timeline of his life from enlisting to now so she'd have a framework for the article. Before she knew it, the alarm on the phone in her purse was lightly ringing church bells to tell her that an hour had come and gone.

She silenced it with a sheepish smile. "I guess it's time for me to get out of your hair."

Was it her imagination, or did he look slightly sorry to hear that? Either way, it was definitely time for her to go. From the moment she'd arrived, she'd been sidetracked, and she needed to get home and get her game plan together in time for Wednesday's visit.

What surprised her the most was that, once they'd situated themselves before the windows with only the less damaged side of his face visible to her, she'd quickly discovered how easy it was to talk to him. She wasn't distracted by his prosthetic hand, which dangled out of sight over the far edge of his chair, or by his mangled skin and missing ear, both of which were mostly hidden from her view. All she could see was the weathered, rugged handsomeness of his left side, the imperfection of his nose, the occasional twinkle in his brown eye, the easy way his long legs crossed in front of him.

He was smart and quick and well-read, and though he'd warned her that he was unpolished, she had yet to see much evidence of it. In fact, if it weren't for the mask of mangled skin on the right side of his face, Asher Lee would be a catch. A massive catch.

But the fact was, despite her best efforts to look into his eyes only when he greeted her, his face was terrible to behold. She'd never seen anything so damaged, so disfigured and awful in all her life. She could barely look at him without wincing, without sympathy, and, much to her shame, without discomfort.

Which served to remind her: she wasn't there to be his friend. She was there to tell his story. And it was best not to get mixed up. *This is an assignment, Savannah, not a potential friendship. Don't forget it.*

As she prepared to stand and say her good-byes, she looked over at him. The way his eyes rested gently, patiently, on the stained-glass windows before them made her pause and turn to look herself. Savannah replaced her bag on the floor and eased back into her chair, staring straight ahead through the rainbow-colored windows as the sun lowered in the distance, bathing them both in color. She stared at the beauty before her, without speaking, without moving, totally transfixed by the reds and blues that danced in the late-afternoon sun. It didn't occur to her to speak, as if disturbing the perfect quiet of the moment was unthinkable.

Only later, at home, did it surprise her that she'd sat so long, so comfortably, in such complete silence, with someone she barely knew.

CHAPTER 4

The first time you realize you enjoy his company more than anyone else's

Despite their moment in the sun, Savannah felt it was important to give her full concentration to the article and was far more professional on Wednesday, arriving on time with chocolate chip macadamia nut cookies and meeting Asher in the study before he had a chance to meet her on the landing. He stood in the doorway of his office as she marched up the stairs, a surprised look on his face, which she forced herself to meet head on. With no-nonsense professionalism, she noted that although the way his right eye drooped was jarring, the scarring wasn't quite as bad as she remembered. She gave him a brief, polite smile, then sailed through his study, situating herself in the wingback chair on the left, in front of the stained glass windows.

"Well, hello to you too," he said as he joined her.

"Hello," she said, distracting herself by setting up her little voice recorder on the table between them. She had made a strict rule not to be distracted by his quasi-handsome half face. In fact, it was probably best if she didn't look at him at all and just asked her questions and took notes as he answered them. Yes, that was better. She scooped up the little recorder, pressed stop, and tucked it back into her bag, taking out her notebook and pen. "Shall we get started?"

His voice was appreciably chilly when he answered. "I wouldn't want to keep you."

"It's for the best, don't you think? That we concentrate on the interview?"

"Of course," he said, crossing his long legs at the ankle.

No long legs. No ankles.

Interview. First installment due Friday. Stop messing around.

"So, Mr. Lee—"

"Asher."

"Asher," she said, losing her train of thought as the name rolled off her tongue. There was something sexy about it. The *sh* sound in it. "That's such an unusual name."

"Forgotten your Sunday school lessons, Miss Carmichael? Tsk, tsk. And here I had it on good authority that your family are strong Methodists."

"Sunday school?" she asked, at a total loss, her notebook falling forgotten to her lap.

"Asher was a son of Jacob and Zilpah, who was the handmaiden of Leah."

"The older, uglier sister, whom he didn't want," she blurted out, remembering the story.

He raised an eyebrow. "I guess you didn't miss Sunday school after all."

"I knew I'd heard the name before. But why did your parents choose it? Arguably he had a checkered beginning."

He smiled at her observation. "The meaning. *Asher* means happiness."

She shouldn't have done it. She shouldn't have turned to face his mostly handsome half face while the sun was low and warm, making the moment magical all over again. But it had been so damn long since Savannah had felt happiness. And that's exactly what she felt when she looked over at him, and smiled.

***

By some stroke of luck, it had just happened again. Savannah

Carmichael had looked over at his ugly mug and smiled. His heart somersaulted like crazy, and he held his breath as he watched her, praying that the moment would last for more than a few seconds. But damn it if Miss Potts didn't burst into the room with her cheerful greeting, offering melt-in-your-mouth cookies and hot coffee. Really he needed to have a word with her. He appreciated her thoughtfulness, but he wanted every possible minute with Savannah to himself.

It's not like he knew her very well. They'd spoken a handful of words on the phone and spent a little over an hour together on Monday afternoon. But she'd totally commanded his every thought since he watched her drive away forty-eight hours ago. Tuesday and most of Wednesday had crawled by in agonizing slowness until she returned, and he couldn't contain his disappointment when she'd been all-business upon arrival. The only bright spot had been that when she greeted him, she'd looked at his whole face, and, surprisingly, he hadn't detected any of the expected revulsion or sympathy. She'd looked him over quickly, then walked to her chair, as though conversing with a mutant was an everyday occurrence in her world. He hated like hell that it gave him hope.

And then, just about when he'd talked himself out of hope, she asked him about his name and offered him the gift of her blindingly beautiful smile. It made him want to weep. It made him want to write poetry. It made him grateful that Miss Potts had encouraged him to rejoin the human race. Whatever happened with Savannah, he'd be forever grateful that she coaxed him back into this small, safe corner of the world.

"Chocolate chip macadamia nut?" he exclaimed with a full mouth. "Oh my God, Savannah!"

"Can this girl cook or what?" asked Miss Potts, winking at Savannah.

"This girl can cook," said Savannah weakly, adjusting her light-pink cardigan over a matching tank top. He'd checked it out the moment she'd arrived. The way it hugged her breasts was criminal, and yes, he was actively trying to look down it every time she bent over her notebook. Contrary to appearances, he was only human, after all.

"What are we talking about today?" asked Miss Potts.

"Mr. Lee's—er, Asher's formative years and high school days," Savannah answered efficiently, putting her half-finished cookie back on her plate.

"Well, my goodness, I'm sure I have his dental records somewhere around here too," Miss Potts teased, but Asher noticed Savannah's cheeks coloring. Her shoulders slumped, and she leaned back in her chair, sighing.

"I'm being rude," she said.

"Not in the least, dear," assured Miss Potts, patting her shoulder before turning to leave. "You're here to do a job. I admire you for doing it."

Savannah turned back to Asher as the door closed behind Miss Potts. "I'm sorry, Asher. I stormed in here like I was working a beat. I keep forgetting this is a *human interest* piece. I guess it would help if I acted a little more human."

Asher's words from Sunday night echoed in his head: *I barely look human. I'm not fit to rejoin the human race*, followed swiftly by Miss Potts's summary of his and Savannah's similarities: *You got your hand blown off; she got fired from the most prestigious newspaper in the country. You both came home to lick your wounds.*

He looked at the way her pretty lips tilted down, the way the hand closest to him gripped the arm of the chair. She was trying like hell to recover from her own pain, her own heartbreak. And he had agreed to help her.

Without thinking, he reached over and placed his hand on hers, struck by the soft warmth of her skin beneath his, before realizing, with a good amount of horror, what a liberty he'd just taken. *She's a beautiful, young, talented writer. She doesn't want some hopeless, deformed man touching her.* He started to pull away, but she shocked the hell out of him by quickly reaching up with her fingers to lace them through his, bending his fingers with hers so they were trapped. He couldn't bear to look at her face, so he stared, with wonder, at their hands, running his thumb gently over her skin as a welcome, long-forgotten heat coursed through his veins, waking him up, making every nerve ending, every cell, focus its attention on the delicious pressure of her fingers squeezing his.

After several moments, he looked up at her, only to find her staring down at their hands, just as he had been. She caught his eyes, her lovely brown ones happy and confused, defiant and worried.

"It's okay," she whispered, as though reassuring herself even more than him. "We're becoming friends."

And just like that, all that wonderfully warm heat turned cool, and he pulled his hand away. Friends. Of course. She'd never be able to see someone like him as an actual man. His heart sputtered and grappled with the unexpected blow. He gave her a tight smile, resting his hand in his lap.

"You had questions about my formative years," he said softly, trying his best to conceal his bitter disappointment. "Fire away."

***

Savannah saw the instant change in Asher's face when she used the word *friends,* and she berated herself for being a coward. She'd been surprised by his gesture but shocked by the way her heart had started pounding from the simple contact of his hand covering hers. The wind had been knocked out of her chest, and a million butterflies had taken over residence in her stomach. She was blindsided by the strength of her reaction. It worried her. Heck, it scared her. She barely knew him. It was impossible that she should already be infatuated with him. So she defused her feelings by taking the coward's way out and calling him her friend.

"Tell me a little bit about your family history," she said in a carefully modulated voice.

As she wrote down his answers, her mind wandered, trying

to placate her unease. *It's better this way. You still have ten sessions after this one, and you cannot fall for him like you did Patrick, you stupid girl. Look how that turned out. Not to mention, could you really fall for someone whose face looks like Freddy Krueger's?* Though shocked by her meanness, she also knew that it was fueled by her desperation to keep business and pleasure separate, and it only worried her more. Like most people, she was meanest when she was scared.

"I guess you could say that there have always been Lees in Danvers, though I suspect I'll be the last." He picked up his coffee cup and took a sip, staring out the windows like she was boring him.

She stared down at the words she'd just written: *I'll be the last.*

"That's ridiculous," she blurted out.

"Sorry?"

"Th-that's ridiculous," she said more softly.

"I think not," he said, taking another sip of coffee, his nose in the air.

"You won't be the last Lee in Danvers."

"Next question," he demanded in a low, tired voice. "Or shall we call it a day?"

She turned over her notebook in her lap. She needed to fix this. Not just because it felt terrible that she'd hurt him, but because she'd meant what she said. They *were* becoming friends. In fact, she could never remember being as excited to see Patrick as she was to see Asher again today. The last two days had crawled by as she reviewed their disjointed conversation and wonderful moment of communion watching the setting sun. She didn't have any friends in Danvers, really, besides Scarlet, and Scarlet was always with Trent, planning their wedding, imagining their future. Meeting Asher felt promising and special, and while Savannah really did need his story for her piece, she sort of wanted his friendship too.

"Friends could just be the opening bid," she whispered,

feeling the heat rush into her cheeks. It felt forward to say the words, but she didn't want him to think she'd sidelined him because of his looks. Damn, but she wasn't good at this stuff.

"Sorry?" he asked in that superior, aloof voice he must have perfected at U.Va.

"I'm not calling at friends."

He turned to her slightly. "Are you speaking in poker metaphors, or am I going crazy?"

Her lips trembled as she tried not to giggle. The whole conversation had become absurd.

"Am I meant to raise?" he teased.

"Just don't fold," she said, smiling now, realizing how much she liked being with him, despite how he looked, despite the fact that he'd barely been out of his house in eight years. She liked him.

He looked confused and bemused and a little delighted as he placed his cup back on its saucer, then turned slightly to catch her eyes. "I wouldn't dream of it."

An hour later, he'd schooled her on every poker trick he'd learned while stationed abroad and when the church bells rang lightly in her bag, she barely knew a thing about his formative years ... but her seven-card stud game would never be the same.

"Next time, leave the alarm at home," he advised, glancing at her bag, but making no move to stand up. He stretched lazily in the rainbow light, running his hand through his shaggy hair.

"Why don't you cut it?" she asked, staring at his hair, then quickly wished she could take it back.

His expression, which had been lazy and content, tightened. "It conceals things."

She turned so that she sat on the edge of her chair, facing him head on, even though he still sat in profile to her.

"Asher," she said gently. "It's not as bad as you think."

"Savannah," he said without looking at her, the right side of his face set in angry granite. "It's every bit as bad as I think. I get the pleasure of looking at it every day."

She reached out, tentatively at first, then with more

confidence, and placed her palm flat on the warm fabric of his denim-covered thigh. "Look at me."

"No," he said, glancing at her hand and making a small groaning sound in the back of his throat.

"Please, look at me. We're friends, remember?"

"Time's up," he said quietly, but firmly, turning completely away from her.

She swallowed, removing her hand and reaching for her bag. As she started to leave, he grabbed her wrist, forcefully, fiercely, adjusting his fingers to a more gentle grip when she didn't pull away.

"You'll come back on Friday?"

"Of course."

His fingers relaxed a little as his thumb caressed the inside of her wrist with slow, hypnotic strokes.

"Good," he said, letting go of her.

Savannah didn't realize she was holding her breath until she was halfway down the stairs.

***

"So how's it going?" asked Scarlet on Friday morning as she sat down across from her sister at the breakfast table. "With "Hermit" Lee?"

"Don't call him that," said Savannah, giving her little sister a look.

"Touchy."

"Not touchy. Just show some respect. He's an injured war vet."

"Lookee, lookee. If I didn't know better, I'd say someone's formin' a crush."

"Shut up, Scarlet."

"Vanna and Asher sittin' in a tree, K-I-S-S-I-N-G ..."

"You're such a brat." Savannah reached for a piece of toast and knocked Scarlet's silverware to the floor.

"Oh my stars!" sighed Judy. "These can't be my grown-up

daughters bickering like schoolgirls."

"She started it," said Scarlet, sticking her tongue out at her big sister. "All touchy about her new beau."

"Katie Scarlet, I could have sworn you had a big wedding order at the shop this morning."

Scarlet looked up at the kitchen clock and burst out of her seat, grabbing Savannah's toast out of her hands. "Criminy, I'm late! Thanks, Mama!"

Judy and Savannah watched her go, then exchanged rolled eyes as Judy took her younger daughter's vacated seat. "You know she's just teasin'."

"I know. It's just ... he's a good man. This town hasn't done right by him."

"Well, if anyone can change that, I'd lay bets on my girl." She pushed Savannah's hair out of her face and cupped her cheek tenderly, before pushing up from the table to check on her batter. Lemon ginger scones. Savannah's mouth watered.

"You know, I knew his mother. Pamela Lee."

Savannah started, slowly lowering her coffee cup to the table and staring at her mother's back in surprise. "You did?"

"Not well, of course. She was Pamela Lee, and I was just Judy Calhoun Carmichael, fresh from the sticks of Big Chimney, West Virginia."

Savannah politely refrained from pointing out that Danvers was also, in fact, the sticks to most people. "She was a snob?"

"Not at all. She was lovely. A real lady. We just didn't move in the same circles, button."

"How'd you know her?"

Judy gestured to the wall that held her framed blue ribbons, to the space between 1995 and 1997 that held a simple white-painted wooden cross. "You ever wonder why 1996's missing?"

"Sure. I've wondered."

"Yet you never asked."

"Figured you had your reasons."

"Pamela Lee and I competed for that ribbon every year, starting in 1987, when your dad and I moved here. Fairgrounds were so close, and everyone always said I made the best baked goods they'd ever tasted. First year, I was informed by some of the other contestants that no one beats Pamela Lee. She sponsors the baking competition, they warned me. Make sure your muffins aren't better than hers. But you know?" Judy smiled at Savannah. "They were. I couldn't help it."

She pointed to the very first blue ribbon on the far left corner of the wall. "It was the first year that anyone could remember that Pamela Lee won the red second-place ribbon. But she was some lady, Savannah. The next morning, she sent me a dozen blue-dyed white roses, with a note that read simply, 'The best baker won.'

"She never gave up. Year after year, my scones beat her scones, my cookies beat her cookies, my muffins beat her muffins. And every year, without fail, those blue roses would arrive on my front porch with some little note of congratulations, so I could enjoy my win. She was all class, Pamela Lee."

Judy smiled affectionately at the blue ribbons, gingerly touching the frames.

"Nineteen-ninety-six," said Savannah softly, with tears in her eyes. "The year Pamela Lee died in a plane crash."

Tears brightened her mother's eyes as she turned and nodded at her daughter. "I couldn't bring myself to bake that year. I just couldn't do it. That poor boy all by himself in that big house, his mama and daddy gone. I didn't enter that year, and that little white cross is in honor of Pamela Lee, the loveliest lady I ever knew. She taught me how to be gracious in defeat. I'll never forget her kindness to me, Savannah." Judy wiped her face with the corner of her apron, as Savannah's own vision blurred with tears.

"Oh, Mama," said Savannah, "all these years I've looked at that cross, and I never knew."

Her mother scooped out a portion of batter and shaped it carefully into a triangle, then placed in on a well-worn, greased baking sheet. "Well, now you do. You do right by that boy, button, you hear? You do right by him."

"I will, Mama."

"And you bring him some of these scones today."

"Yes, ma'am."

Her mother gave Savannah a knowing smile before returning to her scones.

"And when you're ready," she said over her shoulder, "you bring that boy home for supper."

***

A few hours later, Savannah had her notes in order and e-mailed the outline of the piece to Maddox McNabb at the *Phoenix Times*. She was surprised when her phone rang about fifteen minutes later.

"Hello? This is Savann—"

"Carmichael. Maddox McNabb. It won't work."

Savannah blinked, stepping outside and dropping despondently onto the porch swing.

"Won't work?"

"I know you're coming from investigative, so I'll lay this out for you real quick. What you've sent me isn't human interest."

"It's the story of how a town rejected a returning hero."

"It's a downer. It'll make people feel bad remembering all the times they could've been kinder to a vet."

Savannah humphed quietly. And what was wrong with that?

"Nobody wants to read that on the Fourth of July. We want to feel good about our country, about ourselves. We want sexy, or at least all-American, not some exposé about returning servicemen being treated like crap."

Savannah's sneakered toe pushed off, letting the swing sway her into further melancholy.

"Well, I don't know," she said. "I think it's an important angle."

"For the beat? Yes. For Lifestyles? No." He sighed. "I'm

sorry, Carmichael. I just don't know if this is going to—"

That was it. Panic got her back up, and her mouth started working again. "I got you, Mr. McNabb. Sexy and all-American. I'm your girl. Just give me until tomorrow, sir. I'll send you a whole new batch of notes. Same subject. Different angle."

"You might be better off finding an investigative job, Carmichael. I just don't know if—"

"*I* do, sir. I know myself, and I want *this* job, so I'll deliver. Whatever you need. Tomorrow. Look out for my notes."

Then she hit the End button on her phone before he could say anything else.

***

Asher paced his study like a caged bear, whiling away the long hours until Savannah Carmichael showed up at his door again. The problem was, he couldn't concentrate on his beloved books anymore. Even Jennifer Crusie was failing him because every heroine was Savannah and every handsome leading man was, well, not him.

On Wednesday when she said, "Look at me," in that low, certain voice, he'd realized how close he was to considering her request. She was tricking him, in her floral sundresses and bright smiles, into believing that he was a man and she was a woman, and it had been far too long since he'd felt like a man.

Because he wasn't. Well, he was, but he wasn't. He had all of the desires of a man, his body hardening and twitching at the very sight of her, living for her husky laugh and brilliant smiles, wanting the softness of her body beneath his while he touched her and stroked her and buried himself so deep inside her that Afghanistan and IEDs and dead parents and years of solitude never even existed.

But he wasn't a *whole* man. He couldn't leave his house. He still woke up screaming once in a while, drenched in a cold sweat as he felt his hand detach from his arm and Corporal Lagerty's body explode beside him. In the safe bubble of two wingback chairs, bathed in the kind light of the day, he could talk to her, get to know her, even reach for her hand. But his life wasn't *living*, and she was a person of the world. She lived in the sunshine, not shrouded in shadows.

And yet, despite all these thoughts, and perhaps because he hadn't had a friend—let alone a young, beautiful, female friend—in so many years, Savannah Carmichael was special to him. More than special, she was like a miracle. The beautiful maiden who showed up at the beast's castle, only to find there was more man to the monster than she ever could have guessed.

Too bad I don't have an enchanted rose that will change me back into a prince once we kiss. Too bad I will always look like this.

He opened the bathroom door and flicked on the light, staring at himself in the full-length mirror. She had asked why he didn't cut his hair. He shoved it to the side, looking at the place where his ear used to be. Angry, gnarled skin jutted out from the side of his head.

"They're doing amazing surgeries in Maryland now," said Miss Potts softly from behind, edging into the bathroom to hang two freshly-laundered hand towels on a bar beside the sink. "All it would take is a phone call to make an appointment."

"You can't just fix this," he said.

"Not completely. But you should look at some of the photos. They can make a new ear. They can graft skin from your—"

"Enough."

She knew better than to talk to Asher about this, and if she didn't quit, they'd get into a scorcher. Few things bothered him more than discussing his injuries with someone who wanted him to go back under the knife, be it a doctor, counselor or Matilda J. Potts. It was *his* decision. His alone.

Miss Potts put up her hands in surrender. "When you're ready."

"I won't be."

"I don't believe that," she said, heading for the door.

"Don't look now, but whether you like it or not, you've reentered the land of the living. Can't turn back now."

He slammed the bathroom door, walking slowly back to his desk to control his limp, and slid into his desk chair.

On one hand: *Too bad I will always look like this.*

On the other: *They're doing amazing surgeries in Maryland now. You should look at the pictures.*

He stared at the laptop that mocked him, then flipped it open, powering it up for the first time in ages.

CHAPTER 5

The first time you look like hell and he couldn't care less

The problem was, she couldn't think of another angle, because her mind kept reverting to investigative thinking, no matter how hard she tried to think of another way to tell Asher's story. As she walked up the driveway to his front door at 3:55 p.m., she mulled over some ideas. Okay, she wouldn't concentrate on the way Danvers had ostracized him. Maybe she could tell the story of the explosion: How come they hadn't swept for mines, like wire-triggered IEDs? How come a medic was put in that sort of harm's way? And why …?

And then she caught herself. She was doing it again. Hard journalism, not human interest. Damn it.

Miss Potts answered the door with her usual cheer, her eyes taking in the foil-covered plate all but forgotten in Savannah's hand.

"Oh my. What have you brought to tempt me today?"

"Lemon ginger scones," Savannah said, looking up belatedly to give the older woman a tight smile of hello.

"Forgive me for saying so, dear, but you just don't look like yourself today."

Savannah watched Miss Potts's eyes trail down her form before returning to her face. Oh crap! She'd been so distracted trying to think of an angle, she'd forgotten to doll herself up like Scarlet. She was wearing white Keds, denim cutoffs, badly frayed around the thighs, and a black scoop-neck T-shirt that had a smudge of mustard over the left boob. Her hair was in a loose, messy knot at the base of her neck. She looked like a wreck. She also looked like herself.

"This is me," she said, with a sheepish smile, pushing some flyaway strands of her brown hair back into the knot.

"Well, I did wonder when your sister was going to cut you off from her supply of florals and pink."

"Do you miss *anything*, Miss Potts?"

"Very little, dear. I've been alive for a hundred years or so."

"Well, then, this won't come as a shock: I don't bake. Not unless I'm squinting at a cookbook the whole time and making a four-alarm mess in the kitchen. We're lucky when my baking turns out edible. My mother, on the other hand, is a champion baker. My sister isn't too shabby either. Me? I'm a disaster in the kitchen, so how about we lay off that 'Isn't Savannah an amazing little baker?' stuff? It's making me feel dishonest."

Miss Potts's eyes widened, but she grinned before turning toward the kitchen, throwing "Whatever you say, dear" over her shoulder like an afterthought.

Savannah turned to the mirror by the coatrack in the front hallway and looked at her face. Without any makeup, she looked plainer than usual. She took her hair out of the messy knot and smoothed it into a bun, then brought her shirt to her mouth and licked at the yellowish stain, which only served to make it wetter, darker, and more obvious. She rolled her eyes at herself and turned to trudge up the stairs, surprised to find Asher on the landing staring at her. With pressed khakis and a tucked-in oxford, he looked the picture of old-monied grace, whereas she …

"I heard the bell ring. Wondered if you'd gotten lost."

Savannah paused at the bottom of the stairs, waiting for him to scan her appearance, find her completely lacking in florals and Southern charm, call her a fake, and ask her to leave.

"I don't bake," she said.

"I heard."

"Your mom did, though. I didn't know that until today."

Still standing on the landing, backlit by the glare of the afternoon sun, his eyes widened in recognition. "You're Judy Carmichael's daughter."

She nodded, suddenly feeling the insane urge to apologize for all those blue ribbons her mother had won.

"No wonder everything you bring is so delicious."

"My mother sends her regards. She liked your mother. Very much."

"And my mother admired yours."

"I don't like floral sundresses."

"Me either. The cut's all wrong for my limp." He started down the stairs haltingly, carefully, and she realized the limp wasn't very noticeable if he moved slowly.

"This is me," she said as he got closer, holding her hands loosely by her sides as he took in her ratty ensemble.

"I like you," he said, "just the way you are."

She scoffed. "Cutoffs and a stained black T-shirt with my hair in a messy bun."

"Works for me."

"My sister—"

"I don't know your sister, but she can keep her sundresses if they're not your style."

"I look like hell."

He stood before her, angling his body away so that the burned side of his face still faced the stairs and his good eye swept up and down her form slowly, lazily, almost … erotically.

"If this is hell, I need to review my definition of heaven. I've clearly been lowballing paradise."

She didn't mean to do what she did next. She didn't think. She just acted. Reaching up, she gently placed her palm on the smooth skin of the cheek closest to her, searching his eyes. *You were just supposed to be a story.*

"Thank you, Asher," she said.

***

His world spun like crazy, and for just a moment, his eyes fluttered closed as he adjusted to the feeling of another human being touching him voluntarily with gentleness and affection. Aside from Miss Potts's occasional hand on his shoulder or his increasingly infrequent doctor visits, he hadn't been touched by another person in years. The heat of her hand, of her skin pressed tenderly against his, was so unexpected and so mind-bending, his cheek tingled with the electric sweetness of it.

His eyes opened when she moved her hand away.

"I—I'm sorry. I had no right to—"

"I wasn't complaining, Savannah."

Her brows creased, and he perceived an internal battle. "It wasn't professional."

"I thought we'd established that we were becoming friends. I may be out of practice, but I believe friends touch one another now and then."

He saw her shoulders unbunch from around her ears. "I'm a train wreck today."

"Want to talk about it?"

"I'm supposed to be interviewing *you*."

"Friends first. Business second."

He held out his hand, and she took it absentmindedly as he pulled her up the stairs toward his office. Did she realize she'd laced her fingers through his as soon as their hands found each other? Did it make her heart beat like crazy as it did his?

"They didn't like my angle," she said.

"Your angle?"

"Maddox McNabb, the editor of the *Phoenix Times*. He didn't like the story I pitched to him. I wanted to write a piece about the impact of an unwelcoming hometown on the psyche of a returning soldier."

"Cheerful stuff," he said, secretly glad they'd shot down such a pitiful story line, despite its truth.

"They don't think it's sexy enough."

He stopped in the gallery at the top of the stairs and faced her, two steps below, incredulous. "*Sexy*? Have you not mentioned … *me*?"

She rolled her eyes and grinned. "You don't have to be pretty to be sexy. You're plenty sexy, Asher."

For the second time in two minutes, his world was utterly rocked. He searched her face for mockery but didn't find any. She said it so matter-of-factly, like she might mean it, like it could possibly be true. His heart pounded mercilessly against his ribs, and he felt his skin flushing with pleasure. He turned back around, pulling her into his office where he reluctantly dropped her hand to close the door.

Sexy. "Yeah, right."

"Your legs go on forever," she said softly, turning to face him from the center of his study.

His gaze swept down her body, checking out *her* legs, tan and long in frayed shorts that reminded him of summer nights in high school, his once-perfect legs tangled together with some lovely, willing girl's on a picnic blanket. "So do yours."

He watched, immensely pleased, as she blushed, shaking her head at him.

"Have you read all these books?"

Changing the subject. Okay.

"Yes."

"*All* of them?"

"You're my first social visitor in eight years, Savannah. Yes."

She clasped her hands behind her back and walked over to a shelf where the spines were especially colorful. *Romance. It figures.* It occurred to him to distract her by leading her over to his vast nonfiction collection and wow her with his knowledge of obscure world history, but it was too late. She had already figured out what she was looking at. He steeled himself for some teasing.

"You said *all*, right?" she asked, giving him a saucy look.

Oh man, she was something.

"What can I say? I have a soft spot for romance."

"Well, that's … sexy," she said, turning back to the books.

"Maybe I should write my article about an injured war vet who returns home and reads nothing but romance."

He shrugged. It wasn't good, but it was better than the pity piece.

She noticed the ladder by the wall that gave him access to the upper shelves and climbed up a few stairs, pulling out an especially gaudy cover. She read the back, then turned the cover to him. "*The Moor's Maiden*?"

He reached up to grab it away from her, but she raised her arm over her head, adopting the voice of a movie previewer as she read the jacket copy. "'A dark loner from a faraway land … a buxom beauty from the green shores of England …'"

"Give it," he said, reaching again.

She giggled. "'… conquer their warring passions'—warring passions, Asher!—'as they—'"

He reached up again to take the book away from her, and when she leaned away, she lost her balance. His arm went around her waist like a vise as she fell, slamming into his chest, and he held her tightly against him until her feet touched the ground. Even then, he didn't let go.

She panted lightly, out of breath, her breasts pushing into his chest as her eyes searched his face. "S-sorry."

"I'm not," he answered, trying to ignore the way his blood all flooded to one place, leaving him light-headed. His chest heaved lightly, not from the exertion, but from having her so close, in his arms, pressed up against him. If he died right now, he'd die happy.

"Asher," she breathed, licking her lips and pressing them together. "I'm okay now."

He realized what she was saying and loosened his arm, taking a step back, giving her the book. She took it, fanning the pages distractedly, cocking her head to the side.

"When you grabbed me, you used your good arm."

He nodded.

"I've noticed that you barely ever use your other arm."

"That's because I don't … use it."

"Then why have a prosthesis?"

"I only wear it when you come over," he said.

"Why?"

"To make you more comfortable."

"Don't."

"What?"

"Take it off."

"What? Why?"

"Because I don't bake or wear floral sundresses."

Two things happened inside his body at the same time: his heart exploded, and his brain went on high alert. Show her his stump? It was a risk. It was such a big risk to show her the smooth oval stump just under his elbow where his lower arm once existed. He was even careful to conceal it from Miss Potts.

"It's just me," she said, and then, echoing his words from the front hallway, "I like you just the way you are."

***

Without taking his eyes off her face, Asher's good hand moved to unbutton the cuff that clung snugly to the flesh-colored silicon wrist. The button opened with a pop.

"My mother calls me button," Savannah said nervously, without looking away.

Next, he moved his good hand to the neck of his oxford, flicking open the buttons one by one until his shirt was open and the broad muscles of his chest pushed aggressively against the white cotton of his T-shirt. Savannah sucked in a breath, telling herself to behave.

"Help me with this one," he said, extending his good arm to her.

She reached forward, unbuttoning the cuff, feeling the heat thrown off from his wrist, suddenly aware of how much man he was. Not just a wounded veteran. Not just a disfigured soldier. Not just a man who'd deliberately chosen to hide away from the world. But a living, breathing, warm, and totally available human being who was presently making her body hot with awareness. *What would it be like to be with him?*

When she looked back up at his face, the corners of his lips tilted upward and his good eye seemed to twinkle with a mixture of surprise and cockiness. He shrugged out of his shirt, and she noticed the harness that extended from the top of the prosthetic arm and crisscrossed his back.

She swallowed. "Don't wear this for me. Not anymore."

"Okay," he said softly.

As he shrugged out of the harness, the muscles of his chest and upper arms moved in ways that mesmerized her as he freed himself. She watched as he reached over, pulling on the silicon arm until it detached with a quiet pop, and he turned to place the arm and harness on the table behind him. He reached up to where a white sleeve with a bolt hanging from the bottom was still attached to his arm. He tugged until it gave, and he laid it beside the harness. Then he turned to her, probably feeling more naked than he'd ever felt in his entire life as her eyes drifted to the oval stump of smooth flesh under his elbow.

She started to reach out, but then her eyes darted back up to his. "May I?"

Staring at her in wonderment, he nodded. Her fingers trembled they touched down gently on the stump of skin under his elbow, as she learned the textures and contours of his mangled flesh.

"It's so smooth," she said.

He sucked in an audible breath.

"I'm hurting you?" she asked.

"No," he murmured. "Never."

"Is there still feeling?"

"Some," he said honestly. "Mostly phantom sensations."

As her fingers continued to brush gently over his stump, her breasts rose and fell higher and faster than before. She caught him as he lowered his eyes to them, staring hungrily before looking back into her eyes. She raised her eyebrows, feeling heat pool in her tummy, her awareness of him and of her and of them off-the-charts as he stared at her.

The door opened and she yanked her hand away.

"Oh, I see we've *all* gotten a little more comfortable," said Miss Potts, bustling into the room with the silver tray carrying coffee and scones. "What a good idea."

Savannah moved quickly away from Asher, trying to breathe normally as she made her way to the left wingback chair in front of the stained glass windows. Once there, she pressed her palms to her hot cheeks, trying to figure out what was happening between them, trying to convince herself that whatever it was, it was a very bad idea. Asher plopped down in the chair beside her, clearly perturbed by Miss Potts's inopportune intrusion, but Savannah had to admit she was relieved.

Not only was Asher several years older than she—which wasn't actually a deal breaker for Savannah—but he had baggage galore, he was a veritable hermit, and, most important, he was her subject. *Good Lord, Savannah. First a source, now a subject. Try conducting yourself with an ounce of professionalism, for goodness' sake.*

She numbly accepted the cup of coffee from Miss Potts, determined not to be distracted by Asher Lee's amazing chest, amazing voice, amazing sense of humor, amazing, amazing, amazing … anymore. No, she'd be the hard-hitting journalist she was trained to be.

By the time Savannah headed home, at six o'clock, she was feeling much better. The rest of the afternoon had proceeded without incident, Asher answering her questions without reaching for her hand or any other extended physical contact. Their fingers brushed once as they replaced their coffee cups at the same time, but they continued talking without a blip. It had, in fact, been an informative session. Not only had they discussed Asher's grade school and high school years, but they'd been able to cover his childhood feelings about Danvers, about being a Lee, and about losing his parents so tragically.

She'd been especially tempted to reach over and touch his

hand as he related this part of his history, but she held herself back. If they kept distracting each other with their blossoming personal relationship, she'd never get the article done.

Wait, she thought, as she turned the key in the ignition. *Or would she?*

This was supposed to be a human interest piece, right? What would be more human than the unlikely friendship between a down-on-her-luck reporter and a hermitlike war veteran? First-person narrative. Two people who provoked sympathy. She hit the steering wheel once with glee. That was it. The article would be about how she lost her job because of a bad source. How he lost his hand and injured half of his face. How he came home, and she came home, and two misfits found comfort, found friendship, found something that resonated in each other.

She knew, instinctively, that the gritty editor would love it, and as soon as she got home, she typed up a quick e-mail detailing the new angle and submitting a piece, complete with poker tips, called "Asher Lee: An All-American Story."

Savannah paced her small childhood bedroom over the next hour, trying to distract herself without success as she waited for Mr. McNabb's reply. Scarlet poked her head in at one point.

"Come to the club for dinner and dancing tonight."

Savannah shook her head no. "Sort of waiting for an important e-mail, Scarlet."

"I'll cancel on Trent. Dinner and a movie. Just you and me?"

"Tomorrow?" asked Savannah. She wouldn't be able to concentrate on a movie until her story angle had been approved anyway.

"I'm holding you to it. You're supposed to be my maid of honor, and we've barely done any wedding stuff together. I know it's not your thing, Vanna, but the least you can do is spend some time with me before I'm a Mrs."

Savannah held her arms out to her sister. "I'm sorry, hon.

I've been really distracted. If this story gets approved, it could mean a fresh start for me."

"In Phoenix," said Scarlet, glumly.

"Phoenix. New York. What the difference? You'll still be the belle of the ball here in Danvers, and I promise I'll come home more regularly to bounce Trent and Scarlet Juniors on my old-maid aunt knees."

Scarlet pulled out of her sister's arms, sitting down on the bed. "This is the happiest you've been in weeks, you know."

Savannah had a brief flashback to Asher's arm around her and felt her cheeks flush with heat.

"I didn't mean to make fun of Asher at breakfast," Scarlet said.

"It's okay. Just don't do it again, Scarlet. He's a pretty amazing guy."

"Is he?" she asked, and Savannah was too caught up in images of Asher to hear the warning note in her sister's voice.

"Yeah. He's smart and sophisticated. He's really well-read. He's a bona fide war hero. He makes me feel … feel …"

"What? What does he make you feel?" asked Scarlet.

"I don't know. Different. Better. His name means 'happiness.'"

"Vanna, he's lived up in that old house for as long as I can remember. Never comes to town. Never has anyone up, except you. People say all sorts of things about him." She paused. "His hand … and his face …"

Savannah narrowed her eyes, biting her lower lip to keep herself from lashing out at her sister's small-mindedness. "I've hung out with him three times. *Three times*, Scarlet. And I swear to you, I barely notice it anymore. Is it pretty? No. But there's a lot more to him than some facial scarring. He's … remarkable."

Savannah's phone started buzzing, and she reached across her sister to answer it. "Mr. McNabb?"

"Carmichael. Great stuff."

"Really?" She looked up in time to see Scarlet standing in her doorway, a worried expression on her face. Savannah covered the mouthpiece and whispered, "Dinner and a movie tomorrow," and Scarlet nodded before turning away.

"Yup. I really like it. Not to mention, I'm going to do pretty well in my standing poker game tonight." He laughed. "When can I have the next installment?"

"I see him on Mondays, Wednesdays, and Fridays."

"Send me something else next Friday. I'll figure out then if I'm going to serialize it or hold onto the installments for one big piece. You're a good writer, Carmichael. Jones was right about that."

"Thank you so much, sir. I'm going to knock your socks off!"

"You do that. Bye."

"Bye, sir."

Savannah hit End and threw herself on her bed, kicking her feet with abandon as she shouted, "I'm back, I'm back, I'm back!" until she finally quieted, staring at the ceiling and feeling lighter than she'd felt in weeks. Only one thing would have made it better: to share the news with Asher. To watch his face brighten with approval as she told him that she'd figured out the angle.

It was then, and only then, that she realized she had a whole weekend and much of Monday to endure alone before seeing him again.

CHAPTER 6

Contemplating an entire weekend without Savannah's company made Asher feel more needy and more churlish than he'd felt since he started getting his act back together two or three years ago. He strongly considered going on a bender to pass the weekend in drunken numbness, but he hadn't worked on his body strength for the past few years just to toss it to the side because he was missing a girl. As soon as she left, he put his hair in a ponytail, changed into workout clothes, and headed downstairs to his state-of-the-art home gym, where he spent two hours lifting weights to keep building solid muscle mass in his chest, good arm, and good leg. Then he did all of his rehabilitation exercises on his injured leg. Twice. He was sweaty and tired when he came upstairs at eight o'clock, but he didn't miss her any less.

"Dinner's ready," Miss Potts informed him, when he appeared at the top of the stairs.

"I'll take a quick shower."

"It'll get cold," she said. "Anyway, since when do you shower before dinner?"

In just the week he'd been spending time with Savannah, his social graces and manners were returning at a clip. But Miss Potts was right. He could eat dinner now and shower later, when the memory of his recent experiences with Savannah and his general longing for her would be assuaged only by a blast of freezing water.

He sat down at the dining room table, grinning at Miss Potts over the steaming slices of meat loaf and pile of mashed potatoes, both covered with brown gravy, with green beans on the side.

"My favorite," he said. "Thanks."

"Glad you're asher, Asher," she said, and he grinned at the old joke his grandmother used to make. She sat across from him, fidgeting with her hands on the table. "I have to tell you something."

He knew that confessional tone, and his grin disappeared as his fork changed course halfway to his mouth.

"I made an appointment for you. You can cancel it if you want to."

"Where? With whom?"

"At Walter Reed."

His fork clattered on his plate. "I'm not going."

"Okay. Have it your way."

"I swear, Miss Potts—"

"Don't swear. The appointment's for tomorrow." She shrugged. "Sort of thought you might want something to do. You know, to pass the time."

Sly thing. She knew he'd be stalking around for the next three days waiting for Savannah to return on Monday. Damn her, but she knew his weaknesses and zeroed in on them like a tactical missile.

"Then again, you could always pick up the phone and ask to see her this weekend. You don't *have* to wait until Monday."

"That would be presumptuous. She agreed to Mondays, Wednesdays, and Fridays. I don't have a right to ask for more." *Yet.*

"Then you're free to go to Maryland. I also booked you a room at the Naval Bridge Inn & Suites for Saturday and Sunday nights."

Miss Potts knew as well as he did that he'd never consider staying in a civilian hotel, where people would stare and gawk at his injuries. At the military-associated Naval Bridge, no one would even blink as he checked in or ate a quiet meal alone at the restaurant. In fact, at the Naval Bridge, he was likely to run into other injured vets, or at least get respectfully saluted by younger, whole men who had yet to survive a deployment.

"Why *Sunday* night too?"

"First consult is on Saturday afternoon for your hand. Second is on Monday morning for your leg and face."

"Damn it, Miss Potts."

"Don't you swear at me, Asher Sherman Lee," she said, her face reddening. "You don't like it? Cancel it." Then she stood up indignantly and left the room in a huff.

Asher sighed, then picked up his fork and took another bite of meat loaf.

Bethesda. He hadn't been in years. Not since he'd gotten his present, and wildly outdated, prosthesis fitted five years ago. Lately he'd been reading about new attachments that somehow sensed your brain waves and sent signals down the arm to the hand. Bionic arms. He couldn't deny that he'd been intrigued, if not excited, by the new developments.

I've noticed that you barely ever use your other arm.

But maybe he would, if it wasn't just a useless piece of silicon for appearances. He'd be able to keep holding her hand while his prosthetic hand turned a doorknob.

Asher, enough!

But his mind was already reeling with possibilities.

He'd be able to pick her up in his arms and carry her to bed, touching her with his good hand, while he took off his clothes with the other. He'd be able to hold her tightly against him while his good hand traced the lines of her face. He'd be able to wrap both arms around her …

The oil heater in the basement kicked on, and Asher was so lost in his fantasies that he jumped. Damn it, he had to stop thinking like that. He wasn't involved with Savannah. She didn't belong to him. They were becoming friends. That's all.

But he remembered how her body felt pressed against his in the library, and his heart started racing.

"Fine, Miss Potts," he bellowed. "I'll go to Maryland tomorrow."

Without missing a beat, she swung back into the dining room through the kitchen door, a pleased smile brightening her wrinkled face.

"Wonderful. I knew you would."

***

By Sunday afternoon, Savannah considered swinging by Asher's house, but she couldn't come up with a good enough excuse, and besides, he'd committed to being interviewed only on Mondays, Wednesdays, and Fridays. Sundays were his private time for reading or exercising that surprisingly hard, toned body, she mused, feeling a little swoony.

The toe of her shoe dangled off the porch swing, the rubber squeaking against the hardwood floor as she stared at the pitcher of lemonade on the coffee table in front of her.

A sleek, dark-green Jaguar pulled up to the curb and parked, and she watched as Trent Hamilton's coiffed blond head emerged from the car. He winked at Savannah as he opened and closed the front gate and jauntily made his way up the front walkway.

"Got an extra glass?" he asked, leaning against the porch railing.

"Sure," she said, pulling one from a stacked pile and filling it for her future brother-in-law.

"How's the story coming? About 'Ole Asher Lee, the weird war hero?"

Savannah rolled her eyes. "He's a veteran, Trent. Show some respect."

"Ain't good for a town to have some old creep livin' like the hermit of the hills."

"Relax. He's a perfectly nice guy. And he gives Danvers character."

"*Some* character."

"You know how he sustained his injuries? He was headed into a warzone to drag an injured soldier to safety. An IED went off right near him. Blew off his hand and scarred his face and leg." She didn't mean to sound so harsh, but she couldn't help it. "What have you done lately for the good of humanity, Trent?"

He finished off his lemonade and set down the glass slightly harder than necessary. "How you and my Scarlet are sisters ..."

"She got the soft. I got the hard."

"You ain't kiddin'. Hey, how about I stop makin' fun of Asher Lee, and you don't tell Scarlet I got you all riled?"

The thing Savannah would always like best about Trent was how much he loved her sister. Somehow it made everything okay. She stuck out her tongue at him. "Deal."

Her phone vibrated in her back pocket, surprising her, and she waved for Trent to go inside.

"Hello?"

"Savannah, dear, it's Miss Potts."

"Miss Potts! Hello!" Suddenly her heart seized. Why would Miss Potts be calling her? Could something have happened to Asher? "Is everything okay?"

"Oh, yes, dear. It's just that Asher was called out of town. He won't be back until very late on Monday night, so I'm afraid he'll have to cancel your session."

The disappointment Savannah felt almost winded her. She scooted back on the swing, curling her legs under her. She'd been counting down the hours, minutes, seconds until Monday at four o'clock. Finding out she'd have longer to wait made her feel so desperate, so unhappy, she swallowed over the lump forming in her throat.

"Called out of town?"

"I'm afraid so."

"But he'll be back late on Monday?"

"Very late."

"Oh." Savannah stared forlornly at the pitcher of lemonade, watching droplets run down the side like tears. "I didn't know he ..."

"Took off now and then? Well, dear, he's a *man*. Of course he does."

Savannah sat up straight as she perceived Miss Potts's meaning. Of course. He's a man. With *needs*. He was out of town getting those needs met. Someone—some awful, two-bit, floozy who couldn't possibly share Savannah's appreciation for his mind—would be running her dirty fingers over his rock-hard chest all weekend long. She winced.

"I see," said Savannah, working hard to keep her voice level.

"I knew you would. See you on Wednesday?"

"Sure," she answered, feeling her nostrils flare and her eyes burn with … with what? Anger? Check. Betrayal? Not that she had a right to it, but check. Jealousy? Check. Sadness? Oh Lord, *check*.

"Wonderful. Good-bye, dear."

Miss Potts hung up, and Savannah sat stock-still, her heart pounding uncomfortably as she tried to sort through her feelings. Asher Lee. Crippled, disfigured Asher Lee was getting his rocks off somewhere with someone while she sat at home pining for him, imagining him all alone in his brown house on the hill, pining for her in turn. But no. No. That wasn't the case at all. Clearly his schedule was much busier than hers.

She had no right to the sharp way her heart ached, but it did. And inconvenient that, because it told her something important that she'd suspected all weekend long: Asher Lee wasn't just a subject to her anymore, and he wasn't just a friend either. In a very short time, Asher Lee had become much more to her foolish heart, and she hated herself for just assuming somewhere in her head that he'd be hers for the taking if she crooked her little finger.

"Savannah," her mother called from the dining room. "Suppertime."

She hefted herself off the swing, feeling miserable, bracing herself for fabulously happy Mr. and Almost-Mrs. Hamilton sitting across from her while her own brief dreams of someone special went up in smoke.

***

It was a satisfactory weekend, thought Asher, speeding west toward home.

The appointments on Saturday and Monday had gone well, and Asher had learned a lot about his options. If he wanted to be fitted for the i-Limb "bionic" hand he'd read about, he'd need to schedule an appointment for the casting and another for the training, but they estimated he could be up and running by August. As for his face, some new developments in facial reconstruction meant that they could build a prosthetic right ear for him based on the shape and size of his left ear. He would need a quick operation to imbed magnets into the place where his ear used to be, and remove any ancillary tissue. Then the artificial ear could be fitted. They said he needed a few straightforward operations to remove areas of scar contractures and replace the damaged skin with healthy skin grafts, and another procedure to smooth out his jawline with silicone implants. They'd even be able to reestablish the normal contour of his right eye and smooth out some of the burns too.

He'd require one more consult, and then the surgeries could be scheduled for the summer and fall. Probably four to seven procedures in all. The news wasn't as bad as he'd thought it would be, and it had certainly given him a great deal to think about.

As for his leg, that's where he ran out of luck. There were procedures to replace the bones, but the bones were sound. It was the muscle, cartilage, and skin that had been so badly injured, and the only thing that would improve function was his adherence to daily physical therapy. Asher committed to himself to do more, to do better, to lose as much of the limp as possible.

And he'd even run into an old friend from Afghanistan, so he hadn't ended up eating alone on Sunday night, after all. Turns out he owed Miss Potts some thanks because it was a far more productive trip than he'd anticipated, and he felt buoyant as he made his way home to Danvers.

Hell, home to Savannah.

He'd thought of her all weekend long. At every available moment, she was on his mind, in his heart, his feelings for her growing with alacrity as he considered these improvements as a way to make himself more appealing to her. Truth be told, he'd never have considered them at all without the possibility of Savannah in his life. At the thought of her body, warm and pliant in his arms on Friday afternoon, he'd sink into the bliss of fantasy, wondering what it would be like to kiss her lips, to touch his tongue to the curve of her neck, to run his fingers over the sensitive skin of her breasts and watch her eyes close in pleasure.

Someday, he promised himself. *No matter what you have to do. Someday.*

He glanced at the dashboard clock. It was already two thirty. With at least another hour of driving still to go, he stepped on the gas, knowing that heaven's gates opened at four o'clock.

Which is why, when he pulled up in front of his house at three forty-five and Miss Potts explained that she'd canceled the interview, he almost lost his mind.

"What are you talking about?" he growled, standing in the front hall with his duffel bag slipping off his shoulder to the marble floor with a dull thud.

"I didn't think you'd be home in time. I didn't want the poor girl to waste her time. Wednesday's just as well, isn't it?"

"No, it's not. It's *not* just as well, and I don't appreciate your interfering."

"Well, I never. I only meant to help."

"What did you say to her?"

"I told her you were called out of town as men sometimes are."

"*As men sometimes* … " His eyes widened, and his chin jutted forward as he understood her meaning. "You implied that I—that I was—"

"Jealousy *does* make the heart grow fonder."

"Miss Potts," he groaned. "I never asked for your

meddling!"

"This is the thanks I get for helping?" she demanded, then turned on her heel in a huff and headed back toward the kitchen.

"Some help!" he yelled at her back.

Asher ran his hand through his hair, disappointment and frustration driving him to do something he hadn't done in almost eight years: He walked back through the front door, got in his car again, and turned it toward town.

***

Scarlet had gotten off early from work and sat beside Savannah on the swing, reading out of one of those goddamned bridal magazines again, but Savannah barely heard a word. It was almost four o'clock. And there would be no rush of excitement today as she drove up to Asher Lee's house. No teasing conversation. No brush of his strong, warm hand. No rainbow-colored sunsets. No nothing.

He'd figured prominently in her dreams last night, the undamaged side of his face bending to kiss her. And then she'd backed up only to watch some bottle blonde writhe beneath him as his perfect ass clenched, thrusting forcefully forward over and over again. She'd woken up shaking and sweaty and … sad. She hated dreams that didn't wear off as the sun rose. She hated them even more when they lingered late into the day.

"'… and little gift bags for out-of-town guests are always a nice touch,'" read Scarlet. "Isn't that a nice idea, Vanna? Gift bags for the folks comin' in from out of town? It says here to 'make sure you include bottled water, chocolates, directions to the church and reception, and recommendations of things to do.' We could add Virginia Peanuts, too, and maybe some of mama's famous muffins. Charmin'. Vanna? You listenin'?"

"Gift bags," Savannah said listlessly. "Charmin'."

Sitting closer to the porch rail than the house meant she had an unobstructed view of kids riding their bicycles and the odd afternoon car. She sighed deeply, feeling forlorn.

Scarlet made an exasperated sound. "Oh, for Lord's sake, Savannah! Why don't you just go over there tomorrow and give him hell? I can't stand it when you mope. You're too strong and too tough to mope."

Savannah turned to her sister. "I have no right to give him hell, and I'll be done moping in a few more minutes. At four o'clock. When we head to Fowler's Bridal."

"You really like him."

Savannah shrugged. "I don't know him all that well. But, yeah, Scarlet. I liked him. We had a lot more in common than I expected. I guess I just thought ..." She looked away, at a mother pushing a carriage along the sidewalk. "It doesn't matter."

She heard the expensive motor before she actually saw the black sports car pull up in front of her house.

"Who do you know who owns a black BMW?" she asked Scarlet.

Her sister stood up and went to the porch railing, her pink-and-white gingham sundress blowing lightly in the afternoon breeze. "No one."

Savannah propped her elbow on the arm of the swing, watching with tepid curiosity as the engine went silent. For several long moments no one emerged from the car, but her mouth dropped open in shock when someone finally did.

"Is that ...?" asked Scarlet, whipping her face to Savannah's.

"Yes," breathed Savannah, her heart pounding like crazy as her stomach flipped over in excitement. "It's him."

Asher moved quickly, slamming his door and keeping his head down as he made his way around the hood of his car. He opened the little gate and surged forward up the brick walkway, finally glancing up to find Scarlet gaping at him from the top of the steps.

"You're Scarlet," he said, extending his left hand. "Nice sundress."

Savannah couldn't keep a grin from spreading across her face as she heard his voice and choice of greeting. Unpolished. Perfect. She untangled her legs and stood up, wishing the world would stop spinning so much faster than usual.

"Th-thanks," said Scarlet, taking his hand, flashing a worried look at Savannah.

Asher followed Scarlet's glance, his eyes finding and resting on Savannah's.

"I'll just … I'll just leave you two to …" Scarlet turned and headed into the house, letting the screen door slam behind her.

Asher clenched his jaw and Savannah could see the wildness in his eyes. My God, how much courage had it taken for him to show up here? She forgot about the bleached-blonde floozy and her disappointed hopes. She extended her hand to him, and he took it, moving around the coffee table to sit beside her on the swing. Once seated, with his injured side safely facing the side of the house, he seemed to relax. A little.

Savannah turned her body to face him, one knee brushing against his khaki-covered thigh as she moved. It felt like rock and made her shiver.

"What are you doing here? You canceled."

"I *never* would have canceled. Miss Potts canceled. I read her the riot act. I almost killed myself getting home in time to see you … to …" His voice trailed off, and he clenched his jaw, like he'd said too much. He turned slightly to catch her eyes. "I didn't want you to think I'd stood you up."

"So you drove over here?"

At some point, their fingers had found each other, and his thumb stroked the back of hers gently. "It was impulsive."

"It was darling," she said. Then, remembering his activities all weekend long, she wrangled her hand away from his and shifted her body to face front. "Though I'm surprised you could squeeze me in."

She felt him move his arm around her shoulders and she forced herself not to lean back into it, even when his fingers lightly massaged her shoulder.

"I was in Bethesda, Savannah. At the military hospital, where I had a super-sexy dinner with my friend …" Her narrowed eyes whipped around to find his, but she was confused to find his wide and innocent. And, damn it, teasing. "… Lieutenant Barry Stevenson. We served together. In Afghanistan."

"You weren't … I mean, you didn't have … That is, you weren't—"

"I understand Miss Potts made a very innocent trip appear to be more than it actually was. Though I'm incredibly chuffed that you care."

Savannah felt the hot, red flush cover her chest and neck, creeping up to cover her cheeks. "She led me to believe …"

"I don't know why she would have done that. I don't … *keep company* with anyone."

The heat in her cheeks was almost painful now, and she reached forward for the iced tea pitcher, pouring two glasses and appreciating the coolness against her fingers. What a fool. What a complete and utter idiot. Oh boy, would she have some choice words for Matilda J. Potts on Wednesday.

"When did you get home?" she asked weakly, taking a sip of her tea. Though she had poured him a glass, he hadn't moved his arm to take it, and his fingers continued the heavenly rhythm, massaging her shoulder. She never wanted him to stop.

"Fifteen minutes ago."

She turned to look at him, cocking her head to the side. "You came right here?"

He nodded, looking slightly sheepish. "It's four o'clock."

"It's four o'clock." She winced, shaking her head. "When you canceled, I made plans with Scarlet. We're picking out my maid of honor dress today. Did I tell you that my sister's getting married in July?"

"I heard through the grapevine."

"Miss Potts?"

"The one and only."

"We're going to have to keep an eye on her," remarked Savannah, grinning at him, loving how his good eye crinkled when he smiled back.

He finally slid his arm away, shifting forward on the swing. "I guess I'd better be going, then. But Savannah ..."

She didn't know what he was about to ask her, but he bit his lower lip, looking down at his hand on his thigh.

"Stay for dinner on Wednesday?" He looked up at her, and she saw the uncertainty in his eyes, the hope, the warmth.

She nodded. "Do you still want me to come at four?"

"Sure. We'll do the interview first, and then we can just ..."

"Have dinner," she finished, wondering if he could hear her heartbeat. It pounded so thunderously in her ears, surely everyone on her street could hear it.

"Why Savannah," her mother said cheerfully, stepping out onto the porch, followed by Scarlet, who hovered behind, looking wide-eyed and uncertain as she flicked nervous glances at Asher's arm and face. "I didn't know you had a visitor."

Asher stood up immediately, offering his good hand to Judy Carmichael. "Mrs. Carmichael. I'm—"

"Asher Lee. Of course you are." Savannah thanked God for her mother's kindness. She didn't flinch or shudder or gawk as she beheld Asher's imperfect face. She beamed at him. "You have your mother's eyes."

"Yes, ma'am."

"I liked her very much."

"She liked you, ma'am."

"Come for supper on Sunday. Three o'clock."

"Oh, I ..."

"I insist, Asher." She covered his hand with her other hand, patting gently to seal the deal before releasing him. "We'll wait for you in the car, button."

Asher and Savannah watched as Judy and Scarlet made their way around the house.

"Damn," Asher said. "I should've told her I liked her

muffins. And cookies. And scones."

"You can tell her on Sunday," said Savannah, reaching out to touch his arm in farewell.

"Savannah, I ..."

She looked up to meet his eyes as they walked side by side down the porch steps, the back of his hand lightly brushing the back of hers with every step.

"I just ..."

"Me too, Asher," she said softly. And then, because she was so glad to see him, and so glad not to feel so damn sad anymore, she leaned toward him on tiptoe and pressed her lips gently to his left cheek.

His lips dropped open in awestruck surprise as she drew back, and she had a brief fantasy of leaning up to kiss *them,* too, but she was already feeling a little light-headed from that peck on his warm cheek. She turned toward the driveway, sprinting away and turning back only to wave when she heard him call, "Wednesday!" from behind.

CHAPTER 7

The first time you talk until dawn

Asher didn't tell her to dress fancy, but when she arrived on
Wednesday in a skimpy silver top that clung to her breasts,
fancy dark-blue jeans that hugged her ass, and black ballet flats,
his jaw just about dropped. Her hair was pulled into a loose
braid at the nape of her neck, and she wore silver bracelets on
her left wrist that jangled as she handed a small foil-covered
plate to Miss Potts. He'd seen her dressed like a country miss
and a disheveled city girl, but sophisticated was new.
Sophisticated made his blood hot and his body hard. How in the
world was it possible that he had even an outside chance with
such a woman?

He watched from the top of the stairs as she greeted Miss
Potts.

"Well, Savannah Carmichael. Don't you look just lovely?"

"I was invited to stay for dinner." He heard the wariness in
her voice.

"Of course you were. And Asher asked specifically for a
picnic in the grove."

"A picnic?"

"Have you been to the grove?" asked Miss Potts.

Savannah shook her head.

"It's a special spot," Miss Potts said, patting Savannah's
cheek in a motherly gesture. "Oh, and dear, I'm so sorry if I led
you astray during our phone conversation on Sunday."

"I'm sure you are," answered Savannah, her voice level but cool.

"I'm a terrible tease," said Miss Potts winking at her before bustling into the kitchen, leaving Asher to continue his descent down the stairs to welcome his guest.

"It's good to see you," he said, reaching out to take her hand. "You look beautiful."

She smiled up at him, lacing her fingers through his as he led her to the stairs.

"There's more to her than meets the eye," murmured Savannah, looking toward the kitchen.

"True enough."

"She deliberately misled me, Asher."

"I know."

"Why would she do that?"

He shrugged, glad he remembered to leave the office door ajar so he didn't have to drop her hand. "Maybe she didn't want you to think I was out of the game."

She pulled on his hand, forcing him to stop and face her before taking a seat in the wingback chairs. "For the record? I never thought you were out of the game."

He gave her his best "don't kid a kidder" look and raised her hand to his lips, brushing her skin with aching tenderness before releasing it to take his seat.

She seemed surprised by his kiss and lingered behind her chair for an extra moment before joining him.

"Well, even if I did …," she said in a breathy voice, thick with some sort of wonderful emotion that he could easily fall in love with. She raised her eyes to his, and the heat there nearly made him jump her. "… I certainly don't anymore."

***

Asher had stopped in the kitchen to pick up the picnic basket on their way outdoors, and Miss Potts had whispered something to him that made him blush and give her a stern look as he took the basket. Savannah considered asking him what she'd said, but her own nerves were getting the better of her. At no point had he asked her out on a date, or called tonight a date, and yet it was, hands down, the sexiest, most thoughtful, most romantic date she'd ever been on, and it had barely started.

An outdoor picnic? In a place called the grove? Girls would swoon for less.

Which made her feelings about everything more confusing than ever. That she cared for Asher had been well established in her mind over the weekend, but following his perfect-looking body from behind through the woods, she wondered where exactly she wanted her feelings to lead her. To a special friendship? To a relationship? To love?

Yet again they'd had a marvelous conversation in his office, and he'd told her about his decision to attend U.Va. and why medicine had appealed to him as a career. He'd been a member of the prestigious, secretive Delta Kappa Epsilon fraternity, and refused to tell her about his hazing experiences, though he did lift his pant leg to show her a crude tattoo in Greek letters near his ankle, raising his eyebrows merrily when she winced.

It was definitely where she'd start this week's piece—with that little tattoo—though that was another thing. She hadn't told him yet about her new angle: to portray their budding friendship, rather than tell a straightforward story about his life. And aside from the tattoo anecdote, she had no idea what tone to take in this week's piece. Should she mention her fit of jealousy at being misled by Miss Potts? Should she describe the leapings of her heart when he arrived on her doorstep? And what about tonight? Arguably her "story" started now, when the formal interview was over and they continued to explore the budding attraction between them. But was she prepared to share the nitty-gritty of her relationship with Asher? And, most troubling to her, would he object?

She shrugged away her concerns. He'd given her permission to interview him, right? How she chose to portray the content of their conversations was her decision, right? Of course, and of course. Anyway, she hadn't even started the next part of the piece yet. If, at some point, she felt that her story was somehow trespassing on his privacy, she could share it with him then. There was simply no need to bring it up tonight.

All thoughts of her article and her feelings and her confusion and nerves turned to awe as the grove came into view. Much to Savannah's surprise and delight, the grove turned out to be a rustic dining pavilion set in the middle of an apple orchard about a five-minute walk through the woods from the main house.

On a brick patio sat a large wooden table in light wood with six comfortable chairs. Adjacent was a seating area with a love seat, two easy chairs, and a low, rustic table set before an outdoor fireplace.

At each corner of the patio stood an authentic-looking totem pole, and from the tops of the poles, metal bars extended diagonally up to the center, all four bars meeting over the middle of the pavilion, where a deer antler chandelier cast soft light over the entire area. You could tent the whole area with those poles if you chose, but tonight they were wrapped with tiny white twinkle lights that gave the entire setup a fairy-tale quality.

"Oh, Asher," she said, meeting his eyes as he lifted the picnic basket to the table. "It's breathtaking."

***

Yes, he thought, staring at her face in the soft light of dusk. *It is*.

He hadn't been able to hold her hand as they trekked through the woods since he'd been holding the basket, and for the first time since they'd started meeting, he wasn't wearing his prosthesis. It was okay, though. He'd sensed her skittishness as they left his office, and frankly he was feeling a little out of his depth too. He hadn't asked a woman out in over ten years, and though he hadn't called it a date, it was pretty clear that's what it was, wasn't it?

Or was it? He was pretty sure she'd been jealous of his nonexistent lover last weekend. They held hands easily now, and she'd even kissed his cheek on Monday afternoon. But just about all those gestures could fall under the behavior of close friends. And though he loved his growing friendship with Savannah Carmichael, he wanted far more from her, and tonight was his first move toward making that happen.

He took his iPod out of his pocket and plugged it into the docking station that connected to an outdoor audio system. A moment later, soft music filled the grove.

Her face tilted up, smiling in wonder, as she took in the details.

"Did you build this place?" she finally asked.

He shook his head. "Not entirely. My grandfather built the patio and fireplace back in the fifties. My father added the totem poles and beams. There's a mesh tent and a full tent that can be added to the poles to ward off bugs or the elements. I added the electricity and decided to split the patio into dining and lounging."

"You 'lounge' here a lot?"

He shrugged, opening the picnic basket and finding one of two bottles of wine. He checked it out: a decent vintage with a twist-off cap. He said a word of silent thanks to Miss Potts. Corkscrews were not his forte. He removed two wineglasses from the basket.

"Chardonnay?" he asked.

"Sure. I'd love some." Savannah gestured to the table. "Should I …?"

"Why don't we relax first?" He nodded toward the fireplace.

He watched as she walked over to the little sitting area, part of him praying that she'd choose the love seat. His heart dipped when she didn't. She chose an easy chair instead, sitting on the edge, wringing her hands and playing with her rings. She was nervous; he needed to remedy that.

He brought her a glass of wine before returning for his, then sat down alone on the love seat across from her. "Are you cold? I can light the fire."

Savannah took a sip of her wine. "Later?"

Well, at least that's promising.

"Can I ask you something?" she asked.

He nodded. "Anything."

"You never said, and I'm not always very good at reading between the lines. But … is this a date?"

Her directness surprised Asher, but he felt a little relieved to have a chance to answer the question.

"Yes."

"What about friends?" she asked, her eyes luminous in the soft light.

"Friends is good," he answered, putting his glass on the table between them and lifting his arm to the back of the love seat. He stared at her, wanting her beside him, amazed that she was here with him, worried about doing anything that might make her run away from his face and his arm and his leg and his shattered life. His hand patted the back of the love seat. "Come here."

She sat up a little straighter, and, intentionally or not, it made her breasts thrust forward inside her little silver top. His eyes flicked to them before returning to her face.

"I hated the thought of you with someone else last weekend," she whispered.

"I wasn't with anyone else. I was thinking of you."

"We barely know each other."

"Good thing I'm not asking you to marry me."

"If I come sit by you, what're you going to do?"

He swallowed. Unbelievably, she was here. On a date with him. Best not to overthink it, because it was already too dreamlike to be true. All that mattered was that he had a chance with her. He was all in at this point—there was no room for half measures, no turning back.

He held her eyes and spoke firmly. "I'm going to kiss you, Savannah."

Her eyes widened, and he heard her short, surprised intake of breath. After an eternal moment, she stood up and sat down beside him.

***

Asher turned his full face to her, and Savannah was again struck by how little his injuries affected her now, almost as if she were immune to them, almost as if he wouldn't be the same without them. His eyes searched hers as he withdrew his hand from the back of the couch, reaching up to cup her cheek. She leaned into the strong warmth, letting her eyes close as the wine hit her head and the music swelled, and she felt his lips touch hers.

His hand slid backward, his fingers weaving into her hair with more pressure, pulling her face forward, and her heart kicked into a gallop as his lips moved on hers, brushing, nipping, hypnotic. She leaned forward, pressing her hands against his chest, the hardness making her breathless as his tongue gently traced the seam of her lips, coaxing hers apart. Her mouth opened softly, reflexively welcoming him, and when their tongues touched, tentative at first, the wild buzzing in her stomach felt so hot, she moaned softly into his mouth.

His hand skimmed down her face to her neck, down her arm to her waist, which he encircled, jerking her against him with such strength and certainty, her fingers curled against his chest, fisting in his shirt as heat pooled below her waist.

Savannah had been kissed before—clumsily, hesitantly, passionately—but this kiss was on another plane of chemistry entirely. It was as though his taste, his smell, his touch, had been engineered solely for the purpose of making her give in. He kissed her long and fast and slow and wet and deep, and as their tongues twisted against each other Savannah's nipples beaded, and she arched against him, hearing a desperate groaning, growling sound coming from his throat as his iron-like arm tightened around her.

His lips skimmed down her cheek to her neck, his tongue darting out to lick the warm skin where her pulse fluttered wildly, pressing his lips against her while she inhaled raggedly.

"Asher," she gasped, trembling and panting as she rolled her hips instinctively toward him.

"Mmm," he breathed, taking her earlobe between his teeth and making her gasp again from the sharp pleasure of the sensation.

"Oh my," she said, whimpering softly as she wetted her lips, trying to catch her breath unsuccessfully as the world continued swirling around them.

"Your skin's like warm honey," he whispered so close to her ear, she shivered, and she felt him readjust his hand, slipping it under her flimsy camisole to flatten against the skin of her lower back. "So sweet. So damn sweet, Savannah."

She murmured incoherently, letting her hands slide up to his shoulders and loop around his neck. She buried her face in his shoulder, and he held her close as their hearts leaped and pounded against each other, and the strength of Savannah's newfound feelings made her feel invincible and terrified and unsatisfied, and wanting so much more from this man who'd lived his life in the shadows for way too long.

He pulled back, his hot breath fanning her face, smelling slightly of Chardonnay and lust as he rested his forehead on hers.

"Jesus, Savannah," he said in a rough, gravelly voice.

"Yeah," she sighed, her eyes finally fluttering open to find his looking, deep and drugged, into hers.

"That was …" He licked his lips, leaning forward to catch her upper lip between his teeth and tug lightly. "I don't even …"

"I know," she murmured, finally getting her bearings. She tilted her face and closed her eyes to kiss him again, softly, gently, a "see you later," not a "farewell."

"I don't want to stop," he whispered hotly against her lips.

Savannah shivered, pulling on his neck even though there was nowhere else for him to go. She adjusted slightly so that her front was flush with his, her breasts rising and falling into him, every cell in her body wanting more from him, more skin, less clothes, more heat, less of anything standing in the way of release and relief.

He kissed her, then pulled back to find her eyes. "Where'd you come from, Savannah Carmichael? And why me?"

"From across town," she said softly, nestling her cheek against his shoulder and opening her eyes to the thousands of white lights roped over their heads. "Because you said yes."

"Yes to you?"

"Yes to letting me interview you."

"Maybe I was saying yes to your mom's brownies."

"Hey," she said, grabbing a handful of his hair at the nape of his neck and tugging. "I made those."

He laughed, the vibrations of his chest against her stimulated breasts feeling like bliss and torture at the same time.

"Speaking of food, you hungry, baby?"

Baby? Her breath caught momentarily from the unexpected sound of the sexy endearment tumbling from his mouth. *Yes. For more of you. For you calling me baby again. For the weight of your body pressing down against mine. Preferably with no clothes. Just skin and heat and—*

"Savannah?"

"Mmm," she answered with a little whimper. "I'm starving."

***

Asher watched her eyes sparkling across the table as she laughed between bites of cold fried chicken, telling him about her first assignment in New York: an exposé about dog owners who didn't pick up after their dogs. She was a good storyteller, and the material was amusing, so he made himself smile in all the right places, but he was having trouble concentrating. His body was still wired and reeling from what had just happened between them.

It had taken a fair amount of courage to make a pass at her, but his misgivings had been quickly overcome as he watched her eyes close when he reached up to touch her cheek. Her face was so beautiful in the soft light, so trusting and yielding, and when he leaned down to touch his lips to hers, something had given way within him, making space for something old and forgotten, that he'd lived without for too long, that he feared he'd never know again. But it wasn't just about the physical connection to a beautiful woman, it was about Savannah herself, ambitious and driven, brave and jealous and faulted, who seemed to look beyond his injuries—with terrifying precision—and see his heart.

He was falling in love with her. He was certain now.

"… so you can imagine. I'm twenty-three, trying to confidently follow behind this older, balding man with a shih tzu, to pester him about why he was ignoring the 'scoop it' ordinance, and my photographer is following behind me, grumbling about not being paid enough for this kind of stupid-work." She grinned, taking another sip of wine. "Education via humiliation."

"Real-world experience," Asher agreed, raising his glass to cheer her.

"You know what I've been wondering?" she asked, cocking her head to the side in the gesture he was starting to love so much. "Why you deferred Johns Hopkins. I mean, you graduate from U.Va. with honors and have a mostly free ride at med school waiting for you. Then, out of nowhere, you enlist. I admire the service, but I don't understand the motive."

There was the reporter again, and though he liked Reporter Savannah, he liked Friend Savannah and Kisser Savannah a little more.

"I was a senior in college when 9/11 happened. All I wanted to do was help," he said simply, taking a sip of wine. "But, hey, I thought we did today's interview at four."

"Oh," she said, sitting back, rebuffed. "I'm sorry, I …"

He winced. He hadn't meant to embarrass her. "No. I'm sorry. It's a fair question, interview or not."

"I do that," she said, frowning at her plate. "My sister hates it. I forget to be a person. I can't stop chasing the story. Every story. Any story."

"I like that about you," he said, reaching his hand across the table, palm up. It took her a moment to place her hand in his, but he was relieved when she did. "I like how ambitious you are. How focused. I admire it."

"It's not always a plus."

The pad of his thumb reflexively stroked the soft pillow of her palm. "What do you mean?"

"I have tunnel vision. Not just about my job. When I'm into something, *passionate* about it, I can't see the forest for the trees, you know?"

"Are you speaking generally or specifically here?"

She shrugged. "Both, I guess."

"I know you lost your job, Savannah. At the *Sentinel*. And I know why."

She raised her eyes from her plate, a frown souring her expression as she searched his face. She must have decided to err on the side of caution because she pulled her hand away to pick up her glass and take a long sip.

"Like I said," she said ruefully, "I have a tendency to lose perspective."

"It wasn't your fault."

"The hell it wasn't."

"Patrick Monroe is a bastard," growled Asher.

"You talk like you know him."

"Would it surprise you if I did?"

"Very much," she said, confusion narrowing her brown eyes.

"We spent two summers together at Camp Dooley in Upstate New York."

Her lips parted in surprise, but it was clear from her expression she knew of the upper-crust summer camp for privileged boys. "You're kidding me!"

"I'm not. And he was as much of an ass wipe then as now."

Her eyes brightened again, he noticed, with relief and pleasure.

"I smell a story," she said.

"Does it smell like duplicity and cheating?"

"Yes, in fact, it does. What was he like then? Pat?"

"Superior. Charismatic. Spineless."

"So you really liked him," she deadpanned.

"Yeah, lots," said Asher.

"You rich boys and your summer camps."

"Don't lump me in with him. I may live in a cave, but I'm not a snake."

"Why only two years? At Camp Dooley?"

"He got kicked out for fraternizing with a couple of the girls from Camp Kristina next door."

"At the same time?"

"You know Pat."

"Unfortunately." Her eyes went dull as she finished her wine in one long gulp. "He ruined my life."

He winced at her tone—the defeat in it, the quiet surrender.

"Nah," he said. "The *Sentinel's* not the only rag in the country."

"But it's the best."

"That's a matter of opinion. I hear the *Phoenix Times* has won a lot of awards in the past few years. Maddox McNabb seems to get a lot of hot scoops, from what I can gather."

"Well, don't you just have your finger on the pulse of my life."

"Yes, baby," he said, low and slow, remembering the feeling of her pulse beneath his lips. "I do."

The way her cheeks flushed and her tongue darted out to lick her lips, he knew her mind had flown to the same airspace. He refilled her glass as she looked away shyly.

"You researched me," she said, taking the glass and holding it without sipping.

"I had to know whom I was dealing with, Savannah. I've protected my life from the outside world for almost a decade. I couldn't let just anyone in."

"You know I have a weakness for my … sources." Her eyes searched his, and he knew what she was asking: *Did you think I'd be an easy mark?*

"In a million years, I never thought I'd have a chance with you, Savannah." His voice was measured and low, and when she looked up, her eyes were soft. He could tell she knew he was telling the truth.

He watched her breasts move faster as her breathing grew more shallow. He glanced at her neck, where he saw her pulse pounding, and it did terrible, awful, miraculous, hopeful things to his body.

"How about dessert?"

***

As midnight approached, Asher pulled the two easy chairs over to the love seat so they could both put their feet up. Savannah kicked off her shoes, resting her head on his chest in contentment as he held her close with his good arm. They'd barely taken a break from talking since dinner, and Savannah's mother's key lime tartlets had been consumed hours ago.

"What do you want out of life?" asked Asher, his hand trailing up and down her back and making her shiver lightly. "Where do you want to be in five years?"

"I want to be the top investigative journalist at one of the top newspapers or magazines in the country. But I want to report locally on city news, not nationally, because I also want to settle down. I know it's a myth—perfect job, loving husband, 2.3 kids, a cocker spaniel, and a house within an hour of a symphony, stadium, and the sea—but I want it. The myth. Someday. Five years would be good." She took a deep breath and closed her eyes, listening to the beating of his heart. "What about you?"

"Two weeks ago, I would have said nothing."

"Asher, that's terrible."

"But true."

"And now?"

"Now I'm getting grabby."

"It feels good to want," said Savannah.

"It feels terrible to want," he said softly, "when your chances of getting what you want are so slim."

His words made anger surge within her. She leaned away from him, catching his eyes in the firelight. "Stop doing that."

"What?"

"Lowballing yourself."

"I think I'm reality-balling myself."

"No," she insisted fiercely. "You're not."

She reached for his face with both hands for the first time, her palms landing simultaneously on smooth skin and scarred skin. She held him still and deliberately looked into his eyes— his normal eye and the other eye, whose socket had been damaged by the detonation of that goddamned IED. She lingered on that eye until he closed them both and then she leaned forward to press her lips against the mangled skin beneath it. His breath was ragged as she placed a second kiss on the injured skin of his cheek, then on the corner of his lips.

He roared to life, his incredibly strong arm pulling her onto his lap, his mouth opening to kiss her senseless, to kiss her like crazy, to drown her and consume her and make her forget all the kisses that came before.

She rolled her hips against him, lowering her hands to his neck as his hand slid up the skin of her back then around to her front so he could cup her breast through the lace of her bra. He kneaded her skin gently as his growing erection pushed up against her thighs, and she rolled over it again to let him know he shouldn't stop.

He sucked on her tongue as his thumb and forefinger found her nipple, rolling it, teasing it into a hard point before moving to the other. She ran her hands through his shaggy hair, grasping, clutching, arching against him as her insides ran hot and wet with the power of her arousal, her want, her need.

She rocked against him as his hand slipped away from her breasts, reaching up to cup her cheek and mellow out their kiss, slow it down. He nipped at her lips, softer and lighter, murmuring softly, "Savannah, Savannah, Savannah."

"Don't stop," she sighed.

"We should."

"We shouldn't."

"I've never wanted anyone as much as I want you," he said, kissing a trail down her neck.

"Take me," she said, whimpering as he licked a spot where

her neck and shoulder met.

"You might regret it, baby," he said, his voice thick with lust as he continued kissing her neck, the exposed skin of her chest, his fingers grazing her jawline, his thumb a gentle pressure against her windpipe that made her feel vulnerable to him, at his mercy. She trusted him. She loved it.

"I won't. No regrets, Asher. None."

He laughed softly against the warm skin of her chest, before pulling back and gazing up at her face. "We've finished two bottles of wine."

"I'm not drunk."

"I know you're not," he said gently. "But you're not exactly sober either. I wouldn't be much of a gentleman if I pressed my advantage,"

He kissed her forehead, then helped ease her off his lap, breathing deeply, then sighing as she nestled back up against his chest.

"It's not that I don't want to," he said. "You have no idea how much I want to."

"I have an idea," she answered, looking down at where his pants tented aggressively.

He shifted his hips uncomfortably. "Well, what can I say? You do things to me, Savannah Carmichael. I'm putty in your hands."

"More like cement."

"Savannah," he warned.

"But you're not in my hands."

"Savannah!"

"Even though it would be nice if you were."

"Christ."

"Five-year plan," she reminded him saucily. "I want to know what it is. And no more of this crap about not being able to get what you want. I'm here, aren't I?"

His voice was low and emotional when he responded. "You're here, baby."

She snuggled closer, and they talked until the sun came up and she fell asleep to the rhythm of his heart.

CHAPTER 8

The first time you bring him home to meet the family

When Asher woke up the next morning, the first thing he felt was the wonderfully heavy weight of Savannah's head against his chest. The first thing he saw, however, was the disapproving face of Miss Potts, who stood over them with her hands on her hips.

He blinked at her, his arm tightening around Savannah protectively.

"Her mother called."

"Her mother?" he asked, half asleep.

"Wondering where she was since she didn't come home last night."

"She must have forgotten to call. We talked until dawn."

"Her mother was *very* worried."

"She's an adult, Miss Potts. She's twenty-six."

"Tell that to Judy Carmichael." Miss Potts pursed her lips. "What about her reputation?"

"This isn't the 1800s."

"Lucky for you, or Frank Carmichael might be out here with a shotgun in the next little while. And she'd be the next Mrs. Lee."

He refused to rise to that specific bait, regardless of how the very idea made his heart beat faster.

"Humph," said Miss Potts. "Wake her up and come up to the house. I'll make eggs and biscuits before she goes."

She turned to go, and Asher called after her softly, careful not to wake up Sleeping Beauty. "Miss Potts."

She turned, her expression still disapproving.

"I care about her. A lot."

"Caring about someone means looking out for their best interest. Always. Without exception." She put a finger to her chin, tapping thoughtfully. "I'll have to make something special for Sunday. As a peace offering."

Asher grinned. "Mama's peach cobbler?"

"The very thing," said Miss Potts nodding approvingly, before turning to head back into the woods.

Savannah stirred in her sleep, nestling closer to him, and he held her a little tighter, kissing the top of her head. She settled back against him, breathing slow and deep.

He rolled Miss Potts's words around in his head: *Caring about someone means looking out for their best interest. Always. Without exception.*

Savannah was eight years younger than he, young and vibrant and beautiful. Whatever she wrote for the *Phoenix Times* would be a surefire hit, and she'd move on from Danvers, from him. It twisted his heart into knots to think about losing her after sharing a night like last night. And yet it's what she wanted most in the world: to be the best reporter at a big-city newspaper.

And for him, leaving Danvers—leaving the sanctuary of his home—was still unthinkable.

There was no future for them. He certainly couldn't ask her to hide in the shadows with him, nor could he follow her to a city where people would gawk at him like the freak, the beast, he was. It was a long shot that she'd even be interested in him somewhere other than the safety of his house in Danvers. No, there was no future for Asher Lee and Savannah Carmichael.

The thing about surviving something truly tragic is that it changes your expectations forever. You make do with very little. You're grateful for crumbs. You make the best of small mercies. You endure large trials. You understand that life owes you nothing. You expect nothing, and when something wonderful happens, you don't trust it. You know it can't possibly last.

He kissed the top of Savannah's head again with quiet yearning. When the time came, he would let her go. But for now, for the next handful of weeks, she was his, and nothing—nothing—would compel him to walk away from her until it was time for him to let her go.

***

"I've decided," said Scarlet at dinner on Thursday night. "Vegas! Won't it be wild?! Las Vegas, Vanna! For my bachelorette party!"

Savannah raised one eyebrow at her sister, counting down the moments when she could excuse herself from the table and crawl into bed. After sleeping for only a few hours beside Asher last night, she was cranky and overtired today. Not that she wouldn't brighten up in an instant were he to suddenly walk into the room.

She sighed, a little disgusted with herself. She was in *that* stage. The pathetic stage when there's only one person in the world who can make you happy and every moment without him feels like a waste of time. The desperate stage when you long for that person so completely, you can't think straight from missing his touch, remembering the way his eyes softened when they looked at you or the groaning sound he makes in the back of his throat when he—

"Christ, Savannah! Are you listening to me?"

"Language, Katie Scarlet!" chastised their father, Frank, before tucking back into his baked beans.

"Well, cheese and rice, she's my goldarned maid of honor, and I'm plannin' my own bachelorette party. Mama!" she whined, looking to Judy for solidarity.

Judy turned to her older daughter, speaking gently. "Button, what do you think of this idea to go to Las Vegas?"

"Scarlet hated New York. It's tame compared to Vegas. That's what I think."

Scarlet got up and threw her balled-up napkin on the table in front of her sister. "Savannah Calhoun Carmichael, you're the … the *worst* maid of honor … ever!" Then she ran from the dining room, and Savannah had a very strong notion that there would be tears and pillow throwing above their heads in the next few minutes.

Savannah sighed, feeling exhausted, feeling bad for how she'd just upset her sister, but she also felt sorry for herself—seeing Asher tomorrow wasn't soon enough, and she missed him to aching even though he lived fifteen minutes away.

She reached for Scarlet's napkin and folded it slowly, then folded her own. "I'll go talk to her, Mama."

Judy stopped Savannah by taking her hand. "Talk to me first."

"It's nothing. I'm just tired."

Her father, who was an expert at sensing girl talk coming around the bend, cleared his throat and excused himself from the table to watch his programs.

"You were out awful late last night, Savannah. You getting serious about this boy?"

"Asher? Oh, I don't know," she said. "I like him. I know that. I haven't known him long enough to figure out the rest."

"He likes you too."

"I know he does, Mama."

"Then why do you look so miserable?"

"Honestly? I'd brighten like a button if he were here right now."

"Ah," her mother nodded. "It's like that."

"And I have to write this article, and I promised it would be about our friendship—the story of us becoming unlikely friends—but it feels like we're becoming more than friends, and I'm not sure I have permission to write about that. But if I don't, I lose my chance at this job. And I need this job, Mama. I'm out of options. I need to make this work."

"Sounds like you need to talk to Asher. Make sure he's okay with it."

"Does it matter?" asked Savannah, feeling mercenary. "It won't be printed anywhere locally, and he'll never leave Danvers. And I need this story." She cringed, shaking her head back and forth. "It matters. Of course it matters. I know it matters. It matters so much it's eating me up."

Judy patted her daughter's hand. "You'll do the right thing, button. I know you will."

Savannah wished she had her mother's confidence in her. "I'll go talk to Scarlet."

"She *is* gettin' married," her mother reminded her. "And I know our Scarlet's been with Trent Hamilton forever, but she's entitled to some nerves. She just wants her big sister there for her. It's not so much to ask, Vanna."

"I know, Mama. I'll tell her I'm sorry."

"But Vegas is a dreadful idea."

Savannah smiled for the first time since she'd left Asher's house this morning. "Myrtle Beach would suit her much better."

"That's my smart girl!" said Judy, beaming at Savannah and patting her hand again.

***

Savannah sent the next installment of "Asher Lee: An All-American Story" to Maddox by noon on Friday, and she waited, tense, to find out what he thought. Her phone rang by 12:30.

"Carmichael? Maddox McNabb here. I read your piece."

"And?"

"Something's missing. You're holding something back."

"How do you mean?"

"Your general descriptions are just fine. But the way you describe *him*—it's half-assed. It's like you're afraid to say too much. This was a date, wasn't it? This dinner in the grove?"

Savannah grimaced. She'd tried to write the piece as two friends having dinner together. Apparently it didn't fly. "I guess so, sir."

"Let me give you some advice, Carmichael. Give it heart,

or give it up. You falling for this man? Asher?"

Savannah gritted her teeth. She'd promised a human interest story, not her personal business. It felt like whoring herself. Worse, it felt like whoring Asher.

"Your silence tells me all I need to know. That's the story, Carmichael. How you went after an interview and fell in love instead. Like it or lump it, that's the story I want. That's the story I need. That's the story my readers will ooh and aah about on the Fourth of July. The beautiful, hard-nosed reporter who fell for the mysterious, disfigured war vet. It's *Beauty and the Beast* with 'The Star-Spangled Banner' playing in the background. Don't like it? Don't write it. We go our separate ways. You decide, kid."

Her hackles rose. "But Mr. McNabb, I can do a fine piece on Asher Lee's injuries, the way this town turned their backs on him, how he reads any book he can get his hand on, and went to U.Va. and got into Johns Hopkins but decided to serve his country instead. His story is remarkable. *He's* remarkable. I'm nobody. I'm nothing. No one wants to read a story about me."

"Wrong!" bellowed Maddox McNabb. "I hate to tell you, Carmichael, but right here, right now? *You're* the story. Name of the game is human interest. You're human. I'm interested. Either rewrite it by tomorrow, or don't contact me again." And he hung up.

Savannah clenched her jaw, lowering the phone from her ear to her lap, her head spinning. Damn it, she was stuck. And damn it, she hated being stuck. There had to be another way: another person she could interview, another war vet who had a story to tell. But no, Maddox McNabb wouldn't be interested in that story. He already had a humdinger on the line.

She took a deep breath, lying back on her bed and staring despondently at the ceiling. Whatever was happening between her and Asher felt too good, too fine, to be used as fodder for a news story. It felt low and cheap even to consider it. And yet she was a good writer, wasn't she? All of her professors at NYU had told her so, and she'd been the fastest rising reporter at the

THE *Vixen* AND THE VET

Sentinel before her inglorious fall. Couldn't she pull it off in a way that would appease McNabb but not expose the most private man she'd ever met? *There must be a way*, she thought.

And then it came to her: she occasionally used a pen name for articles she wrote at the *Sentinel*. She called herself Cassandra Calhoun after her mother, Judith Cassandra Calhoun Carmichael. Couldn't she do that for this article too? Of course she could! She could be Cassandra and Asher could be … Adam. And as long as she didn't mention Danvers, she could write whatever she liked, Asher's privacy would be protected and no one would ever be the wiser.

***

Asher made sure to greet her, reaching for her hand and pulling her against his chest as soon as she walked through the door on Friday afternoon. The hours had crawled by without her stories and teasing and mind-bending kisses, and all he wanted was to spend as much time with her as possible before she left him again.

"I missed you," she said softly, her breath against his cheek making his body harden everywhere.

"You too."

"It's terrible to be this infatuated."

"I agree."

"I haven't felt this alive in years."

"Me either."

"Screw the interview," she said breathlessly. "Let's make out."

He saw stars. Literally. Stars. How was this possibly his life? Beautiful women did not show up on the doorsteps of disabled vets and proposition them.

"Are you an alien?" he asked.

"Not that I know of."

"Are we on *Candid Camera*?"

She took a quick look around the room. "You never know,

but my guess is no."

"Is someone paying you a vast sum of money to make me feel like this?"

She bit her lower lip, as if deep in thought. "Not that I recall, but if a million dollars suddenly hits my account, I'll give you half."

"You must be for real. Fine. You win. Let's go make out."

He turned toward the stairs, but this time they didn't go left at the split, they went right down the west side of the gallery, past door after walnut door until they came to the sixth and final door on the right. Then he stopped. He dropped her hand and stood back, seizing her eyes with his. "My bedroom. Your decision."

She grinned and turned the knob.

"Just so we're clear," she said, facing him from the center of the room, as he closed the door behind them. "I said 'make out' not 'have sex.'"

His eyes widened as they always did when she shocked the hell out of him.

"I just wanted you to myself for a while," she added quietly.

"It would have been pretty bold of me to just assume we were having sex, Savannah."

She pushed her brown straight hair behind her ear, and his fingers twitched, remembering how soft her hair was. His nose remembered that it smelled like lemons. His body remembered that it was attached to her head, which was attached to the torso that held the most gorgeous breasts he'd ever had the privilege to touch. His pants started to tent again. He sat down quickly at the foot of his bed and crossed his leg over his knee.

Savannah surveyed the rest of his room. "As long as we're on the same page. Oh."

She crossed to his bureau, picking up a picture of him taken the summer he turned sixteen. It was the last picture ever taken of him with his parents. She caressed the glass, turning to face him. "Oh, Asher."

Of course. She'd never seen him as he looked before the explosion. Now she knew. Now she knew just how bad it was. He looked away, ready to follow her to the door and back down the hall to the safety of his study, where they could sit in wingback chairs a foot apart and he could start telling her all about his time in the Army while his heart withered and died in his chest.

When he looked up, she was facing him with tears in her eyes, and he braced himself.

"Your parents," she said.

He couldn't speak.

"This is you with your parents."

He nodded.

"I can't imagine how much you must miss them."

She placed the silver frame gently on his bureau and walked the few steps to sit beside him on the bed.

He turned to her. "Savannah," he started, about to suggest they head to the study, saving her from having to make an excuse out of kindness or some misguided sense of obligation to him.

"Asher," she said, placing a hand on his chest and pushing him back until he was lying on the bed and she was lying beside him. "Kiss me."

Thanking God for yet another reprieve, he rolled on top of her, bracing on his elbows as he palmed her cheek with fierce tenderness. "You terrify me."

She smiled, wiggling beneath him before pushing her pelvis up against his. "I'm harmless."

"You're lethal."

"I'm waiting."

And then his mouth claimed hers, and she didn't have to wait anymore.

***

Savannah reached up to run her fingers over the taut muscles of his back as he kissed her, his tongue reclaiming its captured territory from Wednesday night, and she sighed into his mouth, grateful to be with him again, grateful that everything she'd felt on Wednesday came back in a perfect rush of heat and lust and happiness.

God, what was happening to her? She was becoming this thing that needs Asher Lee. She could barely enter his house without demanding his mouth on hers, his body pressed against hers, his tongue stroking and laving and sucking on hers. She was losing perspective. She was probably being stupid.

But right this minute, with the glorious weight of his body on hers, it just didn't matter. Nothing mattered but being with him and making the most of every moment. She ran her hands down his back to his waist and loosened his shirt and undershirt, pushing both up his back until his skin was exposed, hot and hard beneath her fingers. He pulled away from her mouth just long enough to grab both shirts behind his neck and tug them over his head, finding her lips again as he rolled her to her side, slipping his hand beneath her T-shirt as his tongue sucked on hers.

All she wanted was to feel her skin flush and hot against his, so she reached back, unfastening her bra so that he had an easier time shoving her shirt and bra over her head with one hand. And then there was nothing between his chest and hers. Nothing.

He reached for her breast, gently kneading the overstimulated skin as he kissed her chin, her neck, the valley at the base of her neck. And then his head dipped lower to capture one hard nipple between his lips, swirling his tongue around it before sucking gently.

A bolt of lightning shot from her nipple to the aching flesh between her thighs and she arched her whole body upward to the source of her pleasure. She moaned softly as he moved to the other breast, loving the tight pink flesh with his tongue before lightly sucking it as he had its twin.

Savannah plunged her hands into his hair, flinching and bucking beneath him, praying he wouldn't stop. Her whole body felt electric, tight and hot deep inside where want coiled like an undetonated bomb, waiting for release, praying for relief.

"Asher," she whispered. "Please …"

Still licking and sucking on her nipple, he slipped his hand into the waistband of her shorts, under her panties, over the soft curls and into the folds of flesh where he found her swollen bud and stroked it gently.

A strangled sound came from Savannah's throat as her head bucked back into the pillow, the dueling sensations of his mouth on her nipple and his finger on her swollen flesh almost too sweet to bear. The pressure started to build inside her, and she felt his fingers enter her as his thumb took over the mind-blowing stroking of her sex.

"Oh God, don't stop,!" she moaned, then cried out as his teeth grazed her nipple and her whole body arched upward, convulsing and shuddering, rushing hot and wet and totally undone. He slid up her body and kissed her slack lips tenderly, then pulled her against his broad, bare chest and held her until she stopped twitching, until she could take a deep breath, until she could form a coherent thought once again.

***

"Was that as good for you as it was for me?" he asked, not even trying to conceal the satisfaction and teasing in his voice.

"Better," she said, turning to him with glassy, amazed eyes.

"How are we feeling?"

"Like a goddess." She took a deep breath and sighed. "For someone with one hand, you're strangely like Vishnu. Everywhere at once."

"You've got to work with what you've got."

"Well, you certainly worked it." She paused. "Practice makes perfect?"

"Quit fishing. I haven't been with anyone since …"

"No one? In eight years? Jesus, Asher. How's that been working out for you?"

"As you noted, I still have my hand."

"Gross," she said, trying unsuccessfully not to giggle. "So I'm …"

"The lucky beneficiary of eight years of pent-up lust."

"Holy cow."

"I might start calling you Isis. The cow-headed goddess."

She braced herself on her elbow to look down at him with a withering gaze. "Don't you dare."

His eyes drank her in. "I'm crazy about you, baby."

"Then kiss me again."

An hour later, after plenty of kissing, she pulled her shirt back over her head, but they stayed in his bed, side by side, staring at each other. He pillowed his damaged face against his damaged elbow, imagining that he looked almost normal to her, not that she seemed to notice his disfiguration very much anymore.

"It's Friday night," he said. "You're young and beautiful. Don't you have a date?"

"Yeah. Here."

"No one else in the wings?"

"Do you seriously think there's a better orgasm to be found in Danvers than the one I just had in this bed, Mr. Magic Fingers?"

"I'm serious, Savannah."

"Shut up, Asher. You're annoying me."

"Fine. But don't say I didn't give you an out."

"Do I look like I want an out?"

"I have to hide here. You don't."

She frowned at him. "Do you?"

"Yes. I do. I scare little children. Hell, I scare adults."

"You don't scare *me*."

"You're an alien."

"You sure know how to flatter a girl."

"I told you I was unpolished."

"Unpolished, my foot," she said. "You're more polished than *me*, Camp-Dooley-Deke-at-U.Va. I never met another man so hard on himself." She leaned forward and kissed him gently.

"Tell me about Maryland."

He grimaced. He wasn't ready to share the details of his trip to Maryland with her. It was too heavy, too serious. Skin grafts and facial reconstruction and prosthetic molds. He didn't want her thinking about all of it when she was with him.

He shrugged. "They took a look at everything. It's routine."

"Do you ever think about … having work done?"

Damn, but he didn't want to talk about this. Especially not with her. He tried to think of something to share that didn't have anything to do with blood and gore and skull-splitting pain. "They, um, they have some pretty cool bionic hands."

Her face brightened. "That sounds promising."

"I hate wearing prosthetic limbs."

"Why?"

"The wool socks that go over my arm are uncomfortable. I never got used to the fit of the sleeve, and the suction fit leaves my stump red for hours afterward. Maybe I never had a good fit, or maybe I didn't give it enough of a chance. I worked up the muscle tone and strength of my left hand instead."

"But you sound interested in this bionic hand."

Grudgingly, he realized he was. He'd mostly mentioned it to veer the conversation away from surgeries, but now that they were actually discussing it, he had to admit how cool they were.

"The technology's amazing. The fingers can pick up anything a real hand can pick up. I watched another vet pick up a penny from a tabletop. It has knuckles, you know? And they attach it to the existing nerve so that my brain could actually give the signals for movement. I couldn't believe it."

Savannah smiled. "It *sounds* amazing."

"Yeah. But I don't know. I'd have to be fitted for it, learn how to use it. I do okay, you know? With what I've got?" He was feeling uncomfortable with this entire conversation and defensive about accepting help and treatment, but he was also trying to keep his voice level and calm.

"You do great." She reached up and touched his face with the backs of her fingers, and he leaned into her. "But you sounded excited. I hope you give it a try."

He knew she was just trying to be nice. He knew that, and yet her comment really bothered him, because it implied that he was in need of improvements. And yes, he knew he was, but he didn't like hearing her say it. "Why?"

"Because it might make your life better."

Bingo. "My life's fine."

"Your life *isn't* fine," she said.

He recoiled like she'd smacked him, the sudden adrenaline burst making him feel winded. "What?"

"Asher, you're the bravest, smartest, most interesting person I've ever met. But by your own admission, you hide here. You're letting your life pass you by when you should be living. A louse like Patrick Monroe should be hiding from the world. *You're* a hero."

"You have no idea what it's like," he said, trying to stay calm, reminding himself that she was only trying to be kind, only trying to help.

"Do *you*? When's the last time you went into town?"

"On Monday. To your house," he said tightly.

"I mean to the store or a restaurant. There are a couple of great restaurants in Danvers."

"They deliver," he tossed back.

"It makes me sad. *You* make me sad."

"*Damn it!*" Pity? He didn't want her goddamned pity. His heart quickened in repulsion and he cringed. He couldn't bear for this woman – for Savannah, who made him feel sexy and alive for the first time in years – to see him through that lens, to offer him pity like he was a wounded weakling, like he wasn't a man. His eyes narrowed as he lashed out at her. "God forbid *you* feel sad. If you don't like the way I'm living my life, Savannah, you don't have to be a part of it."

She'd jumped when he cursed, and now she stared at him, shocked, her eyes wide as saucers. "I—I didn't mean—"

"Believe me, I've heard it all before. I don't need to hear it from you, too."

"Oh," she said softly, biting her lower lip. "Oh."

He wasn't looking for someone to change him, and if that's what this was—Savannah Carmichael on a mission of mercy trying to help the poor crippled war hero find his way back to society's loving bosom by way of bionic hands and facial reconstructions?—well, forget it. It was his body and his decision alone, and if that was her goal here, it was best to part ways now.

"Maybe you should go," he bit out.

It was her turn to recoil as tears brightened her eyes. She rolled away from him, sitting up and swinging her legs over the side of the bed. Despite the pain in his head and his heart, he forced himself not to look, to stay focused on the ceiling.

"I didn't mean to upset you," she said softly, and he heard the tears she was trying to keep at bay.

Oh, hell! Was she about to cry? Damn it, he hadn't meant to—damn it!

He just didn't want anyone coming along and fixing him. She had no idea what it was like to have all of those surgeries in San Antonio when he first got home. Weeks upon weeks of agony as they put him under while they sliced and sutured, trying to make him look normal. And it hadn't worked. None of it had worked. He'd still come home looking like a freak.

She stood up, straightening her shirt, with her back to him. He heard her sniffle quietly, and his heart twisted as a new emotion spiked inside of him: panic.

He finally had someone in his life and he was all but driving her away over a few well-intentioned comments that happened to be triggers for him.

What are you doing, Asher? What the hell are you doing? She didn't mean to upset you. This is your *problem, not hers. Say you're sorry. Make it better. For God's sake, don't let her leave like this.*

"Savannah," he started in a softer voice, "Wait. Please.

I—I didn't mean … I just didn't want you to …"

"I'm going home," she said, rushing from the room before he could say another word.

"Savannah!"

He shot out of bed, following her through his bedroom door and running down the gallery as fast as his bum leg would allow. While walking or jogging were good for him, he wasn't supposed to sprint on it, and it ached and burned as he got to the top of stairs only to hear the front door slam in her wake.

"GOD DAMN IT!" he bellowed, lowering himself to sit on the landing as his leg throbbed with pain.

Miss Potts appeared out of nowhere to stand at the base of the stairs with her hands on her hips. She pursed her lips and tsked.

"Somehow I don't think peach cobbler is going to fix this one."

CHAPTER 9

Savannah cried all the way home, and then she cried herself to sleep. When she woke up on Saturday morning, she didn't have any tears left to cry, so she opened her laptop and went to work rewriting her story about their night in the grove. The thing is? It hurt to remember the grove. It hurt so much because all of Asher's sweetness was eclipsed by what he'd said last night: *If you don't like the way I'm living my life, Savannah, you don't have to be a part of it.*

When she thought of the flinty chill in his eyes as he'd delivered that line, it made her want to cry all over again.

She'd heard him call her name as she raced down the stairs, but she was determined not to let him see her cry, hell-bent on making it out of his house before she dissolved into suds. A small part of her was curious about what he'd wanted to say— did he want to explain himself? Apologize? It didn't matter what he'd wanted to say. What mattered is that he had no interest in changing, and the life he lived wasn't one she could join. There was room for only one in the big brown mansion on the hillside. She wasn't interested in consigning her life to the shadows just because he was too afraid to give the world a second chance.

If that's how he wanted to live his life, it was better that they parted ways now.

Her assumption that she was out of tears was quickly proven wrong as her eyes burned with fresh drops. "Parting ways" sounded horrible, sounded like hell. It didn't matter that she'd known him for only two weeks. She cared about him. She cared about him a lot. It was possible that she was even falling in love with him.

Oh hell.

Was she? Was she falling in love with him?

No, damn it. This wasn't supposed to happen again. Not after Patrick. No. Nuh-uh. No way.

She was not falling in love with Asher Lee. She wouldn't allow it. She was infatuated with him and no more. Infatuated with his funny comments and teasing and mind-numbing, one-handed orgasms. A good orgasm could really mess with a girl. Infatuation, not love, sister. Get your facts straight.

Facts. Yes. Facts are comforting.

She ignored the cursor blinking at her, telling her she needed to edit the piece for McNabb, and opened an Internet browser. She typed in the words "infatuation definition" and pressed Enter.

in•fat•u•a•tion (ɪnˌfætʃuˈeɪʃən) A foolish, unreasoning, or extravagant passion or attraction.

Foolish? To fall for a hermit? Check.

Unreasoning? Not based on or guided by common sense? Check.

Extravagant passion? She tried not to think about the way he had kissed her, but she did, and her whole body suddenly felt incredibly extravagant and passionate. Damn. Check.

And yet.

Foolish? To fall for someone bright, well-read, funny, thoughtful, and loving? Uncheck.

Unreasoning? Every cell in her body screamed that Asher was the most stand-up guy she'd ever met. A bona fide hero. A gentleman. A catch. Common sense dictated she do whatever she had to do to not lose him. Damn it. Uncheck.

Extravagant passion? Yes, he'd played her body like a million-dollar Stradivarius, but their passion was not without kindness and discretion. Hadn't he stopped them from making love on Wednesday night? And hadn't she done the same on Friday? They weren't foolish and headlong. Their actions were mature, despite their knee-weakening passion. Un-flippin'-check.

Savannah didn't need Webster's to tell her what she already knew: What she shared with Asher was much more than infatuation.

And she just had to trust … that what she shared with Asher was far from over.

***

Self-loathing is no way to greet a bright and sunny Saturday in June, he thought, rolling over only to release the faint smell of lemons from his sheets, and he wished he could beat himself to a bloody pulp. Of all the stupid, selfish, head-up-your-own-ass things to do. He'd driven away the only woman in the whole world who'd managed to look beyond his injuries and like him for *him*. What a jerk. *You don't deserve her.*

But I want her. I want her so much, it feels like dying to imagine she's gone for good.

He was exhausted from tossing and turning half the night and keeping himself from getting into his car and banging on her front door.

And his leg still throbbed like the devil. So much so, he wondered if he'd actually done something to injure it, though the doctors had assured him that despite the occasional pain, he'd be able to gain full functionality over time. No, he'd just demanded too much too fast.

Much as he'd done with Savannah.

She'd had no idea she was walking into a hornet's nest by asking about his trip to Maryland, and he himself had told her he thought the bionic arm was "interesting." But the part that really bothered him was when she told him his life was "sad." He'd purposely lived his life completely off the grid to preserve the comfort of those around him. To have her walk into his sanctuary and judge him? Tell him his life made her "sad"? It made him see red. No one had the right to make him feel pathetic in his own house.

And yet.

His life *was* sad, the way he hid from the world while other men—assholes like Patrick Monroe—lived their ignoble lives in the sunshine. But how was he supposed to rejoin the human race with any efficacy? New hand? Facial reconstruction? Grafts? Therapy? It wasn't the procedures that bothered him. Although he wasn't necessarily a fan of hospitals, he appreciated that they were a means to an end. And it wasn't actually the work that bothered him—learning to use the new hand or care for his recovering face—he was a fan of hard work. And it wasn't the pain—although he didn't look forward to it, it couldn't possibly be any worse than what he'd already endured.

The problem was hope.

The problem was his body rejecting the grafts. The problem was the new hand failing to live up to its "bright, shiny, new!" expectations, and falling short. The problem was that even after graft operations and therapy and hand fittings and everything, all of it, maybe he'd still frighten people with his face. Maybe he'd still be short a hand.

The problem with hope was that you were required to acknowledge the possibility of not getting what you desperately hoped for.

As long as he didn't consent to the operation or get fitted for the new hand, he could hope. He could lean back on the hope that maybe, one day, if he decided it was the right time, he could have the operation, he could fit the hand, and maybe his life would improve forever.

Yes, hope was the problem, but the most frightening thing of all wasn't the hope. It was the acknowledgment of potential failure.

But none of this was Savannah's fault, and she certainly hadn't deserved his heavy-handed retort. He thought of her sniffles and shaky voice, the way she'd rushed from his room, from his house, from him.

No, goddamn it. He wasn't losing Savannah. Not when they had only two weeks left. Not when the heat of her body and the brightness of her eyes made him feel whole, made him feel invincible and alive. He stood up gingerly, favoring his left leg and hobbling to the bathroom. He had some showering to do … then some flower buying … and then, some very apologetic, very sincere groveling.

***

Savannah heard the doorbell ring, but she didn't pay it any mind. She'd rewritten the piece on the grove, changing Asher's name and her name so that the piece now read like a story about two other people. At first Maddox had insisted she use real names, but Savannah told him that while she'd consider the changes later, she wasn't comfortable using them now, and McNabb grudgingly acquiesced.

Now she was hard at work researching Myrtle Beach, planning Scarlet's bachelorette party while desperately trying not to think about Asher. But she kept hearing his words over and over again in her head, which is why, when she thought she heard the low rumble of his voice from downstairs, she dismissed the thought as mind games.

Knock, knock, knock. She heard her mother's voice just outside her door. "Savannah, darlin'?"

"Yes, Mama. Come in."

Her mother opened the door a crack, then slipped into the room, carrying the largest, most extravagant bouquet of wildflowers Savannah had ever seen. Wildflowers that smelled of lilac and honeysuckle and the outdoors. She breathed deeply and sighed, looking at her mother in question.

"Asher Lee," she said, "is downstairs."

Savannah felt her mouth tilt up into an involuntary smile and her eyes flood with tears. Her mother set the bouquet on her vanity and put her arm around Savannah.

"Whatever he did, he's awful sorry, button."

"He yelled at me and made me cry."

"Guessing he didn't mean whatever it is he said."

"He thinks I want him to change."

"Well, of course you do," said her mother matter-of-factly, swiping at Savannah's tears with the corner of her sunflower apron. "We all want to change the men we love. Leave our mark on them."

"Oh, I don't lov—"

"Of course you don't. I was just makin' conversation." Judy pulled her daughter against her side. "Your father? He used to do this dreadful toothpick thing when we first started going out. After dinner, he'd cover his mouth with one hand and pick at his teeth with the other. Well, one time, he picked so hard the toothpick broke between his two front teeth, and he not only got a splinter, but his gum got so fat he couldn't eat meat for three days. Five days later, there comes the toothpick again. So I said, 'Francis Andrew Carmichael, you stick that wood between your teeth again, I walk.'"

"What happened?" asked Savannah, fully aware of the fact that she was making Asher sweat it out downstairs.

"He told me I had no right to tell him what to do and went right on using the goldarned toothpicks. We didn't speak for a week. When he called to take me out to dinner again, I said yes. And after dinner, he folded his hands in front of him at the table and smiled at me. Not a toothpick in sight, and we haven't bought any in thirty happy years."

"This wasn't about toothpicks. It was about bionic hands."

"You kids and your electronics."

"Mama."

Judy put her hands up in surrender. "Doesn't matter, button. Whatever it is, patch it up. Only person who looks more miserable than him is you."

Her mother kissed her on top of the head, then slipped out of the room.

Savannah looked at the flowers again, wiping away her remnant tears and smiling. He'd nailed the flowers, that's for sure.

She took a deep breath, looking in the mirror. She'd hung out in her room all morning and still had her pajamas on. She needed to change.

Or did she?

She looked at herself through his eyes, taking in her red silky boy shorts with a matching camisole edged in lace. She cocked her head to the side, then turned and headed downstairs.

It served him right.

***

Oh my God.

He'd never seen anything as sexy as Savannah Carmichael standing in the doorway of her parents' living room, hands on hips barely concealed by a handkerchief-size piece of red, lacy fabric that hung flimsy and slippery across her curves. It was the image he'd be grasping for when he breathed his last breath.

"Thank you for the flowers," she said coolly.

"Thank you for the view," he said less coolly.

"You made me cry," she volleyed back, "and I am generally not a crier."

"Well, clearly that makes me an asshole. Ergo, the flowers."

"Not to mention the trip into town."

Was she impressed that he'd come into town again? Please God, let her be impressed. She wasn't giving much away. He, on the other hand, had been reduced to mush the second she walked into the room in her skimpy outfit and mussed hair.

"I owe you an apology. It couldn't wait until tomorrow."

"Tomorrow?"

"Sunday supper. If I'm still invited."

She sighed. "Of course you're still invited."

He opened his arms to her, and she walked to him purposefully, wrapping her arms around his waist, letting him pull her against his chest.

"I'm sorry, baby," he said, kissing her head and speaking

low against her hair. "I didn't mean it." She adjusted her neck so that her cheek rested on his shoulder, and he ran his hand lingeringly over the sleek material on her back, thinking how right and how good and how amazing it felt to have her back in his arms. "I'm just resistant to change."

"Change can be good," she said softly, which made him hold her tighter.

"I know. I'm working on it. I promise."

She leaned back to look into his eyes, and the moment felt incredibly intimate, as though they were connected on a visceral level, like they were the two unlikely pieces of one whole—two damaged people who'd both run home to hide from the world and somehow found each other.

"Asher, I don't want to change who you *are*. I *like* who you are. I *more than like* who you are. And of course I don't presume to know what you've been through, but whatever you want for yourself? Bionic hands? Second chances? I want that for you, too."

He couldn't hold her in his arms anymore without tasting her. He dropped his lips to hers and kissed her longingly, pouring all his fears from last night and relief from right now into the kiss. He memorized the feeling of her in his arms, the way it felt to have her softness pressed against him. Someday, when she boarded a plane for Phoenix, he'd live on these memories, these precious moments with her.

"You're an alien," he whispered in her ear after biting her earlobe and making her tremble. "Admit it."

"Flatterer," she said, her voice low and lust-filled and hitched. "I plead the Fifth on my alien status."

"It's a beautiful day for a drive," he said, resting his lips against her pulse as her fingers laced around his neck, her thumbs doing wicked things to the warm skin she found under his hair. "I could put the top down. We could get out of town. Just you and me? Buy a picnic, find a meadow, make out until sundown."

He had no idea where these words were coming from.

When he drove over to her house, he hadn't the slightest plan or intention to ask her to spend the day with him, let alone spend the day away from home. But seeing her like this and feeling like he felt, saying good-bye until tomorrow afternoon felt impossible. And he wanted to show her he wasn't a hundred percent coward—he might not love mixing it up with the fair citizens of Danvers, but he was perfectly capable of leaving his house for a few hours, wasn't he?

"Your BMW's a convertible?" she asked, raising her eyebrows.

"Yes, ma'am."

"I like fast German cars."

"Riding or driving?"

"Both."

"Is that a request?"

"Mm-hm."

"I love my car, Savannah. I'm not a shallow man, but I love that vehicle. What's your driving record look like?"

"This question from the man who made me cry?"

"I would love for you to drive my car as far and as fast as you like," he amended.

She leaned back and winked at him. "I thought so. Give me a minute to change?"

"Must you?"

"I'm afraid so."

She backed out of his arms, but he called to her as she reached the living room doorway.

"Savannah?"

Her coffee-brown eyes were wide and animated as she turned around to face him, and his heart swelled with love for her. She could have given him a harder time. Could have made him apologize over and over and beg for her forgiveness, but not his girl. Not his Savannah.

"Thank you."

***

The next morning, Savannah stretched languorously in her bed, smiling even before she opened her eyes.

Her dreams had basically rehashed every detail of her country drive with Asher, all in stunning Technicolor. Her body was hot and unsatisfied, but her heart was overflowing with her burgeoning feelings for him. Every minute they spent together only served to fix him more permanently in her life. She tried not to think about Phoenix. She couldn't bear to imagine walking away from him, and yet she couldn't walk away from her career either. She quietly hoped a solution would present itself because letting go of Asher seemed more and more unlikely.

After she'd gotten behind the wheel of his BMW, she turned the car northwest on Route 460 into the Jefferson National Forest, where they'd spent the day driving through Appalachia with the sun on their faces and the wind at their backs. His car handled like a dream, and his hand, warm and certain on her thigh, made her hyperaware of him beside her, as if he couldn't bear letting the car seduce her when he was in play.

They'd gotten sandwiches and coffee at a drive-through and found a secluded spot near a river to spread their blanket.

Savannah had sat with Asher's head on her lap, aviator sunglasses obscuring his eyes but making him so damned sexy, it made her hot all day.

"Let's do this next weekend too," he said as she gently brushed his hair off his forehead.

Her heart plunged. "I can't."

"Oh." A single sound filled with so much disappointment.

"It's my sister's bachelorette party next weekend."

"Vegas?"

"Why does everyone's mind immediately go to Vegas?"

"I guess because what happens there, stays there," he said dryly.

"Not Vegas."

"Thank God."

"Myrtle Beach." She sighed. "We're staying at a three-bedroom condo on the Strand. Nine girls."

"*Nine*? Your sister's having eight attendants?"

"My sister's having *nine* attendants and two readers. Three of them can't make it." Savannah paused for a moment, considering her next words. "Trent and his groomsmen are coming too."

Asher didn't say anything right away. When he did, his tone was clipped. "Lots of bodies in a three-bedroom condo."

"The boys are renting the condo next door."

"Aren't bachelorette weekends generally planned without the groom in attendance?"

"Scarlet said she'd miss him too much."

"So, the Hamilton brothers will be there," said Asher. "And every other good-looking, successful twenty-something in Danvers. I hope you have a great time, Savannah."

He sat up, putting his back to her. "I guess we should probably be heading back."

"I guess so," she said.

She wasn't confused by his reaction. He didn't like it that she was spending next weekend with almost a dozen eligible hot men. She understood. But she didn't apologize because they hadn't promised each other anything. Were they dating? Sort of. Exclusive? Not as far as she knew. She hadn't used the word *boyfriend*, nor had he used the word *girlfriend*. And frankly despite her growing feelings for him, she wasn't sure if she was ready to be exclusive. Discovering new feelings was one thing. Actually changing your Facebook status? That was real.

To his credit, he hadn't pouted for more than a few minutes before slipping back into their easy conversation as he took the wheel and pointed the car back toward Danvers.

She looked at the clock on her bedside table. Church in an hour—the nonnegotiable price of staying at her parents' house— and Sunday supper three hours after that. Just enough time to get her notes in order for the next installment of "~~Asher~~ Adam & ~~Savannah~~ Cassandra: An All-American Love Story."

***

Miss Potts bustled from the kitchen with two foil-wrapped dishes.

"Your mama's peach cobbler and Amish devil's food cake."

Asher grinned. "*Amish* devil's food?"

"I've always loved the wickedness of the name," she said. "You can't use a cake mixer to make the batter since the Amish don't have electricity, and it'd be hell with a hand mixer. They use hot coffee instead, to mix the ingredients and get a good batter."

He had a flashback of himself, as a boy, sitting in the back of his mother's car as she told him about baking techniques. The lifelong friendship between his grandmother Frances Sherman and Matilda Potts meant that Miss Potts often said and did things that resonated so strongly of Asher's mother, Pamela Sherman Lee, it sometimes took his breath away. He leaned down and pressed his lips to her papery cheek.

"She'd be so grateful, you know."

"Your gran was the best friend I ever had, and your mama was like a niece to me," said Miss Potts softly, reaching up to swipe at her eyes. Then she smoothed the collar of Asher's polo shirt. "You look handsome."

"You're a liar."

"Beauty is in the eye of the beholder, Asher. And I've seen the way Savannah Carmichael beholds you."

"It can't last," he said softly, feeling the heavy desperation that he tried, less and less successfully, to keep at bay.

"Don't let's worry about that today," said Miss Potts, urging him toward the door. "You go have a nice time."

"A nice time? I wish I had a mask."

"Not necessary. The Carmichaels are good people. They raised Savannah, didn't they?"

An hour later, sitting beside Savannah at her parents' dinner table, his plate piled high with ham, potatoes, corn, and biscuits, he was surprised to find that Miss Potts had been right. The Carmichaels *were* good people, and after the slight but fairly well-concealed reactions to his face that he perceived upon greeting, they hadn't made him feel uncomfortable again. He noticed that Scarlet Carmichael's eyes occasionally looked away too quickly as he was speaking, and he saw the sympathetic softness in Judy Carmichael's eyes from time to time. But with Savannah beside him, sexy in a black cotton sundress with her thigh pressed up against his? Pretty much he'd say yes to Sunday supper anytime.

The only fly in Asher's ointment was Trent Hamilton, who had looked downright disgusted the first time he examined Asher's face and winced theatrically a few more times for good measure. Only when the Carmichaels weren't looking, of course.

"Vanna, honey, my brother Lance can't wait to renew your acquaintance again next weekend at MB," said Trent, giving Savannah his million-dollar grin.

"If memory serves, Lancey was a little handsy," said Savannah, giving Trent a look.

"That's just because he liked you so well." Trent pulled Scarlet against his side in a big show. "Hamilton boys and Carmichael girls go together like peas and carrots."

Savannah straightened in her chair, ignoring him and turned to Asher. "You ever been to Myrtle Beach?"

Asher nodded, thinking he could take Trent easily if the younger man wanted to keep baiting him. They could step outside, and Asher could rearrange Trent's face lickety-split, see how he liked it. "I did boot camp at Fort Jackson down in South Carolina. Myrtle Beach wasn't but three hours away, so we went several times. You ever been to boot camp, Hamilton?"

"No, sir," replied Trent with narrowed eyes. "You mind if I call you sir? I like to show respect to my elders."

"That's just fine, son," responded Asher smoothly, turning back to Savannah, who rolled her eyes at their antics. "I loved the Strand at night. The way the smells of cotton candy and funnel cakes mix with salt water and sun lotion in the summertime. The twinkle lights. The music."

"Lord, Frank," Judy said, "you remember that week we spent in Myrtle Beach before the girls were born?"

Mr. Carmichael's eyes softened as he gazed across the table at her. "I remember, blossom."

"You're right about the cotton candy, Asher," said Judy. "Did y'all ever see the movie *Shag*? I love that film!"

"It's her favorite," said Savannah, turning to Asher with sparkling eyes.

"In honor of Scarlet's bach next weekend, I think we should have a family viewing," said Judy.

"Oh Lord," sighed Frank.

"Family viewing?" asked Asher, leaning toward Savannah.

"Daddy puts a white sheet up against the house, and Mama makes popcorn, and we sit out on the lawn and watch *Shag*. We do it at least once a summer. Sometimes two or three times. I know every word of that movie."

"Do you know how to shag?" Asher asked, smiling at her.

"'Course! Mama taught us. You?"

"I do. But I can't really. Anymore."

"Sure you can! We'll go slow."

He leaned forward a little more, then stopped himself when he realized that he was on the brink of kissing her at the supper table in front of her whole family.

"I want to kiss you," he whispered.

"Later," she said, shifting in her seat so that her thigh rubbed against his.

"So that's settled," said Judy, beaming at Frank, who looked tired. "Thursday night! A little send-off before you girls hit the road on Friday morning. Of course you're comin', boys?"

Asher looked at Trent, whose eyes narrowed at him with displeasure before looking at Judy and turning on the charm. "Oh, I'll be here, Miz Carmichael. Wouldn't miss it."

She smiled politely at Trent before turning to Asher. "And you, Asher?"

Savannah's hand squeezed his under the table and gave him the courage to agree to another expedition into town. "Thank you, Mrs. Carmichael. I can't think of anywhere I'd rather be."

After supper, Trent and Scarlet left quickly, heading to the neighboring town for a barbecue with friends, and Savannah invited Asher to join her on the porch swing before saying their good nights.

"I love it that you came for supper," she said as he laced his finger through hers. She pushed off to rock them gently on the swing. "I know it must not have been easy for you."

"*You* make it easy for me," he said. "And your family's terrific."

"Scarlet was a little quiet. And Trent ..." Her tone was apologetic, but she shrugged. "He's not all bad."

"I'm sure," said Asher, feeling tight-lipped and annoyed. Trent Hamilton was exactly the sort of narrow-minded, townie asshole that Asher preferred to avoid.

"Really. He loves Scarlet to pieces."

"Seems like it."

"Mama loved having you."

He released her hand and put his arm around her shoulder, pulling her close and loving it when she put her head on his shoulder.

"We're halfway done with the interview," he said. "Have you written any of it yet?"

"Some."

"Going to let me read it?"

"Not yet," she answered quickly.

He squeezed her shoulder. He could respect that—he wouldn't want someone reading his work before it was finished either. They rocked in silence for a few minutes. Lawn sprinklers made for a soothing symphony as children rode their bikes by Savannah's house and the odd car made its way carefully down the quiet tree-lined street. It had been such a long time since Asher spent an afternoon among other people. It felt familiar and new. Comforting and frightening.

"Where are we going with this, Savannah?"

"I don't know," she said, her voice soft and unsure against his neck. After a long pause, she looked up at him. "Do you?"

He shook his head sadly, unable to hold her pretty eyes. "No."

That wasn't entirely true, though. He had a good idea where he *wanted* it to go. He didn't want her to leave Danvers. He didn't want her to leave him behind. The thought of going back to life without her was so painful, it was almost unthinkable. He held her closer.

"Maybe we should slow down a little?" she asked. "Until we figure it out?"

He winced. That was definitely not the answer he was hoping for. Disappointment invaded as he nodded politely, kissing her on the forehead before releasing her and standing up. "See you tomorrow?"

"Of course," she said, surprised by his abrupt good-bye, looking at him with troubled eyes as he stepped off the porch and headed to his car.

CHAPTER 10

*The first time you're naked together and you don't feel a shred
of insecurity*

Savannah spent Monday and Wednesday afternoons
interviewing Asher, but after her "take it slower" bomb on
Sunday afternoon, something had changed between them. Asher
was holding back, and their meetings were confined to the
wingbacks in his office once again. And frankly? She hated it.
Stepping back from a situation always seemed like a sensible
thing to do if you were uncertain of things. But, their chemistry
was so palpable, and her memories of his hand on her body so
real, taking things slower was killing her. Possibly as much as it
was killing him, though he was going out of his way to respect
her wishes.

He didn't put his arm around her or hold her hand as they
sat behind her parents, sister and Trent in the backyard,
watching *Shag* on Thursday night. So when he leaned over to
nuzzle her ear as two of the main characters started kissing on-
screen, her breath hitched in surprise and relief and pleasure.

"Come home with me after," he said softly.

"I leave for Myrtle Beach tomorrow," she whispered back,
trying not to whimper from the feeling of his lips on her ear. The
heat of his breath made her heart race and her skin tingle.

"Come over anyway. I'll drive you home whenever you
want."

She took a deep, ragged breath. She wanted him. So much.
So much more than she'd ever wanted anyone—the eager boys

in high school, the erudite boys in college, the sophisticated men in New York. None of them tugged at her heart as Asher did. None of them made her feel as much as he did. And no, maybe she couldn't have him forever, but whatever happened after the article was published, slow be damned. She wanted this time with him now.

"Okay."

He exhaled beside her, reaching for her hand. She laced her fingers through his and let him settle their hands on his thigh. It was hot and hard, and yearning pooled in Savannah's belly, making it impossible to concentrate on the movie. All she wanted was to hop into his gorgeous car, drive to his house and let him pull her up the stairs to his bedroom.

She shifted slightly toward him in the two-seater Adirondack chair so that her mouth was just a little bit closer to his ear.

"Asher."

"Savannah."

He stared at the screen now, but his chest moved more deliberately than it had a few minutes before, and his jaw was rigid. His hand held hers with more definite pressure, and she leaned into him, her breath brushing his ear.

"For the record, I've decided … that I *hate* … taking things slow."

"That makes two of us," he said in a gravelly voice.

She bit his earlobe gently. "I might stay all night."

He flinched and wet his lips, refusing to look at her, but she felt movement in his pants near her hand and tried not to grin. His mind was just as dirty as hers.

"Fine with me."

"But sex is still off the table for now," she said, as her tongue darted out to lick the sensitive skin where his cheek and ear met.

He groaned softly. "That's a shame."

"Don't get greedy," she said, teasing.

She'd given this some thought. The problem with having

sex with Asher now was that they'd left the airspace for casual sex several days ago and too many feelings were flying between them at this point, intense feelings that hadn't been articulated yet, that could hurt if there were misunderstandings between them. Did they like each other? Yes. Did they have heat? Lord, yes. But the rest was still up for grabs. She wasn't his girlfriend, and they didn't have a commitment in place. Sex at this point could break her heart. And since Savannah's feelings were still raw over Patrick's deception and betrayal, she couldn't risk her heart again so soon. And certainly not with Asher, who meant more and more to her with every passing day. She wasn't sure she could recover from Asher hurting her, and that scared her most of all.

"Is anything else off the table?" he asked, his nostrils flaring as he stayed focused on the screen.

Savannah leaned forward until her lips grazed his ear again. "No."

His breath hitched, and he squeezed her hand, turning to her slowly. "We need to go. Now."

His voice, low and demanding, made the muscles deep inside her body clench and release in anticipation. She bit her bottom lip. "Shouldn't we watch the rest—"

"No."

Even in the dim light afforded by the movie, she could see the fierce desire in his eyes, the longing that probably mirrored her own. They hadn't made out since their picnic on Saturday, and they were about to be separated for three days. She could see it: he was as desperate to be alone with her as she was to be alone with him.

Making the decision for them, he stood, pulling her up with him. They bee lined past Scarlet and Trent, who'd been snuggling on a bench in front of them, and stopped right behind Judy's chair.

"Mama," whispered Savannah, placing her hands on her mother's shoulder and whispering into her ear. "Asher's got a headache. We're going to go."

Judy pulled her eyes away from the screen, looking around at Asher in dismay. "Oh, Asher. I'm so sorry, honey. Come back again real soon?"

"Yes, ma'am, and thanks for having me."

"I'll be home later, Mama," said Savannah smoothly. "Don't wait up."

Before her mother could say another word, Savannah was pulled away, her heart racing as Asher put his car into drive and headed home.

***

They drove in silence, the tension palpable and hot between them as he shifted the car from third to fourth, from fourth to fifth, racing up the dark, narrow roads toward home. Those dreadful words "slow down" had tortured Asher since Sunday afternoon, and with three long days apart on the horizon, he couldn't pass up the chance to have her to himself. He hated the fact that she was headed to Myrtle Beach with a bunch of good-looking men, so the least he could do was ensure that there wasn't any room for anyone else in her head but him.

He finally pulled into his driveway, and when he cut the engine, the silence was overwhelming. He cleared his throat, resisting the temptation to touch her right away.

"I'm glad you came home with me."

She took a deep breath and stared up at the house. "I hate it that I won't see you again until Monday."

He reached for her face, palming her cheek, and turned her to face him. "Me too."

He leaned forward and took her top lip between his, letting his fingers thread through her hair as she moaned softly, leaning toward him. She reached up to cradle his face with her hands, and he deepened the kiss, tasting her mouth and smiling because it tasted like popcorn and butter and he never knew the movies could taste so perfect.

"Even though I saw you, I missed you," he murmured, tracing her jaw with little kisses.

"Me too," she sighed, leaning her head back to give his lips and tongue better access to her throat. "It was hell coming here on Monday and Wednesday and wishing you were kissing me like this. I could barely concentrate on the interview. I just kept wishing you'd grab me and kiss me and tell me 'To hell with taking things slow, Savannah.' It's terrible to feel this much this fast." She breathed heavily against his neck as his hand glided over her breasts and slipped into the front of her black T-shirt. The skin of her tummy was so warm and soft, he flattened his hand, savoring her heat before sliding his hand up to her breasts. He molded the soft flesh under his hand as she gasped into his mouth, stealing his breath.

"Savannah," he groaned, and her teeth bit his upper lip gently as her nipple beaded like a marble under the lace of her bra. "You make me so goddamned hot."

"Upstairs," she murmured. "Your bed. Now."

He pulled back from her, panting, reaching over to open his door without taking his eyes off her, then walked around the car to open hers. When she stepped out of the car, he pulled her against his chest without a word because he couldn't help himself and kissed her slowly and deeply in the moonlight. He'd never known want like this, and he searched his brain to see if it consumed him so deeply just because he'd gone without it for so long. His answer came quickly. It felt wonderful to hold a beautiful girl in his arms, yes, but these feeling weren't about just any girl.

They were about Savannah.

Savannah, who'd walked up to his door with brownies when the rest of the town stayed away. Savannah, who'd offered him her left hand in greeting the moment he met her. Savannah, who smelled like lemons and loved books and had come home to hide. Savannah, who was like flint to his steel, hot and sharp and full of fire. And Savannah, warm and pliant in his arms, letting him kiss her, somehow, miraculously, wanting him just as much as he wanted her.

By the time he drew back from her, he was so hard and so

ready to bury himself inside her, it was almost painful. Why had she taken sex off the table? It bothered him, not because every male instinct in his body was driving him to mate with her, but because he wondered at the reason. Did she not *want* to?

He took a deep breath, pulling away to look up at the full moon before returning his gaze to her lovely, upturned face. He lifted his hand to cup her jaw.

"You're beautiful all the time. But you're an angel in the moonlight."

He winced at his sappy delivery, but his feelings were scary-stupid, quickly changing from admiration and infatuation to love. He could feel it happening. He was driven by them to say ridiculous things.

"I'm no angel," she said softly.

"You are," he said, bringing her hand to his lips, surrendering to cheesy. He was falling in love with her. Cheesy was inevitable.

Savannah tugged him toward the front door, and he followed her inside, pushing the door shut behind them with his foot and letting her pull him up the stairs. It was incredibly sexy—incredibly hot—that she knew where she was going in the near darkness of his house, heading effortlessly to his bedroom. She pushed the door open, and he followed.

***

Her chest rose and fell rapidly, as much from the exertion of racing up the grand staircase and down the gallery to his room as from the force of her feelings and the desperate need to feel him, to taste him, to explore him, to have his hand and lips and tongue on her body. She leaned back against the bedroom door behind her, arching her back as she held his ravenous eyes.

He took a step toward her and put his hand on the door beside her head. He leaned in close, his forehead grazing hers softly, his breath coming in short pants, teasing her lips. The inside of his legs brushed the outside of hers as her short, quick breaths made her breasts rise and fall, her nipples skimming his chest over and over as she inhaled. The friction made them almost unbearably hard, and desperate for his hand or lips to soothe them. His eyes stared deeply into hers in the dim light of his bedroom. The moonlight cast shadows over his face, making it seem, for the moment, uninjured.

"Asher," she sighed, looking up at him with wonder as her fingers traced the lines of his face. "You're beautiful in the moonlight too."

His eyes flashed with heat, and his mouth descended on hers. His arm hooked around her waist, backing up until his legs hit the bed behind him and he fell backward, dragging her down with him, cushioning her fall with his body. He flipped her over without leaving her lips, keeping his body flush against hers as he plundered her mouth, his hand slipping under her shirt to grasp her breast.

She moaned, arching up against him, and he pushed the bra up and over her aching flesh, then dropped his mouth to her nipple, sucking it fiercely into a sharp point and making her insides slippery with arousal and need. She wove her fingers through his mane of hair, frustrated then relieved as the warmth of his mouth moved from one breast to the other. His thumb and forefinger pinched the slippery wetness of one as he loved the other, flicking his tongue over it, then licking in slow circles until she thought she'd lose her mind.

Her hips moved rhythmically beneath him, pushing up into the hardness of his erection as he sucked her with more force, his hand sliding down to her stomach to slip under the elastic of her panties. She gasped with surprise as he slipped two fingers into her, then closed her eyes and whimpered in pleasure, clenching her muscles around the welcome intrusion.

"God, Savannah, you're so wet. So tight."

His words turned her on even more, and she bit down on her bottom lip as his lips trailed down her body, kissing her torso and tummy lightly, licking a ring around her belly button. She ran her hands over her aroused breasts, teasing the damp nipples with her fingers before skimming to the skin of her waist. She wanted him to have total access to her. She arched up and pushed her shorts and panties down, wiggling a little so they fell past her knees. Asher withdrew his fingers, dragging her shorts and panties down over her heels, before yanking her to the edge of the bed and kneeling on the floor before her. He took her left leg and kissed a trail from her ankle to her knee, then threw the leg over his shoulder and did the same with her right.

Oh, my God, she thought. *He's going to ...*

And then Savannah's mind was officially blown.

Once she was wide open to him, his fingers gently spread her lips and his tongue found the throbbing bud of her sex. As he lapped at her feverish skin, Savannah bucked off the bed, her fingers curling into his hair as she whimpered and moaned his name, her heels pushing into his back.

Savannah had barely experienced more than a few awkward moments of oral sex in her life, so when he placed his lips around the erect nub and sucked, stars began to flash and burn behind her eyes. Just as she was about to fall over the edge of sanity, he thrust those two fingers back into her wet heat, and she felt his teeth graze her turgid flesh.

"Asher!" she screamed as her entire body convulsed up against his mouth, then throbbed and relaxed in repeating waves of pleasure. Every muscle inside her body clenched, vibrating rhythmically against him as she experienced the most mind-bending orgasm of her life.

She lay limp and lifeless as he climbed back onto the bed and pulled her up with him until her head hit the pillow. He reached around his neck to take off his shirt, then gently pushed her blouse and bra the rest of the way over her head. Savannah vaguely realized that she was completely naked now, spent and sated on his bed, and couldn't remember ever trusting another man this much before. Asher touched her the way a man touches a woman he loves. He touched her like she was precious to him, and though they'd made no formal declarations of their intentions, she wanted to believe that she was. His arm pulled her securely against his body, and she nestled instinctively into the hard, smooth warmth of his chest, and that's where she rode out the remaining shivers and shudders of awesome.

***

Her breathing finally started to return to normal.

"My God," she murmured, shimmying up a little, the drag of her breasts against his chest a specific kind of torture. He still tasted the salty sweetness of her in his mouth, which made him so hard, it surprised him there was any blood left in his head for coherent thought.

"Asher's fine," he answered tightly, her lemon-scented hair teasing him mercilessly.

"How did you learn to do that?" she asked, her eyes wide and impressed. Her hair was all messed up, and it looked so sexy it made him breathless. *I did that. I made her look like that.* "One-handed, no less."

"I wasn't just using my hand."

"No kidding."

Her tongue darted out to his neck, and darts of pleasure shot down his neck to his groin. He waffled between getting up to take a very, very cold shower, or waiting to see what she'd do next. The anticipation was killing him.

"Asher?"

"Yeah?"

"Only one thing's off the table tonight, right?"

His breath quickened. "Unless you've changed your mind."

"No. But everything else is fair game?" she purred, as her teeth caught his earlobe and tugged.

"Pretty much," he groaned.

"And if we're being *fair* ..." Her lips trailed down his neck, leaving little kisses and blowing lightly on them, which made the hairs on his arms stand up as shivers ran down his back.

"Fair?" he murmured breathlessly, losing the thread of conversation.

"... then it's your turn, isn't it?"

His pulse picked up as all the rest of the blood in his body rushed to his hips, strengthening his already rigid erection which throbbed painfully for her attention.

Savannah pinched his nipple, then peppered kisses over his pecs, which flexed under her mouth. She kissed the tight six-pack of his abs, running her teeth lightly over his skin as her hand slid down his torso. His breath caught as he felt her hand push down gently against the bulge in his pants.

Her other hand worked the zipper, while he reached down reflexively to push at his jeans, a gesture less helpful than demonstrative—he wanted to be bare to her. He wanted her to do whatever she wanted to do with him. He felt her fingers hook under the waistband of his boxers, and he arched, lifting himself off the bed so she could yank them down his legs with one strong tug.

"Oh my," she said, her voice thick and low. "Look at you."

His eyes clenched shut, and a guttural moan released from his throat as he felt her breath touch the tip of his sex. Her nose gently nuzzled him all the way down and all the way back up, and then ...

"Oh God," he groaned, bracing himself.

"Savannnah's fine," she teased.

And then her tongue touched him, licking him from the base to the tip, slowly—ridiculously slowly—so that he felt the heat of her breath mixing with the wetness of her mouth. Goose bumps scattered across his skin as she finally took him into her mouth, her wetted lips sliding slowly down his hardness until he felt the back of her throat against the throbbing knob.

"Savannah ..." He threw his arm over his eyes as the pressure built between his legs. He wanted this to last, but damn it, it had been so long, and she was so hot, and his feelings for her were off the charts.

Her head bobbed up and down slowly as she cupped the soft sack of skin under his massive erection with her hand. He felt it tighten and strain, and he winced from the pleasure, biting his lip until he tasted the metallic tinge of blood. She dragged her lips back up to the tip, slowly, exquisitely, tasting him, kissing him, then repeating the motion again.

He couldn't hold on anymore. It felt too good, and it had been way too long since someone loved him like this.

"Baby, I'm going to …" he said to warn her, and he felt her free hand slide up his thigh, over his hips, until it rested near his heart where he claimed it with his. And in the end, it was that connection—the intimacy of her fingers twined through his— that pushed him over the edge.

With a low, guttural roar of surrender, he gave himself over totally to the pleasure of her touch, climaxing into her mouth, pumping himself into her over and over again. As his muscles flexed, his upper body leaned forward, trembling, until his shudders relaxed and her mouth released him gently. He fell back on the pillow, physically exhausted, drained. She'd taken everything he had to give, which made him breathless with appreciation and love for her, and when she slid back up his body, he roused himself from his pleasure coma and flipped her over, gasping and groaning as he hungrily found her mouth with his.

He tasted himself on her tongue, which made him immediately start to harden again, his erection cradled against the soft warmth of the curly hairs between her hips. He rocked against her, and she moaned softly into his mouth, weaving her hands into his hair and kissing him back.

"Savannah," he said, "I want you so badly … so badly, baby …"

"No. Not all the way," she said, breathlessly, her hands skimming down to his hips. "But like this we can."

He braced himself on his elbows, kissing her as he pushed against her softness, hardening quickly to rub back and forth against her mound. He pressed his hand against her cheek, leaning back to look into her eyes, as she arched up against him. He moved rhythmically, stroking the bud of her sex with every upward thrust until she reached up and grabbed his face, pushing her tongue into his mouth as her fingernails curled into his cheek.

She was wet and slick, and he slid effortlessly back and forth, drawing moans and whimpers from her throat as their kissing started to mimic the motions of their bodies.

Her cries became louder and closer, and he drew back to watch as her eyes clenched shut and her head fell back, thrashing against the pillow. Then she fell apart beneath him, shattered and shuddering as tremors racked her body.

It was the most beautiful thing Asher had ever seen in his entire life.

"Asher, Asher, Asher," she whispered, and he felt the contractions continuing beneath him, vibrating from her core, radiating out from the depths of her body through her skin to massage his hard length, which continued to move back and forth over her still-throbbing sex.

He quickened his pace, feeling his own release imminent, and looked down at her, surprised when her heavy eyes suddenly opened, bright and luminous in the moonlight. She whispered, "Now."

And his heart burst, galloping against hers, as everything tightened then exploded at the same time, fireworks bursting behind his eyes as he came hot and slippery between them, melding their skin together with the force of his release. And when he finally stopped shaking, he rolled onto his side and clasped her against him, desperately, totally, certainly in love with her.

***

"Shower," he finally muttered into her ear after a long moment of silence and complete contentment in each other's arms. "We definitely need a shower."

Savannah didn't want to move. Her naked body felt like jelly against his, warm and liquid under the down duvet. She pushed against him slightly so that he fell on to his back, and she followed him, lying across his chest, still connected intimately by the hot slickness between them.

"Soon," she murmured. "Just keep holding on to me for now."

His arm tightened around her as she gazed at him. She reached up, gently stroking the damaged skin of his right cheek as her eyes held his. "Tell me about this. Tell me what happened."

His eyebrows furrowed together as he looked at her, uncertainty making his features hard as he searched her eyes. "I thought we did interviews at four o'cl—"

"No interview. No reporter. Just your girlfr—"

Heat seeped into her cheeks as she realized what she was about to say. Despite what they'd just shared, he hadn't called her his girlfriend yet. She dropped his eyes and lowered her chin to his chest, feeling mortified.

Then she felt his hand in her hair, stroking gently. "If my *girlfriend* was asking, I'd consider telling her."

She laughed softly against his chest, then raised her head, relieved. "She's asking."

"Wait a second." He smiled back at her, then shook his head as if amazed or bewildered. "How did *that* just happen?"

"My boyfriend loves to change the subject," she answered dryly.

"Can I just have a minute to process this? Because I've lived up here by myself for eight years. I'm Asher Lee, Danvers' Hermit of the Hills, and you're gorgeous, amazing Savannah Calhoun Carmichael, the most beautiful woman who ever landed back in Danvers by way of New York, and without coercion or threat of torture, you just voluntarily called yourself my girlfriend."

"Pretty much," she said, tangling her legs with his.

"I have to know. You have to tell me what planet you're from."

"That's top secret."

"So you admit it."

"I admit nothing," she said in a credible Russian accent.

He laughed, and her exhausted muscles roused themselves, ready to report for more of Asher's attentions.

"I'm crazy about you, baby," he said.

She kissed the warm, hard skin over his heart. "You already told me that. I want to know what happened to you."

"It's heavy stuff, beauty. It's not light reading."

"I read nonfiction too, *beauty*," she replied. "It's part of you. And I'm part of you. So it's time for us to meet."

His grin faded, and he reached down gently to push her head back onto his chest, like maybe he'd have an easier time telling his story if Savannah wasn't staring at him. He ran his fingers through her hair, and she waited patiently, letting him take his time.

"We were in the Zhari District and some guys had been out on a dismounted patrol. There was a man down, Staff Sergeant Williams, who'd stepped on an IED, and since I was the closest field medic on duty, I'd been rushed out from base to help him. When I got there, he was still in the field, and I was met by a corporal from his unit, a guy called Lagerty. We were talking as he led the way to Williams. Just walking along side by side, and suddenly he stepped right on another IED. Right next to me. Blew him fifteen feet in the air and killed him.

"I didn't feel anything at first," he said. "It's not as loud as you'd think it would be, but there was a big cloud of dust and sand, and I'd been thrown a little distance. I knew I wasn't dead." He paused for a second, and she felt him swallow. She pressed her lips to his chest and waited. His voice broke when he continued. "I wished I was. I'm ashamed of that now. Lots of guys got it worse, losing both legs or three limbs, and they fight to stay alive. I didn't know how bad it was at the time. I didn't know my hand was gone and my face looked like chopped meat."

He pulled his hand from her hair and Savannah suspected he was wiping tears from his cheeks. Her own tears were soaking his chest, but she let them fall and kept her hands flattened on his warm skin. His hand returned to her hair, but it rested now, not stroking, as he continued.

"The shrapnel in my face … I didn't feel it. And my hand, I didn't even know it was gone until one of the other guys pushed me back down—I was trying to get up—and he was saying, 'Face, severe shrapnel.' And someone else was saying, 'Single amputee, effing mess, three men down,' and I was wondering who the hell they were talking about. The only man down was Williams. Amputee? Who lost a limb?

"I kept trying to sit up. I wanted to sit up. I wanted to sit up and help the amputee, but they just kept telling me, 'No, no. Stay down. Stay down.' And I tried to open my eye, but the lids weren't … I just …"

"No more," said Savannah, softly but firmly, pulling herself up to look into his face. She used the backs of her hands to dry her eyes, then looked at him, at the horror and hopelessness that had taken over his eyes. "Asher? Asher, look at me."

His breathing was fast and shallow and a little ragged, like it would be if he woke up from a very bad dream. When he looked at her, his eyes were glistening and uncertain. "Are you leaving now?"

"Leaving?" she asked, shaking her head back and forth. "No, I'm not leaving you."

He swallowed, looking bereft. "I told you it wasn't pretty."

"Asher," she said, her heart breaking for everything this extraordinary man had endured. "I promise you I'm not leaving."

She leaned forward, pressing her lips to his, tasting the saltiness of his tears, peppering tiny, gentle kisses against the uneven contours of lips that should have been smooth but weren't anymore. And she loved them, just the way they were.

His hand slowly slid up her naked back to her neck, holding her head in place as he captured her lower lip between his. She threw her leg over his body to straddle him. He sat up, and his arm went around her, tightening her to his chest as her ankles locked around his back and he deepened the kiss, his tongue tasting hers, his hand kneading the skin of her hip as she sucked on his tongue.

She felt his erection against her inner thigh, rigid and

throbbing, and her decision was quick and fast, and she knew—in her heart, in her soul, in an instant—that it was right.

"I want you," she murmured into his neck.

"I want you too," he answered, breathlessly, trembling in her arms. "Next time you come over, I—"

"Not next time," she said, leaning back to look into his eyes. "Now."

He furrowed his brows, his panting breaths hot on the skin of her lips.

"Is this you feeling sorry for me?"

"A pity screw? I should smack you for that, Asher."

"Then what changed?" he asked, and she softened when she saw the confusion in his eyes.

"For one, I wasn't your girlfriend when I got here."

She licked his lips, and they parted for her, his tongue swirling around hers as she adjusted on his lap, pushing the folds of her sex directly up against the base of his erection, and swallowing his groan when her slick heat pressed into him.

"Also …"

"Also?" he asked numbly.

"I'm falling so hard for you, Asher, and …"

"And?"

"And you're falling so hard for me."

"I am," he said. "I've never felt like this about anyone. Not in my whole life."

"Neither have I," she said, pushing her pelvis forward and watching as his breath hitched and he winced in pain and pleasure. *God, it was so sexy when his face looked like that.* She rolled her hips against him just to see him do it again.

"Savannah," he warned.

"I didn't want to have sex with you because I wasn't sure where we stood, but now …"

"You are?"

"No. Not totally. But I know you care for me. And I don't know … it's enough." She searched his eyes, still wrapped around his body. She couldn't wait anymore. She didn't want to wait anymore. "I'm on the pill. Are you clean?"

He looked into her eyes. "You know I am."

"I had to ask," said Savannah, and leaned forward to kiss him again.

She cradled his face between her hands and rocked forward against him. They kissed madly as she slid her hands down his cheeks to his neck and finally to his shoulders, where she flattened them, bracing herself. She raised her whole body up, then leaned back to catch his eyes.

"Help me," she said softly, gazing at him with all the love that was growing in her heart for him.

His hand trailed down her back, then reached to line up his erection with her entrance.

"Are you sure?" he asked, ready to pull back if she said she wasn't.

"I'm sure," she said, and then slowly, achingly slowly, she lowered herself onto him.

***

He stayed completely still, holding his breath as her tight wetness sheathed him in agonizing perfection. He could feel every ridge of silky flesh inside her, every muscle that adjusted to his length and width. A euphoric rush drained the blood from his head as he pulsed within her, his skin hot, then cold, then hot again as she lowered herself onto him. Not until the tip of his shaft touched her womb did he exhale.

"Asher?" she moaned.

"You feel so good. So good, baby. Sweet Savannah."

He reached for her face, pulling her toward him to kiss her as she pushed down on his shoulders, raising herself, then lowering again. He shuddered, trying to remember to breathe as he grew impossibly thicker and harder inside her. She rocked against him, and he sucked on her tongue before she pushed down on his shoulders again, raising her body. But this time, as she slipped down, his pelvis thrust up and she gasped into his mouth.

He groaned as she braced herself again, pushing up again as she slid down, until they created a rhythm of their own. She leaned forward, and her teeth scraped against his neck, making him so incredibly hot, he felt the tightening, the way he wanted to get as deep as possible, so there was no telling where he started and she began.

"Savannah," he said, palming her cheek to look into her face She moved up and down on him, meeting him stroke for stroke, her eyes closed and her neck bent back in ecstasy. "Come for me, baby. Come for me now."

She bit her lip, panting and gasping as her palms gripped his shoulders and her fingernails curled into his upper back, drawing blood. "Asher, I … I… Ohhhhh!"

Her ankles tightened around his waist, and she threw her head back. He pressed his lips to her throat and felt the walls of her sex clench around him so intensely, he lost any control he thought he had, thrusting into her as deeply as possible one last time. He came harder than he ever had, bellowing her name as the world slipped away and no one—no, not anyone—existed except for him and the unbelievably beautiful, tender, brilliant girl in his arms.

Savannah, whom he loved.

Savannah, whom he would love forever, long after she was gone.

CHAPTER 11

The first time you realize that you don't want anyone else but him

Asher pulled up in front of her house just as the airport van arrived. He leaned over the bolster to pull Savannah's face to his, then swept his tongue into her mouth, branding her, wanting her to remember every detail of their lovemaking all weekend long so that no other guys could possibly live up to the scorching intensity of their time together.

Damn it, but he hated letting her go.

She smiled at him shyly, then blushed and dropped her eyes. "I feel like everyone will know what we've been up to. I feel like it's written all over my face."

"Good." He kissed her hard again. "I want them to know. Especially the dozen guys in the condo next door."

"Oh, Asher. I've been in New York for years now. I wear black and curse too much. I'm not what any of the Danvers Country Club set is looking for. I'm not what they want."

He looked at her face—her full pink lips, flushed cheeks, bright eyes, and shiny brown hair. "You're what *every* man wants."

"But I'm *your* girlfriend."

And he had no choice. He had to kiss her again, only pulling back from her when they heard a sharp rapping on the glass beside her. Asher let his hand slide down her face and pushed the button on his door to open her window.

Scarlet Carmichael stood outside the window with her hands on her hips and a very sour expression on her face. "Really, Savannah? *Really*? The night before my bach you do a disappearing act?"

Asher leaned over the seat, looking up at Scarlet. "Sorry, Scarlet. It was my fault too."

Scarlet pouted. "Nobody ever made Savannah Calhoun Carmichael do a thing she didn't want to do, Asher Lee. Hush up."

"Don't you speak to him like that," said Savannah, reaching for Asher's hand.

"SA-VAN-NAH! The van is here! My attendants are inside drinkin' Bellinis. We are leavin' in *ten minutes*, and no one had any idea where on God's green earth you were!"

"Well, I'm here now, I'm already packed, and I'll be right in for a Bellini." Savannah made a whisking movement at Scarlet's face with her free hand. "Go on. Go on, now. I'm sayin' my good-byes."

"Well, say them … FASTER!" growled Scarlet, turning, well, scarlet. She stomped back into the house, her aqua-blue-and-white-striped sundress swishing angrily in her wake.

Savannah turned back to Asher. "I guess I have to go."

"I'm sorry I got you in trouble."
She shrugged, lifting his hand to her lips and kissing it softly. "It was worth it."

He leaned forward, swapping his lips for his hand and gently kissing her with all the love in his heart. "Be good now, ya hear?"

She nodded, giving him a sweet smile as she opened the door and walked through the white picket fence.

Asher's heart ached as he watched the front door closed behind her. Then he turned his car around and pointed it east, toward Maryland.

***

Savannah sat in the far back corner of the van and rested her head against the window glass, ignoring her sister and her seven sorority sister-style friends from high school: Lynnie, Jenny, Goosey, Bonnie, Millie, Minnie, and Ginny. When Christy and Kelly joined them for the rehearsal dinner and wedding, the group would be complete.

They'd all bonded for two key reasons: one, they were all thin, beautiful, and very Southern, and two, they loved the way their names sounded all together, preferring to call Scarlet by her actual first name, Katie. In fact, in high school, they'd once entered the talent show all together and sang the whole Britney Spears song "Oops! … I Did It Again" a cappella, using only their ten names for words.

When they first got in the van, Jenny said they should all call Savannah Vanny.

"Y'all, Vanny is a perfectly sweet sobriquet," said Jenny, who'd once spent a week in Paris.

"It's precious," agreed Goosey, whose little-known real name was Hortense. Her mother had called her "little goose" when she was a baby, and the nickname had stuck. Between Goosey and Hortense, Savannah was fairly certain she would have chosen Goosey too.

"All in favor of Vanny?" asked Minnie distractedly, reapplying her lip gloss ten minutes into the car ride.

They all raised their manicured hands and said, "Yea," in unison. Except Savannah.

"Nay. Not in favor," she said. "And since I won't answer to it, what's the use, girls?"

Scarlet shot her a look, and Savannah shrugged. She would go to Myrtle Beach and make the best of it with Scarlet's silly, well-meaning friends, but she drew the line at ridiculous nicknames.

"Well, Savannah *is* a lovely name," said Ginny, who'd always been the peacemaker. "Like Magnolia."

"Or Tulip. Like the honey," said Lynnie, the dim queen of non sequiturs.

Savannah's head spun. *Tupelo*, like the honey. Not to mention, they were naming flora—for heaven's sake, a tupelo was a tree—when Savannah was actually a city. She bit her tongue nearly hard enough to taste blood, then turned her attention, and forehead, to the cool glass of the window, stopping just short of banging her head against it.

And of course her thoughts turned to Asher.

How in the world would she write up the next installment of "Adam & Cassandra: An All-American Love Story"? Was she actually supposed to share some of what had taken place in Asher's bedroom last night? She clenched her thighs tightly together as her memories heated her cheeks and her eyes glazed over with lust. She'd ended up with five orgasms, all told, and the one this morning, as Asher made love to her when the sun was coming up, was the most beautiful of all.

Waking up spooned together, with her face turned toward the sunlight streaming through the windows, she'd felt Asher push her hair aside and bury his face in her neck. She sighed, warm and languorous, her body aching both from use and from want as she felt his growing hardness against her lower back. Her breathing sped up, hitching as she realized how much she wanted him again, how right it felt to be filled by him, how this was her last chance until next week.

She bent her top leg in invitation, pressing back against him, and he ran his hand lightly from under her breast to her side, over her waist, down to her hip, which he grasped gently. He moved closer, and she felt the tip of his hardness linger at her entrance. She covered his hand with hers, to give him permission and let him know she was ready. He eased himself inside her, inch by inch, slowly, lovingly, taking his time and stretching her gently until he was fully sheathed within her.

Despite his care, she still gasped as he entered, clenching her eyes shut as his velvet heat swelled inside of her. He reached around to caress her breasts, rolling a nipple tenderly between his thumb and finger as she kept her hand on top of his, and pressing kisses to the back of her neck.

"More," she murmured, leaning her head back against his shoulder.

He pulled back gently, then slid back into her again, deeper this time.

"Savannah," he groaned, his breath hot against her neck. "It's so good ..."

"More," she said again, raising his hand to her mouth. He slipped two fingers between her lips so she could suck on him, rolling her tongue around his fingers as his hips pulled back and rocked into her again.

Savannah's hand skimmed down her sensitive breasts to her tummy, slipping between the slick folds of skin, and whimpering as her fingers rubbed the throbbing bud of her sex while he gradually increased the rhythm from behind.

He withdrew his slippery fingers from her mouth, reaching for her nipple and pinching until it was hard and aching. Savannah arched back against him, feeling the pressure and heat pooling in her belly, beneath her fingers, tightening around his erection, which continued to slide and throb within her.

"Asher, I'm so close," she panted. "I'm so ..."

He pulled out of her almost entirely, lingering at her entrance, clutching her against his chest, and whispered, "I'm falling in love with you, Savannah." Then, he pushed back into her hard and fast and as deeply as possible. She cried out, her body exploding, the sweetness of his words making her breath catch. Her inner muscles clamped around his strong, hard length, holding him tightly, keeping him deep, as they found their release together—a climax so strong and so complete, it was like dying and being reborn in each other's arms.

Savannah's body trembled in her quiet corner of the van as she relived every perfect detail, her eyes dampening as she heard his words in her head again, *I'm falling in love with you, Savannah.*

For as much as she'd dated several different men, some quite seriously, Savannah had never been comfortable with the "I love you" stage of those relationships. It always felt fabricated or forced, like something that was expected— something that was supposed to come next in the relationship and that she could check off once the words were said. It had never felt real. It had never felt sacred. Until now. Because she heard it in his voice and felt it in his touch and knew it from the look in his eyes when they caressed her face: this was the real deal. Asher Lee was falling in love with her.

And for the first time in her life, because it was, in fact, the first time the words actually meant anything, they scared her. This wasn't checking off a box or saying words she didn't mean in a "Sure, love ya too" sort of way. He was braver than she was because even though she couldn't return the words this morning, she felt the same. She was falling in love with Asher too. The act of falling in love with someone was singular in her life, and wholly uncharted.

Her heart pounded relentlessly against her ribs.

Savannah didn't like uncharted.

And yet, as she gazed out the window with watery eyes, she realized that she didn't feel uncomfortable with Asher's declaration. She realized that there was little in her life that meant more to her than making room for Asher. She wanted him to love her. She craved his body and mind and heart. But she didn't know how to have them and keep them when there were other things she wanted too.

She forced herself to think about the piece that still needed to be written at some point today and sent to Maddox. She blocked out the group of singing, chattering girls around her and listened to the words in her head: *I'm falling in love with you.* Her reporter's mind insisted that, to nail the piece, she'd start with that line, then tastefully backtrack to how they got there. It was exactly what McNabb wanted. A honey of a love story. A crowd-pleaser. The "ooh, aah" moment that would make voyeuristic eyes mist with tears for the wounded vet who managed to find love in the arms of a reporter.

She frowned at her reflection in the glass as the green hills rushed by.

It wasn't about anonymity; she could easily protect Asher's privacy by changing their names. No, this was about a new problem that Savannah had never experienced. Their love affair might be great news, but it was also … *theirs.*

Asher had said those words to *her.* Only to her. Whispered them into her ear while their bodies were intimately connected, holding each other tenderly and reverently. They were sacred and powerful, and yes, they'd make a good story, but they belonged to her and Asher. They belonged to stolen moments during the most vibrant sunrise of her life. They belonged to her ears alone, not 100,000 more listening in.

And yet, even if she and Asher could figure out a way to meld their worlds, could she live a satisfying life in Danvers knowing she had thrown away her chance to restart her career? Would the safe glow of Asher's love be enough as she left her dreams dead by the roadside?

"Vanna," said Scarlet, throwing a small foiled packet and hitting her in the forehead. "You are far too serious for my bach weekend!"

Savannah picked up the condom from her lap and shook her head at her sister, who at some point had donned a plastic silver tiara that read "Bride-to-Be" in pink plastic rhinestones with a short white veil in the back. Three silver flasks were making the rounds, and Scarlet grabbed the nearest one and thrust it over the seats toward Savannah, then grabbed another and yelled, "Cheers!" with a big grin.

Savannah sighed. For once, Scarlet was right. Her thoughts were too heavy. She'd deal with them later.

"Cheers!" she cried, beaming at her sister and tilting back the flask of vodka and lemonade until it was empty.

***

"Well, Asher," said Colonel McCaffrey, M.D., as he entered the consulting office and sat behind the desk across from Asher. "Let's get down to it, eh? We can do the cast for your prosthesis today, but you'll have to come back in a week for the fitting, and then two weeks after that for final delivery. And when you come back for it, I advise you to stay on for a little while and really learn how to use it. I know you were hoping to get it all over

154

with in two visits, but it just doesn't work that way."

"I understand, sir."

"Do you still want to go ahead?"

Savannah's face appeared in his head, and his answer was quick and easy. It was time for him to make plans to live *in* the world, not outside it. "Yes, sir. Yes, I do."

The colonel slid a stack of forms across the desk. "A little light paperwork. You know the drill. Need it all back ASAP."

"Yes, sir." He placed his hand on the stack for a second, then looked up, meeting the doctor's eyes. "And my face, sir?"

McCaffrey opened a file and looked at it with furrowed brows before closing it and handing it to Asher. "Now wait a minute, son, before you go looking at that. Never liked these digital projections, because medicine, especially reconstructive procedures, is not an exact science. I'd hate for you to look at that and feel excited or disappointed because the reality is that there are no guarantees. It's just a guess based on the procedures the doctors would be trying. But, well, it's our best guess of what you'd look like after the initial surgeries."

Asher stared at the manila file that held the answers to whether or not it would ever be possible to live a normal life again. He took a deep breath, surprised by the burning behind his eyes, and opened the folder. What he saw inside made him gasp, and he blinked repeatedly so he wouldn't cry in front of a colonel.

No, the man looking back at him wasn't perfect. His skin had an irregular texture and tone. His nose was still slightly misshapen. But he had two symmetrical ears, his cheek and jaw looked almost normal, and his right eye socket didn't droop. If you glanced at him for more than a second, you'd notice he'd been through something, but he would mostly blend into a crowd. He wasn't beautiful, but he'd mostly be able to lead a normal life.

"Sir, I … I don't know … I mean …" Asher looked back down at the picture and blinked.

"It's all right, son. I know." The doctor paused, then spoke gently. "There are no guarantees. This is a forensics rendering based on what you've got and what we've been able to do in the past. Could be a little better; could fall short. Only way to know is to try."

"How many procedures?" asked Asher.

"They think four, minimum. Possibly up to seven."

Asher winced. "How many years?"

"That's the good news. If all goes well? About six months. We'd start with your ear. They're building ears out of cartilage these days, but I'd start with a prosthesis. We'd have to smooth out what's there, but then we could do an operation to implant a magnet so that the ear stays in place. We'll take a graft from your forehead to reconstruct your right eye socket. Mend your cheek and even out your jaw with silicone implants. Smooth out some of that burned skin on your lower cheek. I know your leg bothers you too. You may opt to have something done for that as well."

Asher shook his head. "Seven's enough, doc. I can live with my leg as is."

"You'll be back and forth a lot, son. Four hours each way to Virginia during some pretty traumatic reconstructions."

Asher thought of Savannah again, her sweet face and bright eyes. He couldn't ask her to join him on this hellish six-month journey, and he couldn't ask her to wait for him either. He'd have to let her go. She'd head to Phoenix, and he'd head to Maryland. And whatever the future held in store for them would reveal itself later.

For now, he still had two weeks left with her, and he wouldn't let anything get in the way of that time.

"What's our time frame?"

"First available OR table opens up in three weeks."

Asher nodded, feeling relieved. "Thank you, sir."

"You'll rent a place here in Bethesda? You'll need to be local for most of July, August, September. You might be able to commute back and forth by October. And if all goes well, you'll be finished completely by Christmas."

Christmas. Damn. That felt like an awfully long time. He had no right to ask, but he couldn't help but wonder if she'd still want him, still be available, by Christmas. It made his heart clench to think that she'd have moved on by then.

"I'll arrange for housing, sir."

The colonel nodded, gesturing for the file. "Can't let you keep it."

"I know, sir."

"Any questions, Asher?"

"No, sir."

The colonel stood up, extending his hand. "Well, I guess we'll see you next week. For the fitting. Don't forget, you've got the casting at four o'clock today."

Four o'clock. Everything important in my life happens at four o'clock.

"Yes, sir." Asher shook his hand and followed him from the room.

"I'm glad you're finally taking this step, Asher. Mind if I ask what changed your mind?"

Asher felt the phantom touch of her hands on his skin, her body pressed against his, her cries as they climaxed together this morning. What happened in private between him and Savannah was too special, too sacred, even to share with his doctor, whom he trusted and liked very much. "I'm sorry, sir. Personal reasons."

Colonel McCaffrey slapped him lightly on the shoulder and gave him a knowing grin. "I bet she's beautiful."

"She is," said Asher, grinning as he pulled the door behind him. *She's the most amazing girl in the world.*

***

A few hours later, in Myrtle Beach, the most amazing girl in the world had definitely had too much to drink. Savannah looked at the half-finished steak on her plate and felt her stomach rumble in protest.

They'd arrived in town by lunchtime, spent the afternoon sunning on the beach, and found the boys next door barbecuing when they finally walked back up to their house at dusk.

Trent had grabbed his bride-to-be around the waist and invited all of them to come over for dinner, promising steak, sausage—the Beavis and Butt-Head style chuckle after this menu item wasn't lost on Savannah, though she could have sworn Lynnie looked confused—and plenty of cold beer. How could they say no?

Also not lost on Savannah was the smoldering smile she was given by Lance Hamilton, Trent's older brother, whom Savannah had briefly (and disastrously) dated in high school. She later heard that Serena Shepherd had lost her virtue to Lance. According to what she'd gathered, Lance had been sipping Rum and Cokes without the Rum all night, and Serena had been an easy mark.

Lance Hamilton had since married some sweet thing he met at Chapel Hill and settled back down in Danvers, only to be caught with his secretary in a compromising position a few years later. The sweet thing turned out to be not so sweet in the wake of his betrayal, packed up their three-year-old daughter, and returned to Tennessee for a divorce and a fresh start. Which left Lance, unfortunately, available.

At dinner Savannah took the very last seat at the very long picnic table, beside Goosey, since they were the last two to arrive. Then Lance weaseled his way between the two women.

"Hey Goose, let the old folks sit together, huh?"

Goosey shrugged apologetically at Savannah and slid down to make room. Savannah rolled her eyes. "You always did know how to kill a compliment, Lance."

"You're lookin' real good now, Savannah Carmichael," he said, his face turned to her in all its blinding beauty. He had perfect lips, high cheekbones, and an Old South patrician nose. His dirty-blond hair was slicked back like a Wall Street banker's, and he wore a polo shirt of deep cerulean blue, the same color as his eyes.

"Again, bowling me over, Lance. I guess I looked shabby before?" She looked down at her scoop-neck black sheath dress. It wasn't exactly a floral sundress, but she knew Scarlet wanted all the girls to be fanciful this weekend, and this was about as close as Savannah could get. She took hold of the chunky silver necklace around her neck, playing with the large links.

"Hard to tell under the one-piece you were wearing when you walked up from the beach. I like my women in *bikinis*." He ran his index finger down her arm. "You have a bikini, Miss Savannah?"

"If I did," she answered sweetly, "I wouldn't be paradin' around in it for *you*."

"Whew! So cold. That time up in New York made you frosty, honey. I'd like to warm you up a little."

She picked up her beer and downed it in a gulp. It was her third or fourth, and she was light-headed, but being a little drunk also meant that she could keep thoughts of Asher and articles at bay, which—if she couldn't have Asher with her and if she couldn't decide how to write her story—felt better right now.

"Come on now, honey. You and me had a good thing once upon a time."

He cracked open another beer from the large iced basin on the table in front of them and handed it to her.

"*A good thing*? We went out on three dates, Lance. You tried to grope me. I called it quits."

"We were just gettin' to the good part." He licked his lips and smiled at her, putting the beer bottle to his mouth and throwing back his head. Okay, Savannah had to admit, though she wasn't sure if it was the beer talking or the sight of Lance's throat sucking down those suds: he *was* awfully pretty.

Asher's face flitted through her mind, and she grasped for it, taking a long draw on her own bottle. "I'm seein' someone, Lance."

"Now, I think I heard somethin' about that, but I didn't imagine for one moment it was true." His eyes narrowed as he cut off a chunk of steak, chewing thoughtfully.

"Well, despite your tawdry imaginings, it *is* true."

"Asher Lee? The old war hero? The cripple?" Lance turned to Savannah, laughing. "You that hard up, Savannah? You have to date circus freaks?"

She stared at her half-finished steak as her stomach rolled over. She'd had enough. She didn't have to sit here and be polite as Lance Hamilton ripped into the man she loved. "You always *were* an asshole, Lance."

She swung her legs over the back of the bench and stood up. *Oh Lord. Spins.* She dropped her hand to Lance's shoulder to steady herself, and he covered her hand with his, bolting up and put his arm around her waist.

"Oopsie, Miss Daisy."

Goosey looked up from Lance's other side. "You okay, Savannah?"

Savannah didn't much like the way Lance was holding on to her, but she feared she'd fall over if he let go, so she patted his hand gratefully. "Just fine, Goosey, honey."

Lance tightened his arm around her and gave Goosey his most panty-melting grin, flicking his eyes down the table where Trent and Scarlet were holding court before smiling at Goosey again.

"No need to trouble everyone, silly goose. If they ask, just say Savannah needed to walk off the spirits and I was lendin' some moral support."

Savannah looked at Goosey's worried eyes and smiled reassuringly before hiccupping rather loudly. She giggled, putting her hand over her mouth.

"Don't tell Scarlet I'm drunk, Goose," she said in a conspiratorial whisper.

"You be careful now, Savannah."

Savannah rolled her eyes at small-town Goosey. Savannah had lived in New York City, for heaven's sake. She could handle Lance Hamilton for a quick, bracing walk on the beach, couldn't she? Of course she could.

Lance started leading her away, and when they'd rounded

the house, she jerked away from him. "Keep your hands to yourself, Lance."

"I was just tryin' to be a gentleman. Help out a lady in distress."

"The day *you're* a gentleman …," said Savannah, missing the way his eyes narrowed at her criticism.

He grabbed her hand and pulled her toward the rapidly darkening, deserted beach. "You be nice, now. I heard you. You're with Lee. I'm not gonna make a move. We can just go a little closer to the water and look at the lights. You can take some deep breaths of sea air, and I bet you feel right in a snap."

His words were friendly and reassuring, and aside from holding her hand, he wasn't being Handsy Lancey, so she relaxed.

"Breathe in," he said, slowing their pace. "Smell that sea air?"

"Mmmm." Asher was right. Even a quarter mile from the Strand, she could smell popcorn and cotton candy, funnel cakes and suntan lotion. "It's just like he said."

"Just like *who* said?" asked Lance, slipping an arm around her waist.

She didn't like that, but she still didn't feel too steady either, so she ignored it.

"Asher." She smiled, thinking about him. "He used to come here."

"Before his face got all blown off? Is it true what they say? That he's all deformed?"

Savannah tried to yank away, but Lance held her tight against his hip. She looked back toward the house, but they'd walked a considerable distance now and the house was much more than a stone's throw away.

"Don't talk about him like that," said Savannah, starting to feel anxious. She wiggled against Lance to free herself, but his grip was strong.

"Or you'll what?"

"Let go of me, Lance."

He didn't. He put his other arm around her waist and jerked her up against his body, pressing his lips to her neck as his erection pushed aggressively against her belly. "No, I don't think so. I think you owe me after I helped you get away from that dinner without embarrassin' yourself. I think you owe me a few kisses at least."

Savannah hauled back her free hand and slammed it into Lance's face with all her might, connecting with his nose.

"HELL!" he cried, letting go of her to reach up and cradle his bleeding nose.

Savannah didn't wait to see what happened next. She turned and ran, as fast as she could, toward the light of the houses. She was panting and sweating, and her flip-flops fell off in the heavy sand, but she kept running until her legs were pulled out from under her. She fell hard on the sand, tasting grit on her tongue as the wind was knocked out of her lungs.

"You low-rent Northern slut! You punched me?" Lance's weight was crushing her already depleted lungs, and Savannah panicked, grappling at the sand as he straddled her back. "I tried to be nice."

Suddenly he moved to the side, then rolled her over and was upon her again, straddling her hips as he shoved her dress up. "Look at me, Savannah. I want you lookin' in my eyes when I take you."

The change in position allowed her lungs to release, and she sucked in a gasp of air, reaching up with her fists to pummel whatever part of Lance she came in contact with, but he was strong and had her at a disadvantage. He grasped both of her wrists with one hand roughly, pinning them over her head, hurting her.

"You're gonna stop that right—"

Before he could finish his thought, Savannah cleared her throat and spit into his face, covering one eye and part of his cheek in slick saliva, which slid down his face, mixing with the blood of his still-bleeding nose. His eyes flared with fury in the dim light afforded by the nearby houses, and he smacked her face hard, his palm connecting with her lips, which slammed into her teeth. Her head reeled with shock as she tasted the metallic flavor of blood on her tongue.

"Whorin' around with a cripple when a perfectly good man wants to take a crack at you, you ungrateful tramp." He reached up under her dress, and she felt him grab the waistband of her panties when she heard someone calling her name.

"Savannah? Savannah, you out here?"

"Hey, now, Savannah? You here?"

Two voices. Goosey's and Jenny's.

Lance sneered toward the sound of the voices. Then he looked back down at Savannah, removing his hand from under her dress and kneeling at her side so he wasn't straddling her anymore.

She half rolled, half jerked to her stomach, then to her hands and knees, coughing and sobbing, and started throwing up on the sand.

"Oh, no!" Goosey's voice was closer now, drawn by the sounds of Savannah's puke.

Suddenly Jenny was kneeling beside her. "Oh, Savannah, honey, you drank too much."

Lance spoke from beside her. "Poor thing hooked me in the nose when she leaned over and started retchin'."

Neither Goosey nor Jenny addressed Lance, but Savannah felt small hands under her shoulders, helping her up.

"Come on now, Savannah," said Jenny. "We have to get you cleaned up."

Savannah stood up, brushing the back of her hand over her mouth.

"Oh, honey," said Goosey, zeroing in on her bleeding lip. "You hurt yourself!"

"I … I, uh…" Savannah tried to catch her breath, but latent fear and fury still made it hard to breathe. She looked down at Lance, who sat on the sand, pressing a handkerchief to his bleeding nose and looking up at her with mean eyes.

"We were havin' a little fun. Wrestlin'," he said, challenging Savannah with his glare.

"*Wrestling*?! You were about a minute away from raping me!" shouted Savannah, pressing the back of her hand to her mouth, then drawing it away. A thin strip of blood stained her hand. Tears ran down her face, but she barely felt them, and she didn't wipe them away. She stared down at Lance until he turned from her, looking out at the water.

"*That* is an ugly word. And I think I look worse than you do, Miss Savannah," he said. He was trying to be light about it, but she could hear the uncertainty in his voice.

"I'm filing charges," she said, and both Jenny and Goosey gasped. Filing charges was an aggressive, Northern way of handling differences, but Savannah didn't care. Lance Hamilton was a menace, and every girl in Danvers should know to beware.

"Drunk girl goes for a walk on the beach. Both she and her companion end up bloody. Looks about even steven to me. Maybe I should file assault charges too."

He was right. He hadn't actually done anything to her that she hadn't done to him. They were both bleeding, and there hadn't actually been a rape. What good would it do for them both to file assault charges against each other? "You're trash, Lance Hamilton."

"Savannah, you come on back up to the house now," said Jenny quickly, pulling on Savannah's arm.

"You are a snake. A rat. A lowlife rapist," snarled Savannah, throwing her sandy hair over her shoulder and shrugging off the girls.

"Now, now, Miss Savannah. Ain't becomin' to call names," said Lance calmly, still seated on the sand, looking out at the ocean.

"Come on back to the house, honey," said Goosey. "We'll get you cleaned up."

"You two know what he is. Just as well as I do."

Neither young woman said anything. Jenny reached out and took Savannah's hand. "You've had a time of it. Come on back to the house now, Savannah."

Savannah bent down close to Lance's ear. "If I ever hear of you touching another woman the way you touched me tonight, I will write the biggest, baddest exposé that ever hit Danvers, and *everyone* will know the scumbag rapist that you are."

Lance chuckled smugly without looking up, and Savannah turned, walking back up to the house arm in arm with Jenny and Goosey.

CHAPTER 12
The first time you see a future with him

Asher drove back into Danvers late afternoon on Saturday, wondering what time Savannah was getting home from Myrtle Beach the next day. They had a regular planned date for Monday afternoon, but that was forty-eight hours away, and after everything they'd shared on Thursday night, it felt like forty-eight million years. Urgency had always been a strong component of his relationship with Savannah—he'd wanted her from the start, from the first moment she arrived on his doorstep in her sister's sundress holding a plate of brownies—but what he felt now had grown into something visceral, an all consuming feeling for which you might change the course of your life.

He pulled into his driveway and rounded the car, taking his small duffel bag out of the trunk before heading into the house. Miss Potts opened the front door.

"Afternoon, Miss Potts!" he exclaimed.

"How was Maryland?"

"They're making the mold. I go back next weekend for the fitting. Weekend after that, it'll be finished."

"And your …?"

"My face?" He sighed, walking past her into the front hallway. "Not quite as simple."

"How many?" asked Miss Potts.

"At least four," he said. "Maybe seven."

"And what are they planning to do?"

He let his bag fall from his shoulder onto the marble floor and faced her. "Ear. Nose. Jaw. And some of my cheek."

"That's a strong start," she said. "Your leg?"

He shook his head. "I'm leaving it alone."

"Couldn't they—"

"No. My face only."

She gave him a grim smile and nodded once, looking away as though there was more to say, but she didn't know how to say it. "Can I, uh, can I get you some food?"

He looked closely at her. "Is it me, or are you acting funny?"

She looked away quickly, bustling toward the kitchen. "Why I …"

"Miss Potts," he said, following her. "What's going on with you?"

She stopped in front of the kitchen sink, turning to face him.

"Now, before you blame me," she said, "I'll have you know I had nothing to do with it this time."

"With what?"

"I… I admit that I led Savannah astray the weekend before last, but that was only because I wanted her to see you as a man, not an invalid."

"What did you do?" he asked, worried now.

"Nothing, Asher. I swear. Nothing." She shrugged helplessly. "She canceled Monday. No explanation. Just canceled."

"What do you mean?"

"Savannah called here this morning and canceled your meeting on Monday."

His heart fell, and his hand started sweating. He clenched it into a fist. Myrtle Beach blared in his mind like a neon sign.

"What did she say?"

"She said she wasn't able to make it and to tell you sorry. She hung up quickly."

Asher's mind reeled. It didn't make any sense. He combed

through their last interaction in front of her house, and he could think of nothing that would indicate her pulling away from him. *The boys are renting the condo next door.*

He turned away from Miss Potts so she wouldn't see the confusion in his eyes.

"Did you hear a lot of noise in the background, like she was having a great time? At the beach? At a party?"

"No. No, I didn't."

He swallowed, reaching up to scratch an itch, and was surprised to feel his uneven skin under his fingertips. It still surprised him sometimes to realize how badly injured he was. And she'd been at Myrtle Beach with a bunch of good-looking guys. His breath hitched as he thought of her with someone else. But no. That wasn't Savannah. She'd just been with *him* on Thursday night. *She wouldn't ... I mean, she wouldn't ...*

"When did she call?" he asked sharply.

Miss Potts took the phone out of its cradle and handed it to Asher. "Look for yourself."

He pressed the menu button to look at recent calls, scrolling back two calls to find Savannah's. 11:23 a.m. Then something occurred to him. His brows furrowed together as he stared at the phone.

"*Savannah* called to cancel? Or her mother called to cancel for her?"

"Oh, no, dear. It wasn't Judy. It was definitely Savannah. If my memory's right, Frank and Judy are away on mission weekend for Stone Hill Methodist."

He turned to look at Miss Potts. "But the call came from her parents' house."

Miss Potts nodded.

"This morning."

She nodded again.

"But Savannah's in Myrtle Beach."

Miss Potts stared at him, seemingly at a loss, then shrugged her shoulders.

As his mind scrambled to figure things out, he absently dropped the phone back into the cradle. Then he turned on his heel and headed back toward the front hall.

***

Savannah winced at her reflection in her bedroom mirror. There was a crust of reddish-brown blood, and a little bruising under the place where Lance had split her lip, and it was puffy and discolored. She'd stopped by the local clinic on her way back into town, and the doctor told her it would go away in a couple of days, but for now she looked like she'd been in a bar fight.

After Goosey and Jenny had walked her back to the beach house, Savannah asked them to bring Scarlet inside without alarming her. Scarlet flounced into the bedroom, annoyed to be pulled away from the barbecue, but her face fell when Savannah looked up from where she sat on the bed.

"Vanna! What happened?"

"Your future brother-in-law got a little fresh with me," she said, making a decision to downplay what had happened. She wasn't interested in ruining Scarlet's entire weekend. She could explain in further detail once they got home.

"What? Lance?"

"The very snake."

"Oh, Vanna, are you okay? I'm sure it was a misunderstandin'," she said weakly. "Why, Lance is just a big ol' flirt."

"No, miss," said Savannah, with flint in her eyes. "He's not."

And something in her tone must have conveyed the seriousness of the situation, because Scarlet didn't argue. Maybe she knew Lance was dangerous. Maybe she'd even been on the receiving end of his untoward attentions once or twice.

Savannah took a shaky breath, walked to the closet, and rolled out her still mostly packed suitcase.

"I'm going home," she said, heading into the bathroom for her bathing suit. "I can't stay."

"No! No, Vanna. Don't go." Scarlet ran to her sister, took her hand, and pulled her up against her. "Vanna, I'm sorry. I'm so sorry this happened."

"Me too. But I'm still going home," said Savannah, her nerves still a little shot from what had almost happened on the beach. "I'm not pressing charges. When you see Lance, you'll know why."

Scarlet's eyes widened.

"But if he ever goes near another girl again, I will fillet him, Scarlet. So help me, I will end him in print."

Savannah called a cab and made it to the airport by ten o'clock, for the last flight from Myrtle Beach to Washington, D.C. She spent the night at an airport motel in Washington and arranged for a private car to take her home in the morning. She'd be sending the bill to Hamilton & Sons. That was for certain.

She gazed into the mirror and touched the discolored skin gingerly, grimacing as pain shot from her mouth to her brain, worsening her headache. There's no way it would be healed by Monday. Maybe Wednesday, if she was lucky.

Miss Potts hadn't pressed her for more information when she told her she wasn't coming on Monday, but Savannah heard the disappointment in the older woman's voice. Savannah hated that she was letting Asher down. She hated not being able to see him, but she was embarrassed by what had happened on the beach, and she didn't want for Asher to think, even for a moment, that she'd been after alone time with Lance. It was just best to wait until Wednesday and not open the whole can of worms.

She sat down on her bed to check her e-mails. The quiet afternoon in her parents' empty house had been productive, at least. She'd sent the third installment of her article to McNabb, and he called her almost immediately to tell her how much he liked it.

"I've decided to print the whole thing at once, Carmichael. A big, beautiful Lifestyles piece on the Fourth of July. How a local girl and wounded soldier found love. It's going to be a smash."

Savannah had smiled weakly at the phone. Even with Asher's name changed to Adam, Savannah employing her pen name, Cassandra Calhoun, and Danvers never mentioned, she still didn't feel entirely comfortable sharing the intimacies of her time with Asher. The latest story had been about family supper, movie night, and Asher telling her he was falling in love with her.

As she'd written the story, she typed the words, then erased them, then retyped them, staring at them for a long time:

```
In the early-morning hours, I
woke up beside him, bathed in
rising sunlight. I pressed my
fingertips   to   his   scarred
face  as  he  looked  into  my
eyes  and  told  me  he  was
falling in love with me.
```

She declined, of course, to add that they'd both been naked and that, as soon as he'd said these precious words, he went on to thrust so far and deep into her that he ended up giving her the best early-morning orgasm she'd ever experienced. She moved the cursor over the words "falling in love with me," highlighting them and staring at them for a long moment. She was falling in love with him too, and she hated that their story was the only way for her to dig herself out of the professional hole she found herself in. She wished there was another way, but there wasn't. She just had to hope that Asher either (a) wouldn't read the article at all, or (b) would forgive her for using parts of their story.

She rolled onto her back, staring at the ceiling, wondering what he was doing right now. Was he at home, reading a book in the grove? Or having a late lunch in his study? Taking an afternoon nap or chatting with Miss Potts over chess? She longed for him brutally, wishing she could jump in her car and drive to his house. They could spend another weekend together and just let the days melt into Monday. And the nights. Oh God, the nights. Her breathing quickened, and her pulse hammered. She'd never had a lover as patient and passionate as Asher. It was as though he couldn't get enough of her body, and she certainly couldn't get enough of his.

At some point, she'd stopped seeing his injuries entirely. They certainly didn't shock her anymore. His lips, his hand, his strong arms and beautiful torso ... He loved her as she'd never been physically loved in her entire life. She was addicted to him. It was harder and harder to imagine the future without him.

The doorbell had probably rung twice before she heard it, cutting unwelcome into her lazy daydreams. She made her way downstairs. Her mother had told her that a friend from church was dropping off bridal magazines for Scarlet. It couldn't possibly be anyone here to see her; she was supposed to have been in Myrtle Beach all weekend.

As she opened the door, she gasped, reaching up to cover her injured mouth as her eyes slammed into Asher's.

She was too late. He'd already seen.

His face, which had, in an instant, changed from surprised to happy, now showed confusion and worry. Reaching forward, he wrapped his fingers around her wrist gently and pulled it away from her mouth. As he stared at the ugly contusion, he sucked in a gasp, and his chest swelled as he held it. She tried to pull her wrist away, but he held on tightly, so her efforts only managed to pull him inside. He pushed the door closed behind him with his foot.

"What happened?"

"I ..." She panted lightly as he still held her wrist. "I, um ..."

"Don't bother lying," he said softly, lowering her wrist and releasing it, so he could brush her lips with the feather touch of his thumb, examining the small contusion. "I'll know."

His gaze found her eyes, which searched his desperately, and, to her horror, she felt herself crumple against his chest, weeping into his shoulder as his strong arms encircled her.

***

I'm going to kill him. I'm going to kill Lance Hamilton.

Savannah sat curled up next to him on the couch. He had his arm around her shoulder, and she burrowed her head into his neck with her legs tucked under her body. She'd stopped crying a little while ago, but his fury had grown white-hot and dangerous despite the calming way he stroked her shoulder as she told him what had happened in Myrtle Beach. Every muscle in his body longed to find Lance Hamilton and smash his fist into his face.

God, if Goosey and Jenny hadn't followed her … if they'd waited another few minutes to go looking for her … It was bad enough that Hamilton had touched his polluted lips to Savannah's neck and reached under her dress. Asher felt the adrenaline rush that made every protective instinct rise to the fore, and pulled her closer, pressing his lips to her hair. Hamilton would get his. Asher would see to it. For now, he needed to concentrate on Savannah.

"I'm so sorry that happened to you, baby. I'm so sorry."

She sniffled, one of her hands clutching at his shirt, and he felt her breath hitch.

"I shouldn't have been drinking so much," she said in a soft voice, full of self-recrimination.

"No!" he said sharply, leaning back to look down at her face. "Don't do that. You didn't do anything wrong. He's a goddamned pig, Savannah. You didn't do—"

"I knew who he was, Asher. I had no business being alone with him. I knew what he did to Serena Shepherd."

"What?" he asked. "Jock Shepherd's little sister? What did he do to her?"

"Best I know? He raped her. When we were seniors."

"Rape," said Asher, hating the taste of the ugly word in his mouth.

"Minimally there was very strong coercion." Savannah paused. "No, that's total crap. It was rape."

"You're sure?"

Savannah nodded against his chest. "I overheard her in the girl's room talking to her best friend. I didn't want to leave the stall, so I lifted my feet up and pretended I wasn't there. I heard the whole blow-by-blow. But she was drunk, and he wasn't. And she said no, but he kept going."

Asher's mind reeled. Serena had been the youngest of the four Shepherd siblings, littlest sister of Jock Shepherd, with whom Asher had played lacrosse in high school.

"Jock and Tim Shepherd would've beat him stupid if they'd known." Actually he knew Jock and Tim would've killed him and wouldn't have said sorry either.

"It's not something a girl advertises." She took a ragged breath, and her hand on his chest flexed again. "If I'd known you were coming over, I'd have …"

"What? Tried to cover it up?"

Savannah leaned up, looking into his eyes and nodding. "I was drinking, Asher. It was a bad decision to walk on the beach with him."

Maybe she'd been flirting with Lance? Given him the wrong idea? It felt like she was holding something back. "Did you *want* to be alone with him?"

"No! I swear it. I called him an asshole just before I stood up to leave. But then the world swam, and he steadied me with an arm around my waist. I didn't want Scarlet to know I was so buzzed, and he offered to take a walk with me so I could clear my head, so I—"

"Wait. Why'd you call him an asshole? What was happening just before you got up?"

He watched a tear roll out of her eye and travel down her face. And then he knew. He knew what she was holding back, and it felt like someone had just sucker-punched him in the heart.

"He was talking about me," he said quietly.

She stared down at her hands and nodded.

"He was talking about me, and you called him an asshole, and he attacked you on the beach ten minutes later."

Savannah didn't say anything, but one of her shoulders shrugged lightly, and he knew he was right. It made sense. Someone with the ego of Lance Hamilton wouldn't be able to handle the fact that Savannah was sleeping with a cripple, a freak, and not with him. Asher clenched his jaw so hard it ached. The woman he loved had been assaulted because of his presence in her life. It made his heart twist, and he fisted his hand so hard, his short nails bit into his palm.

Savannah's shoulders crumpled forward, and he could tell from the way they were shaking that she was crying again, so he shoved thoughts of Lance Hamilton to the back of his head and gathered her against him, lying back on the couch and pulling her down beside him.

"No, darlin', no. Don't cry. It's okay. You're safe now."

He kicked off his shoes and lay flat on his back with Savannah on her side sandwiched between him and the couch cushions. She reached up and pulled a blanket from the back of the couch, spreading it over them, and let her head drop wearily to his chest. He rubbed her back in soothing strokes, whispering that she was safe, and within minutes he heard her breathing normalize, deeply in, deeply out. She was asleep.

It tugged at his heart that she was so exhausted. She must not have slept much last night between her abrupt departure from Myrtle Beach and early-morning car ride back to Virginia. Come to think of it, she hadn't slept much on Thursday night either. He stroked her hair gently, and knowing she couldn't hear him, whispered, "I love you, Savannah. I'm so sorry, baby."

He would deal with Lance Hamilton on Monday. For now, all that mattered was Savannah, and all he wanted to do was take care of her.

***

Savannah's fingers curled around the soft blanket, and she sighed as her eyes fluttered open. The light was weak and dying in her parents' living room, and she was alone on the couch, wrapped up carefully in a blanket. But the most heavenly smells were coming from the kitchen.

She sat up, remembering that Asher had been by and she'd told him everything before crying her eyes out and falling asleep on his chest. She took a deep breath and realized she felt better than she'd felt in two days, like a weight had been lifted in telling her story to Asher. Just being with him felt safer and better than being anywhere else. She tried a smile and found that her lips still hurt, but the pain was fading.

"Well, that's a good sign," he said from the living room doorway. "Waking up with a smile."

"I feel so much better now that I told you."

He crossed the room and squatted down in front of her, taking her hand and bringing it to his lips. "Wish *I* did."

"Sorry to burden you with it."

His eyes shot up and held hers, intense and angry. "You think I'm upset with *you*? Nuh-uh, darlin'. But I'd like to kill Lance Hamilton. He's a goddamned menace."

Despite the hot, hard, genuine anger infused into his words, her brain got stuck on the way he said *darlin'*. It was the second time he'd used that endearment, and the way he drawled it sounded so sexy and so right, it made her swoon inside a little.

"You're my girl, Savannah. You're not burdening me. Nothing's off-limits. I love—I love it when you talk to me. About anything."

She took a deep breath, letting the blanket fall from her shoulders.

"Anything?" she asked, lowering her voice just a touch.

He nodded. His eyes didn't give much away, but she could have sworn she saw a bit of heat flare up behind them.

She leaned forward. "Asher, I don't want to talk about Lance Hamilton anymore." She licked her lips and looked up at Asher. "Call me darlin' again."

His eyes darkened, capturing hers as he leaned forward until she felt his breath on her lips. "Darlin'."

Shivers cascaded down her back. "How gently do you think you could kiss me?"

"Oh," he sighed, smiling at her with his lips opened softly. "I think I could try."

His fingers threaded through her hair, pulling her closer, and she closed her eyes and felt the feather-light brush of his lips across hers. For such a tender caress, a surprisingly strong bolt of heat shot down from her face to right between her thighs, which opened to him.

He dropped to his knees, scooting forward, then sitting back on his haunches as his arms wrapped around her waist and he pulled her down onto his lap. She straddled him with her back against the couch and her ankles locked around his back as their lips touched. She bowed her body forward, into him, as the kiss deepened, still gentle, but their tongues were touching now, swirling and circling.

She nudged her hips forward, brushing over his erection, and he groaned into her mouth. Savannah swallowed the sound, threading her fingers through his hair, gathering it all at the nape of his neck and tilting his head back to brush her lips against the exposed skin of his throat.

Ding-ding. Ding-ding. Ding-ding.

"Fuuuu…," he growled as she ran her tongue over his skin, tasting him. "Baby, that's the oven," he said through gritted teeth.

"The oven?" She pressed her breasts against him as her hands laced behind his neck and her lips lingered on the warm spot at the base of his neck.

Ding-ding.

"I made you dinner," he said in a strained voice.

"What?" She was snapped out of her lust coma by his words and leaned back, slack jawed, to stare at him.

"Dinner," he said, panting against her cheek. "I made you a casserole."

"You made me a *casserole*?" she asked, trying to get her head around this information. No boyfriend had been sweet enough to make dinner for her. Never. It was a totally new experience.

"French toast casserole," he explained, his hand gently rubbing her back. "It's the only thing I really know how to make, and I thought you might be hungry."

I am hungry, she realized. *For food first, then for you.*

She wiggled off his lap and stood up, then dangled her hand by his face to help him up too. He took her hand, and once he was standing in front of her, she took his face between her hands. "No one's ever made me dinner before, Asher."

His face transformed from slightly confused to very pleased, and he grinned at her.

"My gratitude." She kissed his lips. "Might be." She kissed him again. "Endless."

"Endless?" he asked, staring at her almost like he was surprised he managed to speak at all.

"Mm-hm," she said, pushing her hips into the hardness behind his jeans as her tongue flicked out to lick his lips one last time.

"How, um, how endless?" he asked, his eyes dark and wide and a little drugged.

"The sort of gratitude that lasts … All. Night. Long," she whispered with a healthy bit of saucy. Then she bit his lower lip, stepped around him, and headed for the kitchen.

CHAPTER 13

When he woke up in her bed the next morning, it took him a few seconds to figure out where he was. The early-morning light filtering through the gauzy white curtains made her whole room feel sweet and dreamy, and he pulled her closer, hardening on contact when the soft skin of her backside shoved into his hips.

She sighed lightly, but he could tell she was still asleep from the way her chest swelled and relaxed under his hand beneath her breasts. He kissed her hair, breathing in the familiar scent of lemons, thinking about last night.

They'd eaten his French toast casserole at her parents' kitchen table, smothering the golden pieces with warm maple syrup and talking about whatever popped into their heads. At one point, she'd gestured to a white cross on the wall, surrounded by blue ribbons, and told him it was his mother's cross. Damn if his eyes didn't burn a little looking at it. The casserole was his mother's recipe, and he felt how pleased she would have been to see him sitting in Judy Carmichael's kitchen with her beautiful daughter. He felt his mother's hand on his life, in his growing love for Savannah, and it made her seem even more like a missing puzzle piece, like something he didn't even know was missing until she arrived fully formed in his life.

He'd asked her about the article, and again she demurred, telling him she'd show him when it was all done. It didn't bother him that she was shy about it, though his curiosity was starting to get the better of him. Anyway, she'd quickly distracted him, taking his hand and pulling him upstairs to her bedroom, where she demonstrated what "endless gratitude" looked like.

Their physical relationship was practically mind-bending. Before his injuries, he'd had a healthy sex life, but nothing he'd ever experienced compared to sex with Savannah. She blew everything that had come before totally and completely out of the water. It touched him deeply that she didn't seem to see his imperfections and disfigurement—she either saw beyond them or simply accepted them—and it made him want to kneel at her feet in gratitude and devotion after so many lonely years.

But second to their scorching chemistry was how easily he could talk to her. Growing up in provincial Danvers had its benefits: safety and community, fresh air, green grass, and kissing behind the bleachers. He'd had the typical all-American childhood, complete with doting parents and the additional promise of a sizable trust fund. But spending time in Charlottesville and in the Army had shown Asher a lot more of the world than sleepy little Danvers could offer. He'd been exposed to so many different ideas and cultures, alternate ways of looking at things. Even upon returning to Danvers, he'd read copiously, keeping himself—mentally, at least—of and in the world as much as possible. Not that it really mattered at this point in Asher's life, but even if he wanted to mix it up with the locals, it was unlikely that the sensibilities of small-town Danvers would jibe very well with the man he had become.

Which is why Savannah, who had studied in New York, reported on important world events and kept her mind sharp and current, was so amazing and bewildering and exciting to him. In a very small pond, they were two alike fish, and it drew him to her. She was his lover, yes, but in a surprisingly short amount of time, she'd also become his best friend.

"What're you thinking about?" she asked, arching back against him and making shivers run down his spine.

"You," he said, leaning forward to kiss her neck. "How much better my life is with you in it."

A long moment passed when they simply lay together in the quiet of her bedroom, skin to skin, his heart pumping against her back and his lips resting lazily on her shoulder.

"I'm falling in love with you too," she finally said quietly with her back to him.

Her words ricocheted in his brain like too much awesome to bear. He didn't expect them, didn't anticipate them, and his heart—which had quietly longed for the words for days—didn't know how to believe it was possible that a creature as lovely as Savannah could fall for a creature as broken as him.

"Say it again," he whispered, closing his burning eyes so that all that existed was her voice in his ears.

She rolled back, and he moved slightly so that she could lie on her back beside him. He opened his eyes to look at her, and with her messy hair and fat lip, she was the most beautiful girl he'd ever seen. "I'm falling in love with you, Asher."

Without breaking eye contact with her, he reached out to push her hair gently off her forehead. "You take my breath away."

"I need you," she said, her breasts rising and falling quickly as her nipples puckered under his intense gaze.

"What do you need, darlin'?" he asked, as his fingers traced the side of her face, pausing briefly on her lips, which opened for him. He slipped a finger between her teeth and her tongue cradled him from underneath while she sucked strongly. Heat shot unerringly from his finger to his groin, swelling his erection as he remembered what it felt like when she hadn't been sucking on his finger.

"You." The sound was low and gravelly, delivered from the far back of her throat.

"Savannah," he breathed, withdrawing his finger.

"I need you to touch me," she said, wetting then biting her lower lip.

"Where? Here?"

His fingers trailed down to her breasts, one slick digit slowly circling her nipple, while he watched her eyes.

"Mm-hm. More," she said breathlessly, and he dipped his head to take her swollen flesh between his lips. He suckled deeply, greedily, just as she had, and her back bowed, lifting off the bed, pushing her breast into his mouth.

She whimpered, and he switched to the other breast, kneading the abandoned one passionately, almost roughly, rolling her erect nipple between his fingers until she cried out.

"More?" he panted.

"More," she dared him, her eyes dark and wild as she leaned up on bent elbows to watch him kiss a trail from her breasts. He lingered on the soft, warm skin of her tummy, kissing and nuzzling as she grew impatient beneath him.

"Please," she sighed. Her knees were bent and spread, inviting him, waiting for him.

"Here?" he murmured, sliding down between her thighs, kissing the soft white skin before spreading her nether lips with his fingers. He paused.

"Please, Asher," she gasped.

He took the entire bead of swollen sex between his lips.

She cried out as he sucked on her, swirling his tongue around the inflamed nub of nerves as she wound her fingers in the sheets by her sides, twisting them. Her muscles bunched and tensed beneath him as he laved the sweetness of her skin, sucking on her until he knew she could barely stand it another instant.

"I ... I have to ...," she whimpered, thrashing her head on the pillow, and he lifted his mouth, sliding his body up quickly and thrusting deeply into her with one smooth stroke. She was so hot and so wet, he groaned, the strangled sound from the back of his throat almost inhuman.

"Come for me, darlin'," he rasped.

Savannah opened her eyes to look into his and bucked off the bed to slam her hips into his, her fingernails drawing blood from his back as she climaxed beneath him. Her muscles flexed and released like a storm around his sex, pulling him deeper and milking him into the fastest orgasm he'd experienced in his entire adult life. He cried out as he shuddered and pulsed within her, demanding her lips and kissing her until they were both languid and spent. Their bodies bound by sweat and exhaustion, they held each other close until they both fell back to sleep.

***

"Vanna? Vanna, you here?"

Savannah's eyes flew open, and she looked over at Asher, naked beside her, asleep on his stomach. She pushed on his back, and his arm reached for her.

"Scarlet's home," she hissed, swatting his hand away. Good lord, her parents would not understand about her having a man overnight in their house. She'd hoped to have Asher on his way before Scarlet or her parents got home.

"So what?" he asked, looking up at her before closing his eyes and nestling back into her pillow.

Savannah slipped out of bed and grabbed a pair of panties off the floor, found some jeans on her window seat, and quickly wiggled an NYU sweatshirt over her head.

"Asher! Will you get dressed?" she whispered loudly in his ear.

"Vanna?"

There was a light rap on her door, and Savannah tripped over Asher's shoe and opened the door a crack to look out at Scarlet. "Just waking up, Scarlet."

"Lazybones! We ended up taking the eight a.m. flight instead. Trent had a last-minute conference call today."

"Oh."

Scarlet furrowed her brows as she looked at Savannah through the crack of the door. "Are you going to let me in?"

"Umm ... well, I—"

"Morning, Scarlet."

Scarlet's mouth shaped into a surprised O before looking back at Savannah with curiosity and amusement. She flicked a quick glance beyond Savannah. "Mornin', Asher."

Savannah looked around to find Asher standing behind her, wearing nothing but jeans and a smile. He wrapped his arm around her waist and pulled her back against his chest, kissing the top of her head. As he dragged her back, she opened the door for Scarlet.

"Mind I don't tell Mama and Daddy, now."

"You wouldn't!" said Savannah, feeling like a teenager.

"Wouldn't I?" Scarlet teased, walking into Savannah's room. She sat down at her sister's dressing table, and her face grew serious, as she pointed to her own lip. "You okay, honey?"

Savannah peeled herself out of Asher's embrace and sat on the edge of the bed.

"We have to talk, Scarlet. About what happened on the beach."

Scarlet glanced toward Asher, who watched the girls with his arms crossed over his chest.

"Asher stays," Savannah said, reaching her hand to him.

He took her hand and laced their fingers together. Scarlet watched this interaction with interest and … what else? wondered Savannah. Envy? Yes. It looked like envy.

"Scarlet," Savannah started.

"Now, honey," said Scarlet. "Trent talked to Lance, and they already explained everything to me. You were a bit in your cups and clanged heads as you were bendin' down to vomit on the sand. Poor Lance, caught in the crossfire of you feelin' sick—"

"Stop it!" Savannah's fingers gripped Asher's like iron. "You know it didn't go like that. And if you ask Goosey and Jen—"

"Oh, honey, Goosey doesn't want to get involved in some little ol' family quarrel." Scarlet had shifted slightly to fuss with the brush and comb on Savannah's vanity, unable or unwilling to meet her sister's eyes. "You were drunk in the van, Vanna. You drank too much beer at the barbecue. You can't go blamin' someone else for your poor choices. Why, if—"

"Have you gone utterly, completely insane? He would have raped me, Scarlet, if Goosey and Jenny hadn't come along. That's all there is to it."

Scarlet still stared down at the brush and comb, but her hands had stilled, and her chest heaved with the force of her breathing. "Well, now, I—"

"Scarlet. You tell me right now—right the hell now—that you believe me, that you know what was about to happen, what *would* have happened if those girls hadn't come along. You look at me and tell me you know that Lance Hamilton would have assaulted your own sister, because you know it's the truth. You *know* it is, Katie Scarlet Carmichael!"

Asher moved slightly so that his hip was pressed against hers, and he pulled their hands into his lap protectively, but he was otherwise silent. He was letting her know he was on her side, that he believed her and believed *in* her, but he was also giving her the space to work things out with her sister, and she loved him for it.

"He is a letch and a pervert and a *rapist*, Scarlet."

Scarlet's eyes rose to meet Savannah's, and to Savannah's dismay, they were cold and furious. "You are talkin' about the brother of my fiancé, Savannah. Trent's brother. Trent. The man I'm going to marry."

"And I am your *sister*," said Savannah in a quiet, almost disbelieving voice.

Scarlet stood and said, "I wasn't there. I didn't see what happened, honey. Lance says one thing. You say another. You were both a little drunk and both ended up bleedin'. Can't we just leave well enough alone? Even if he got fresh, you got a swing in, didn't you? I'm sure he learned his lesson. Let's just leave it be."

Savannah stared at her sister, slack jawed and shocked, as though she were looking at a stranger. There had always been a significant age difference between them, and Scarlet had always been a hometown girly-girl next to Savannah's more independent, sophisticated woman. But never did Savannah believe that a scumbag like Lance Hamilton could drive a wedge between them.

"Scarlet," she said, wincing at the anguish in her voice.

Scarlet smoothed the skirt of her sundress. "It's in the past, Vanna."

"That's all you have to say?"

Scarlet shrugged but didn't meet Savannah's eyes. "Nothing else *to* say."

"Right." Savannah turned to Asher with tears in her eyes. "I can't stay here."

He unlaced his hand from hers and swiped at her cheeks with his thumb, first one, then the other. "Then you're coming home with me for a little while, darlin'."

"Vanna!" exclaimed Scarlet, turning in the doorway to stare at her sister. "That's ridiculous."

"What's ridiculous is that you won't sort this," Savannah said in a calm, measured voice, encouraged by Asher's gentle support. "Your future brother-in-law tried to assault me. And you want to act like it didn't happen. But it *did* happen. And it needs to be sorted."

"So what do you want me to do?" demanded Scarlet in a shrill, out-of-patience voice, her little manicured fingers curled up in tight balls by her sides.

Savannah jumped up with her hands on her hips. "I want you to tell me you believe me. I want you to talk to Trent, and I want him to talk to Lance. I want Lance to admit he was out of line and apologize to me and tell me it'll never happen again. You want to do this the Southern way? No police? Fine. But we still *settle accounts*. And if you won't settle them, I can't be around you."

Scarlet stared at Savannah for a long moment. "I'm sorry, Savannah. Truly, I am. But I just don't feel it's my place." Then she slipped out the door, closing it carefully behind her.

Asher stood up, wrapping his arms around Savannah from behind, and she turned in his arms to weep against his chest.

***

Settle accounts. They were the only words that buzzed through

Asher's head as he drove into town the next morning.

Not that he didn't love having Savannah staying at his house. He loved waking up beside her this morning and knowing that she'd still be there when he got home. He loved knowing that they'd have all day together: to walk in the woods, to make love in the grove, to have dinner together at the long dining room table that had been so lonely for so long.

But he loved her too much to take any pleasure in her rift with her sister. He could see how it was eating at her, but he also knew that Scarlet would need to admit what had happened for Savannah to return home. Further, she'd need to secure a proper and contrite apology from her fiancé's brother. Nothing less would do. Hamilton was lucky that Savannah hadn't pressed charges, though Asher silently agreed it would have been a tough case. Assault without witnesses and resulting in near-equal injuries wouldn't be easy to prove. And if Scarlet wouldn't even stand up for her own sister, there's no way Goosey and Jenny would agree to be involved. Not that they'd seen anything anyway. According to Savannah, Lance had already rolled off her when they found her.

Settle accounts. Savannah was right. It was the Southern way. And while Savannah and Scarlet had their own accounts to settle, so did Asher. Another man had violently put hands on his woman. And he'd be damned if he let it go without a scene.

It would mark the first time he'd gone anywhere in town, aside from the Carmichael house, in eight years. That reality barely crossed his radar as he pulled into the parking lot adjacent to the small white clapboard house that acted as offices for Hamilton & Sons Financial.

Hap Hamilton, Lance and Trent's father, was the executor of the Lee family trust, having inherited the job from his father, Henry Harvard Hamilton. Although Asher didn't know Hap very well, they'd spoken on the phone now and then over the years, and until now, Asher had had no issues with the Hamiltons. That had changed. After settling matters with Lance, he fully intended on moving his business to a different financial firm and cutting ties with the Hamiltons permanently.

He parked his car and walked as briskly as his leg allowed to the front door, entering the small reception area. A young woman looked up from her keyboard, and Asher braced himself.

She gasped, then winced, her face contorting as she showed her teeth and narrowed her eyes in horror. "Oh dear," she whimpered, then closed her mouth, trying to recover. She dropped her eyes from his face quickly, taking in his pressed oxford shirt, crisp khakis, and expensive shoes. She finally exhaled, and he saw her shoulders relax.

"Which way to Lance's office?" he demanded in a low, clear tone.

She didn't look up, but pointed. "T-to the left. L-last door on the left."

Asher turned without another word, walking down the tastefully decorated corridor past a conference room and a small lunchroom. When he got to the final door on the left, he turned the knob and threw it open.

Lance Hamilton sat in a tall black leather chair with his back to the door, talking on the phone. "I can't guarantee it, Miz Simmons, but I sure will try."

At the sound of the door slamming shut, he swiveled in his seat, his eyes growing wide as he took in Asher standing before his desk. He stared at Asher's face in fascination for a moment, then grimaced in distaste, wrinkling his nose.

"Miz Simmons, I'ma need to call you back. Somethin' unexpected and unpleasant has just found its way into my office. Uh-huh. In a jif. Bye, now."

He placed the phone back in the cradle, never taking his eyes off Asher. Then he leaned back in his chair, tenting his fingers under his chin. "See now? I thought you were just a children's story, Asher Lee."

"I'm not," said Asher, clenching his fist.

"Can I help you?" asked Lance, with a curious expression.

"You laid hands on something that belongs to me."

"Oh. Oh, ho, ho." Lance rocked lightly in his chair, a smarmy smile spreading across his face. "Now, this wouldn't be about that cold Northern slut, Savannah Carmichael, would it?"

Asher saw red. Raw, raging red. He leaned over the desk and grabbed Lance by the knot in his tie at the base of his throat and jerked him forward until his face hit the desk. Lance was so shocked, he didn't have a moment to react.

"Call her a slut again," snarled Asher.

"She's just a cheap piece of Northern tail."

In an instant, Asher yanked Lance up, let go of the knot, drew back his muscular, corded arm, and smashed his fist into Lance's already bruised nose. Blood spurted onto Lance's desk and down his shirt as he drew back his fist to hit Asher, but Asher blocked the hit with his palm and pushed Lance backward. Lance crashed unsteadily backward into his desk chair, which tipped over, causing Lance to crash onto the floor.

Asher rounded the desk and pounced, straddling the younger, less fit man, pinning his arms to his sides. His fist connected with Lance's nose one more time, and the sickening sound of cartilage snapping preceded Lance's shrill scream.

"You broke my nose, you asshole!"

"You want to roughhouse with someone? Fight with me."

"I was raised better'n to fight a cripple."

"The hell you were."

Lance tried to free his arms where Asher had them pinned to his sides, but Asher's legs were too strong.

"You're garbage. You get off on hurting women, you sick twist."

"I never touched her. She's a lying slut."

Asher spat on the bloody mess that was now Lance's face. "I told you not to call her that."

He raised his fist again, and Lance whimpered, clenching his eyes with fear as a tear rolled down his cheek. *Coward*, thought Asher. *You're just a bully and a coward.* He stilled his hand and lowered his fist, speaking in a low, lethal tone.

"You listen to me, Lance Hamilton, and you listen good. If

you *ever* go near Savannah Carmichael again with anything but the utmost respect, I will come back here with my Army-issued sidearm and I will shoot your balls off your body. That is a bona fide goddamned promise. Nod if you understand me."

Lance had opened his eyes, but most of the fight had left them. He was breathing heavily, probably from the pain of the broken nose, but he managed to nod.

Asher climbed off him and headed to the door. When he looked around, Lance was crawling to his knees and using the side of his desk to support himself as he stood up. He clutched his nose, hands covered in blood.

"I'm filin' assault charges!" Lance shouted from behind his desk.

Asher had opened the door, but now he whipped around, crossed the room and had his fist back in Lance's face before Lance knew what hit him. He fell back into his chair, whimpering from the pain as Asher grabbed the sides of the chair, trapping Lance.

"Boy, you don't know when the hell to shut up!"

Lance sat back miserably, staring up at Asher, every bit of piss and vinegar gone.

"Listen up, Lance. This is the last time I'll talk nice to you before I make your face look like a copy of mine. You're not filing anything. Not against me. Not against her. If you *ever* dare to bother Savannah again, I will find Serena Shepherd, and I will pay whatever it takes to bring her back to Danvers and have her corroborate every word Savannah Carmichael says about you. So unless you want to be known as the county rapist and be taking it up the ass in lockup for the next decade, you will leave this alone and you will *never* go near Savannah Carmichael again. You hear me, you goddamned rapist?"

"I hear you. I hear," Lance mumbled, slumping back in his chair, utterly defeated. As Asher exited the office, he found Trent Hamilton standing in the hallway, looking pale and shocked. He'd obviously overheard everything.

"Your brother's a *menace*," said Asher, wiping his

bloodied knuckles on his pants. "Get him under control before you marry into that family. I mean it. Or I'll be back for you too."

Trent swallowed, looking at Asher with something new in his eyes. Respect? Admiration? Yeah. It was there behind the shock and awe. Maybe girls weren't the only people Lance Hamilton had bullied in his lifetime. Maybe Trent had been a victim too. Trent finally nodded once, never taking his eyes off Asher's.

Asher reached out to squeeze Trent's shoulder before turning to head back down the hall.

***

"Oh my," said Miss Potts. "Oh! You don't say! Is that right?"

Savannah knew it wasn't polite to eavesdrop, but she was dying for a cup of coffee. She pushed the kitchen door open and gave Miss Potts, who held the phone with rapt attention, an inquiring glance. She waved Savannah into the kitchen, pointing out the coffeemaker in the corner of the counter. Savannah took a mug down from the cupboard and filled it, leaning against the counter.

"That is just shocking, Sophia. Oh my. Just shocking."

Savannah looked up, and Miss Potts gestured to the kitchen table, where a covered cake stand rested on the center of the table. Savannah uncovered it to find biscuits and muffins. She took one and sat down.

"The ambulance? Oh my. Couldn't someone have just driven him to the local clinic for a stitch? Oh, really? Broken that badly? Oh my."

Savannah bit into the muffin and tried not to grin. She was familiar with these sorts of conversations. She'd heard them in her mother's kitchen a thousand times. Someone in Danvers had gotten into a tangle with someone else and the whole town was abuzz.

"Well, I have to say, I always thought he'd turn out bad. I

had him in my class and he was a troublemaker from the get-go. Worried a storm his brother would be the same, but Trent was a much sweeter child. Anyhoo, I imagine he had it coming. Does anyone know why?"

Savannah's ears perked up as soon as she heard Trent's name, and she started concentrating more carefully on the conversation, trying not to look overtly interested. Miss Potts caught Savannah's confused eyes and beamed beatifically before turning her attention back to the call.

"Yes. Yes, Sophia. You're right. Well, wonders never cease. I'm sure he'll be back any minute. Oh, yes. Yes, I will. Bye now."

Miss Potts replaced the phone and turned to Savannah, resetting her face into a kindly smile. "How's your muffin, dear?"

"It's very good," said Savannah, searching Miss Potts's face, trying to figure out what was going on. "Miz Lee's recipe?"

Miss Potts grinned. "Of course."

"So, uh, something big must've happened for Sophia Henry to have the gossip mill running at this early hour. Is it even 8:15 yet?"

"Yes, dear. It's almost 9."

"Did I hear Trent Hamilton's name? And something about Asher?" Savannah looked around the kitchen. "Where *is* Asher?"

"Well, I suspect he'll be back any minute."

"Back?"

"Seems he had business in town."

"What business?"

"The kind of business that gets Lance Hamilton's face beat in," she said sweetly.

"W-what?"

"Yes. In fact, it seems Asher Lee showed up in town for the first time in almost ten years. Parked at Hamilton & Sons, walked right in, broke Lance Hamilton's nose good, and left."

"A-Asher?" The muffin hung from Savannah's limp fingers. "Asher went to—"

"Asher," confirmed Miss Potts, taking the muffin from Savannah and placing it daintily on a napkin.

"Oh no," said Savannah, slumping down in her chair. "Oh no. What did he do?"

"My best bet?" Miss Potts gestured to the spot on her own lip where Savannah's was still scabby and bruised, then reached across the table to take Savannah's hand. "He fell in love. Someone tangled with his girl. He settled accounts."

A primitive thrill shot through Savannah, and her heart beat a tribal dance behind her ribs. She chastised herself that she would applaud such barbarism, but the idea that Asher had actually ventured into town to defend her honor was so hot and so dear, she didn't know what to do with herself. "Miss Potts."

"Yes?" Miss Potts chirped, her face bright and satisfied.

"He went into town. He …" She stared at the older woman in bewilderment.

"Why, of course, dear. He's a man. He loves you." She patted Savannah's hand before releasing it. "He hasn't been to town in almost ten years. And now? He's been to your house more times than I can count, and he just broke Lance Hamilton's nose." Miss Potts shrugged her shoulders and giggled like a schoolgirl, beaming into her coffee cup. Savannah stared at her like she had a screw loose, but Miss Potts smiled back at her, as serene as the Queen of England. Eventually her smile changed from gleeful to grateful as she stared back at Savannah.

"You're changin' his life, Savannah. Can't you see that?"

"He beat up a man. That's uncivilized. I shouldn't approve."

"But you do, and so do I." Miss Potts chuckled, bracing her hands on the table and standing up to freshen her coffee. "That's honor, honey. We're Southerners. It's our way."

Savannah's own words from yesterday echoed in her ears. *You want to do this the Southern way? No police? Fine. But we still* settle accounts. *And if you won't settle them, I can't be around you.*

"I didn't mean him," she whispered, her heart racing with love for him. He'd gone into town to defend her honor, and she couldn't remember any man, not in her whole life, doing something so romantic for her. It made her feel loved and cared for, safe and adored. Protected. Claimed. And for such a modern girl, she found she loved it. She needed to see him, needed to hold him, needed for him to know how much it meant to her that he'd put his own fears and worries to the side just so he could settle accounts for her. "Oh, Asher."

"What, darlin'?"

The kitchen door had swung open, and Asher stood in the doorway, blood spatter on his shirt, his dark, possessive eyes focused on Savannah.

"I'll just be going," muttered Miss Potts, sidling around Asher into the dining room.

"Asher Lee," said Savannah breathlessly, standing up at the table, her knees wobbly from the force of her feelings. "What did you just do for me?"

"Savannah Carmichael," he said, his face softening with the most tender, loving smile she'd ever seen. "I love you. Don't you know I'd do *anything* for you?"

She raced across the room, throwing her arms around his neck as he pulled her close. As her lips found his, she vowed she would figure out a way to never, ever let him go.

CHAPTER 14
The first time you take a trip together

Living with Asher wasn't something Savannah had planned on, but by Friday morning she was so comfortable in his home that it had started to feel just right. Her father had objected at first to her decision to temporarily shack up with Asher, but after hearing about the scene at Hamilton & Sons, neither of her parents uttered another word. Though the rumor mill wasn't entirely clear on the details, everyone seemed to understand that Lance Hamilton had crossed a line with Savannah Carmichael, and Asher Lee had come to call.

Both Savannah and Asher had long been considered oddities: born and bred Danvers folks who'd left the quiet comfort of their hometown to seek their fortunes in the wide world, Asher in Charlottesville and the service and Savannah in New York City. Though no one quite understood what a pretty girl like Savannah saw in a cripple like Asher, it made a certain amount of sense that they'd end up together.

Two odd ducks finding each other like that. Ain't life strange? Ain't love grand?

After the beating, Scarlet had texted her sister three words: *Accounts settled now?* Savannah wrote back: *Only between Asher and Lance. Not between you and me.* There had been no word from Scarlet since then.

What bothered Savannah most was Scarlet's inability to accept her version of events as the truth. She suspected that Scarlet knew Lance was a pig, but she didn't understand why

Scarlet wouldn't admit it. How could they spend holidays with the Hamiltons if Savannah didn't feel safe? How could she and Lance share nieces and nephews if she couldn't be alone in a room with him? Minimally she needed a truly-sorry apology from Lance, or she needed to know that Scarlet and Trent would never ask her to interact with him again. Until one of those two things happened, she couldn't be a part of Scarlet's life. It hurt. But it was right.

It also felt right to stay with Asher, who had become the focus of her world. They talked and took walks together, they read books snuggled on couches and lying side by side on picnic blankets. They shared bits and pieces of their lives with each other, and Savannah marveled at how much they had in common and how much they didn't. And how much it didn't matter that not every avenue of their lives intersected, because that would just be boring, and Asher was anything but boring.

And the nights, when he touched her, rocking into her and claiming her so completely. She'd stopped wondering what life would be like without him. Her heart had convinced her mind that their love for each other was so genuine, so strong and sure even in its newness, that they'd overcome whatever lay ahead and figure out a way to be together. They avoided the actual conversation, but the easy way they spent day after day together meant they were becoming devoted, more and more bound to each other.

Her game plan was simple: she would finish her article, and then she and Asher would have a long conversation about what came next, and as long as it included being together, everything would be okay.

On Friday afternoon, he suggested lunch in the grove. Later they lay tangled together on the love seat reading on their Kindles. With a full belly and the sun on her face, Savannah was just starting to nod off when she heard Asher sigh.

"What's up?" she asked.

"I've been putting off telling you ..." His eyes were serious, like he had big news or bad news, and Savannah's pulse quickened. "I have to go away tomorrow. To Maryland."

"Away?"

To her mortifying shame, she was not only surprised to hear he was going away for the weekend, she was sad. Genuinely. Annoying-whiny-dependent-girlfriend sad. She might have even pouted.

He traced her lips with one finger, gently lingering on the almost-healed skin of her lower lip for an extra moment. "Just for a night."

A whole night? She pouted more. "Oh. Why?"

His gaze darted away from her, and he dropped his hand from her face like he'd prefer not to say. "Medical stuff."

She bit her bottom lip. The last time they'd discussed "medical stuff," he'd flown off the handle and made her cry. She swallowed, looking back at him. They'd evolved since then, hadn't they? Weren't they close enough now that she could ask about this part of his life too? She gathered her courage. "What kind of medical stuff?"

He rubbed his chin, staring at her. "You don't want to hear about this, Savannah."

"What?" Her face must have registered confusion as he stared back at her. "Of course I do."

"It's depressing."

"It's not depressing. It's part of who you are. I want to know all about it."

"The reporter?"

"The girlfriend."

He closed his Kindle case with a slap. "I don't want to burden you."

"It's not a burden. I … I … You know how much I care about you."

Savannah wasn't sure why it was so difficult for her to return Asher's many "I love yous," but it was. Although she'd managed to tell him that she was falling in love with him, and although she felt love in her heart, she'd also felt those things, to some extent, for Patrick, and she was hesitant to use the words again so quickly. She wanted to say them to only one more person in her life. More and more, she thought she wanted Asher to be that person, but she just needed a little more time to be sure.

"Care about you" and "love you" didn't live in the same neighborhood, and Asher was looking to upgrade his real estate. She knew it. She could feel it. His eyes went flinty for a second before relaxing.

"I could probably make it in a day, if you were uncomfortable staying here on your own."

"That's eight hours of driving in one day, Asher!" Then she had an idea. "I could go with you."

"As you just observed, it's an eight-hour trip."

She shrugged, gaining a bit of bravado. He hadn't said no, after all. "But we'd be together. I wouldn't mind *eighty*."

He blinked at her as her meaning sank in, right before his face exploded into a broad smile and he pulled her closer. "Eight hours round trip, just so I can be fitted for a new hand."

"Bionic?" she asked.

"Uh-huh. I'll be a partial bionic man when they're done with me," he said in a happy voice, kissing her hair.

"As long as you're *my* partial bionic man," she said, leaning up on his chest to snag his lips for a kiss, "I'm in."

***

They sat in companionable silence as the Virginia countryside passed in a blur, Savannah in the passenger seat, her fingers click-clacking on her laptop. They were just about halfway to Maryland.

Asher was surprised that she'd offered to come with him. After so many years alone, it seemed unbelievable that in the course of a few short weeks, he'd come this far—he belonged to someone and she belonged to him. And though it probably should have alarmed him how quickly everything was happening between them, it didn't. More than anything, he wanted it to all happen even faster—he wanted a guaranteed forever with Savannah.

And yet, Asher's trip into town had reminded him of how fearsome his face was to strangers. The receptionist at Hamilton & Sons had barely been able to look him in the eye without horror. The problem with discussing the future was that it was impossible to plan one when he couldn't even blend in with humanity.

He saw the multiple surgeries as his one real shot at a future with Savannah. But he hadn't mentioned the procedures to her yet, and it was eating at him. He didn't know how to say it. Here is how it usually sounded when he thought it out:

After you write your article, I'll be moving to Maryland for half a year to have my face operated on multiple times. And I know you're planning to go to Phoenix if they offer you a job. And I know we've only been together for a little while, but I'm in love with you, and the idea of being away from you for that long makes me want to die, so ...

He'd get to the *so* and no further. There was no good way to have the conversation. So ... he'd tell himself to live in the moment and enjoy what time they had together because that time was quickly running down.

He glanced over at her, feeling a little self-conscious because his bad side was on full display as they drove along. Didn't it bother her? Why didn't she cringe when she looked at him? How was she able to welcome his advances, his affections, without disgust or horror? It bothered him that he didn't trust her, because he wanted to so badly. He decided not to sit on these thoughts, but to ask her outright.

"Savannah?"

"Hmmm?"

Though her fingers had stilled, she was staring at her screen intently, likely rereading what she'd been typing.

"The way I look ..."

He had his eyes on the road, but he saw her neck snap up out of the corner of his eye.

"What about it?"

"It's bad. And sometimes I don't understand how you can … I mean, why you—"

"Pull over," she said softly, but firmly.

He did as she asked, watching as she closed her laptop and put it on the floor. He felt her eyes on his face, on the very damaged—grievously injured—side of his face, which had made a receptionist gasp a few days ago. They sat in silence for several minutes, with Asher staring out the windshield and Savannah staring at Asher.

"Look at me," she finally said.

He twisted his neck to face her, frightened by what he'd see there, then felt close to weeping when he saw the compassion and affection brightening her eyes.

"Did you ever watch *Boardwalk Empire* on HBO?"

"Uh, no," he said, surprised by the question.

She gazed at him as she started speaking softly. "There was a character on that show until last season when he died. I don't think of myself as a crier, but I cried when he died. A couple of times, actually. He'd been my favorite part of the show since the day it came on; I lived for his scenes. I'd do whatever I had to do to be home on time to watch on Sunday nights. Leave a party early. Cut a phone call short. And after watching, I'd rewatch all of the scenes with him. I'd watch them all week long. It held me over until the following week. If you can fall in love with a character on TV, maybe I was even a little bit in love with him."

Was it totally irrational that Asher felt jealous of this character? Because he did. He took a deep breath and watched as Savannah's eyes sparkled and her lips turned up, talking about a handsome TV actor with whom Asher could never compete.

"His name was Richard Harrow on the show, and he was played by Jack Huston. He was tall and lanky, not as built as you. He had thick black hair and a—" She touched her upper lip. "—a mustache. He had this gravelly voice that I thought was so sexy, I'd rewind every scene he was in just for a taste of that voice. He was probably in his early thirties, and there was something about him. He was confident and uncertain, fierce and tender, protective, wistful, loyal, vulnerable. Attractive. Complicated. He'd give up on his life in one episode, then fight for it with his last drop of strength in the next. And he would do anything, *anything*, for someone he loved. Every Sunday night, I'd turn on *Boardwalk Empire* and watch it just for him—for Richard Harrow."

Asher took a shaky breath and sighed. "Well, that's great, Savannah. I ask you about my face, and you tell me about some gorgeous actor on TV. Thank you for the reality check of what you want as opposed to what you have." He reached for his keys to turn on the ignition. "If you don't—"

"Shut up, Asher," she said, fumbling with her phone, then placing it on the bolster between them. "Here's a picture of him."

Attractive. She'd said attractive, right? Asher looked out his window, unwilling to look at the *attractive* actor on her phone, confused as to why she'd share all this when all he really wanted was some reassurance about why a girl as gorgeous as Savannah Carmichael was wasting her time with him. He wanted to trust her, and instead she was rubbing this actor in his face.

"Let's just get going, huh?"

She reached out for his arm, clasping his stump in the palm of her hand and wrapping her fingers around his skin. "Not until you look."

He turned and looked down at her perfect fingers on his imperfect arm. He was starting to feel angry now. If she was teasing, it wasn't funny. He was about to tell her so—tell her to pick up her goddamned phone and shove it up her ass—when his eyes flicked to the picture lit up on the screen. He stared, disbelieving, as her fingers gentled around his arm.

"This is him?" he asked, reaching for the phone and drawing it closer. He looked at the picture for a long moment, his eyes glassy and burning, before looking up to find her brown eyes trained on his. "This is … this is the actor, the character, you were talking about?"

She smiled gently and nodded.

He looked back at the picture on the phone. The right side of the man's face was almost totally normal. But the left side. Oh God. The right eye socket was a maroon-colored, gaping hole with no eyeball. Underneath, a red, angry gash of a scar surrounded by melted, mottled flesh led to his lips, which had been torn open and left mostly unrepaired. His upper jaw had suffered grievous structural injury. In fact, his front facial injuries were just as bad as Asher's. He stared, breathless, at the picture before raising his eyes back to Savannah's.

She sniffled, releasing his arm to swipe a tear from her cheek, and giggled softly like she would if she was making fun of herself.

"He was a World War I vet on the show. You never actually knew how he got the injuries. He was wonderful. Everyone who watched that show fell in love with him. Everyone loved him best.

"Don't you see? I was primed for you. Except you're so much more than a character on a TV show, Asher. Not only are you confident and uncertain, fierce and tender, protective, wistful, loyal, vulnerable ... *attractive* ... complicated like the character, but you're mine. You belong to me, and your warm body presses up against mine at night, and what you do with that body makes me ... makes me wonder how I ever lived without you."

It was exactly how he felt too. Every moment he spent with Savannah made him wonder the exact same thing. To know that life could be so much sweeter, so much better, with someone in it, made it practically unbearable to think of all the time before, and all the uncertainty ahead.

"So, *that's* Richard Harrow," she said, pulling her phone out of his hand and looking affectionately at the screen before placing it on top of her computer on the floor. Looking back at Asher, her small grin faded. "That's who I might have been a little bit in love with ... right before I fell in love with you."

Her last words were spoken so softly, his breath hitched, and his heart stopped for a second, like maybe he hadn't actually heard her correctly. He searched her eyes, and in their depths he saw the truth of her words and her story, and he knew, in his soul, that he could trust her, that he didn't need to worry about the veracity of her feelings anymore. He could trust her. He could believe in her.

"So don't ask me again about your face. Don't wonder for a minute if I feel like I'm being shortchanged by choosing to be with you. Just know this: you walked out of my dreams fully formed. I wasn't about to let you walk away."

He didn't know what to say. He doubted he could make the words even if he knew what they were. He reached for her, pulling her against him as tightly as possible and pressing his lips to her hair. He felt the tension ebb slowly from his body as she held him, rubbing her hands gently up and down his back.

"I don't deserve you," he said against the warm skin of her neck.

"After what you've been through? You deserve whatever you want. And if that's me … lucky me."

"It's you I want," he said, overcome. "But I'm the lucky one."

"Okay, Harrow," she said, leaning back to palm the bad side of his face as tears dried on her cheeks. "If it means so much to you? You can be the lucky one. As long as you promise to keep being my fantasy."

In answer, he leaned forward to press his lips against hers, swallowing her sigh and running his hand up from her back to her neck. She'd reassured him in the most amazing, genuine, believable way possible, and as he kissed her, he felt it: the shift from wondering why such a beautiful girl wanted him, to being the man such a beautiful girl wanted. He felt it in the way his heart beat stronger, in the way his fingers cupped the soft skin of her nape, in the way he demanded more from their kiss, and in the way he took from her with confidence, because he knew she wanted him to. Because he trusted that they belonged to each other wholly and equally.

In that moment, he reclaimed himself again. For the first time in almost a decade, who he was and what he wanted took precedence over how he looked. The man inside, who'd hidden from the world in hurt and anger, was almost completely gone now, and in his place sat Asher Lee—confident and uncertain, fierce and tender, protective, wistful, loyal, vulnerable, attractive, and complicated—made whole again by the love of Savannah Carmichael.

***

While Asher went to have his hand fitted, Savannah sat cross-legged on the bed in the large, comfortable motel suite, typing the final installment of her article for the *Phoenix Times*. With the Fourth of July only a week away, Maddox needed the entire piece finalized so it could be edited and placed for the special edition.

She crunched on a handful of Pringles and looked at the header again—"Adam & Cassandra: An All-American Love Story"—and grinned.

With the pseudonyms in place, Savannah had decided to use actual bits of dialogue from conversations she'd had with Asher. As she scanned the thirty-page document, different quotes jumped out at her:

> "I'm, um … I'm unpolished." … "Are you speaking in poker metaphors, or am I going crazy?" … "If this is hell, I need to review my definition of heaven." … "I wasn't with anyone else. I was thinking of you." … "It feels terrible to want when your chances of getting what you want are so slim." … "I'm crazy about you, baby." … "I would love for you to drive my car as far and as fast as you like." … "It's heavy stuff, beauty. It's not

light reading." … "I'm falling in love with
you, Cassandra." … "I love you. Don't you
know I'd do *anything* for you?"

Her eyes sparkled with tears as she skimmed the pages.
These words that were so precious to her, so dear, jumping out at
her in black-and-white, were a living testimony of the days
Asher Lee had spent falling in love with her. And suddenly part
of her was grateful that it would all be preserved under a
carefully anonymous facade: how they fell for each other.

She scrolled to the final page, rereading the conclusion
carefully before sending it off.

> Adam would still be
> considered agoraphobic, but I
> am encouraging him to get out
> into the world more and more.
> As for me? I've found my very
> own modern-day Richard
> Harrow—and in my eyes, no man
> was ever so beautiful.
>
> Adam and I haven't discussed
> the future yet, but I hope
> that forever is in the cards.
> It's not every day you fall
> in love with the man of your
> dreams. When you do, you want
> forever to start as soon as
> possible.
>
> We still have a ways to go,
> but I believe in us and I
> know we'll find our all-
> American happily ever after.

Over the last week, Savannah had gotten more comfortable with the idea of protecting herself and Asher via pseudonyms, mostly to avoid worrying about Asher's reaction to the story. But now, seeing the entire piece in black-and-white, she felt uncertain. She'd purposely avoided telling him much about the article, because she was worried about his reaction to it. Asher was a private person—the most private, reclusive person she'd ever met, in fact—but he *had* agreed to be interviewed, and he trusted her to write a story for publication about his life. *Under the pretense of a story about an injured soldier and the cold welcome home that followed,* her worried heart reminded her.

She shushed it. Asher's privacy had been protected, hadn't it? Yes. Yes! Besides, the article was being printed in Arizona, for heaven's sake. No one he knew would ever have the chance to read it, right? Right.

She shrugged off her feelings and started an e-mail to her editor.

Dear Mr. McNabb,

Please find the completed Lifestyles piece attached. I know you've been reading the weeklies, but this is the entire piece, nuts to bolts. I've edited a few places to improve the flow.

I wanted to reiterate how important anonymity is to me. Although Asher Lee gave me permission to share his story, this isn't exactly the story I led him to believe I'd be writing. He has lived his life in veritable seclusion for more than eight years, and I am anxious to protect/respect his privacy.

As such, you'll notice I've changed his name and employed the use of my pseudonym, Cassandra Calhoun. Thank you for understanding the need for this sort of discretion.

If you feel that I would be an appropriate candidate to lead up the Lifestyles section of your newspaper, I hope you will consider giving me a crack at the job. I
promise you will not find anyone more driven,
devoted, and committed to her work.

Thank you, sir.

Savannah Calhoun Carmichael

She reread the e-mail one last time, and then, satisfied with everything just the way it was, she pressed Send.

***

After getting his hand fitted, Asher walked around the hospital grounds for half an hour before returning to the hotel. He needed to tell Savannah about his surgeries and then give her some space to share her feelings about what happens next between them. Neither of them was planning to stay in Danvers, but did she want to give a long-distance relationship a try? Her in Phoenix, him in Maryland. Lots of texts and e-mails and phone calls, and he'd pay for her to come out every other weekend. Maybe she'd say yes. Maybe she would.

His hand sweated as he unlocked the motel room door.

"How'd it go?" she called to him as he walked into the dim vestibule of the motel suite.

"Fine. It'll be ready next week. Savannah, I need to talk—"

Savannah knelt in the center of the bed wearing the same red pajamas that had completely sideswiped him the day he stopped by her house to apologize for yelling at her. A flimsy, silky little top held on with tiny straps over her creamy shoulders, and barely-there red silk bottoms. She sat back on her heels, her hair braided loosely over her shoulders, her breasts thrust forward. She looked sweet and pliant and sexy as hell.

"Breathe," she said, grinning at him.

He sucked in a huge breath of air, blown away by the sight of her waiting for him. Aw, hell. How was he supposed to talk to her now?

"What were you about to say?" she asked, her eyes lowering seductively to the spot below his waist where he was hardening like cement in the sunshine.

"I'm pretty sure I was going to say we both need to get naked and stay in bed all afternoon."

"Only in bed?" she asked, sucking on her finger and then tracing her nipple through the silk. The filmy fabric darkened from the moisture as her nipple beaded. Oh. My. God. She was going to kill him.

He glanced around the room. Shower … floor … sofa… "You're not going to be able to walk tomorrow."

"Is that a promise?" she asked, tracing the other nipple.

"Yeah," he said, reaching behind his neck to pull his shirt over his head. "Now lie down."

Her eyes widened a fraction at his tone, but she maneuvered her legs out from under her, lying back on the pillows. He watched the way her breasts rose and fell more urgently now.

Asher unbuckled his belt and pushed his jeans and boxers over his hips, then climbed onto the bed.

"These," he said, his hand gliding up her leg to touch the lacey edge of her pajama bottoms, "need to go."

"You don't like them?"

"I love them," he said, tugging them down forcefully and rubbing them between his thumb and forefinger before tossing them on the floor. "God, you're soaked."

"I've been waiting for you," she murmured.

"Spread your legs, darlin'."

He held her eyes unwaveringly and kneeled on the bed as her knees opened for him. His erection was almost painfully hard as he leaned forward to place his palm over the warm curls at the apex of her thighs. He pressed lightly, and her hips pushed up to greet him.

"Open your eyes, Savannah. I'm going to taste you, and I want you to watch me."

She whimpered, panting as she watched him lower his head closer and closer to the throbbing bud hidden between folds of aroused flesh.

"Asher," she gasped as his fingers spread her lips and his tongue landed exactly where he knew she wanted him. He licked the salty sweetness, swirling his tongue over her swollen skin, his own appetite growing from the way her body rose to meet him, the soft sounds coming from the back of her throat. He slipped his hand under her ass to hold her in place and locked his lips around her sex, letting his tongue flick faster and faster until she bucked up against his face and cried out his name. He felt her body tense, then turn to jelly, felt the contractions rack her as she murmured, "AsherAsherAsherAsher," over and over again, his name melting together like a litany.

"I want you," he said, his voice taut and hot as he knelt between her legs.

"Please, Asher," she said, her eyes opening again. "I need you so much."

It was all she needed to say. Her response to his body was almost enough to push him over his own ledge. He leaned forward and slid into her hot wetness with one smooth stroke, groaning as she took his entire length within.

"Don't close your eyes," he said, keeping himself still. He throbbed within her, swelling and lengthening as the warm walls of her sex tightened around him.

Her eyes fluttered open, deep brown and slightly drugged. Lips that he loved to kiss more than anything else tilted up, and she swallowed through shallow breaths. She moved her pelvis up to press against his, and he felt the way her relaxed muscles flexed.

"They're open," she murmured.

He leaned back, pulling almost completely out of her, then buried himself inside again with aching tenderness. He had no idea how he was controlling himself from pounding into her like mad until he found a release to match the one she'd just had.

"They're beautiful," he whispered.

"They're just brown … ahhhh," she moaned as he pulled out and pushed forward again. She panted, a sexy moan at the end of each breath. "… eyes."

"They're yours," he said, feeling the gathering inside, feeling his self-control coming to an end, as he thrust into her again, gaining momentum. "Which means they're mine."

"Yours," she murmured against his lips, and he plunged his tongue into her mouth, the rhythm mimicking the rhythm of his hips.

When he drew back, she whimpered.

"Come with me, darlin'," he urged her. "Come again."

He felt her tighten up that much more at his command, squeezing him, gasping into his mouth before throwing back her head as her body writhed and trembled in ecstasy. He watched her face with wonder, reaching for the back of her neck and pulling her limp, shuddering body against his as he rocked into her one final time. His feelings of possession and belonging, of wanting and loving, pushed him over the edge of reason, and he cried out, "I love you!" into the damp skin of her neck before collapsing on top of her in a tangle of limbs and requited longing and love.

CHAPTER 15

Savannah ran her fingers over the smooth, hot skin of his back, coming down from her high, loving the weight of Asher's body covering hers, loving that he was still inside her. For so long she'd felt alone—an ambitious girl in a small southern town, a Virginia country girl in New York, a hardheaded Northerner in Virginia. Here, with Asher, she was just Savannah, a girl who loved a boy, a woman who loved a man, a person who was loved completely. And that's exactly how she felt with him: complete. Finally whole.

"Asher," she said near his ear, wanting to tell him, wanting him to know that she'd been only half a self before finding him.

He stirred, starting to move away. "Am I crushing you?"

"No." Her fingers stilled, and she pushed down on his back, wrapping her ankles around his legs. Flexing her internal muscles, she felt him hardening again. "Stay for a minute more."

He relaxed, dropping his weight back on her. His arms dropped to either side of her head, where his elbows rested by her ears. He reached up to brush the tendrils of hair from her forehead, looking into her eyes.

"Savannah," he said, quietly, seriously. "What if I needed to be here longer? In Maryland?"

"You mean go home on Monday instead?"

He shook his head slowly, focusing on where his fingers touched her tenderly. "No. We'll go back to Danvers tomorrow, but what if I had to come back here for more than a weekend? And stay for a while?"

She opened her mouth to say something, then closed it, biting her bottom lip in a gesture he recognized as thoughtful but upset. She was sorting this out in her head. "You mean *move* here?"

He nodded, finally looking into her eyes. "Temporarily."

"For how long?" she asked, moving her hands to his shoulders and pushing gently.

He kissed her forehead and rolled onto his back beside her. She leaned up on her elbow, her cheek against her palm, searching his eyes.

"About six months."

Her eyes flashed with worry. "Why? Are you sick?"

"No, baby. Oh, no, nothing like that. No, I ..." He leaned up on his elbow, mirroring her. "There are more procedures I should have. You know, I haven't told you a lot about the explosion and ... what came after. Are you ready to hear about that?"

She nodded, leaning forward to kiss him. She sensed that this was a turning point in their relationship; this was Asher finally opening up completely, finally telling her the most visceral, most intimate truths of his tragic accident. And suddenly Savannah felt quietly grateful for the timing—that the article had already been sent in—that this part of Asher would always stay safe with her.

"I was always ready, Asher."

His eyes told her how much he loved her. But she watched as his face hardened bit by bit until a crease formed between his eyebrows.

"Okay. So I told you about the explosion. Hand gone. Ear gone. Part of my face ... gone." He swallowed and clenched his jaw before continuing. "It all happened in a moment, you know? So fast. Some noise. Some dust. And you're left ... destroyed. A monster that makes children cry. A beast that makes grown men cringe and look away in horror." She started to protest, but he jerked his head no, before giving her a rueful smile. "Not you, darlin'. But everyone else, yes." He leaned forward and kissed her lips before continuing. "They, um, they're talking to you to keep you from going into shock while they run an IV line. And then suddenly you're in a Black Hawk, a helicopter, maybe twenty-five minutes later. You're not really aware of what's going on. You're kind of trying to piece it together. Anyway, they took us—me and Williams and Lagerty—to KAF, to Kandahar, to the hospital there. It's a NATO hospital, multinational, good trauma center."

Her eyes filled with tears, which she tried to keep in check, breathing deeply to maintain control. Her heart was breaking for him as his story unfolded, but she didn't want him to think he was upsetting her. She wanted him to keep talking, but his voice had tapered off, and he appeared to be lost in thought. She leaned forward and pressed her lips to his cheek. When she drew back, he looked at her—stunned and stricken—and she worried for a moment that he wasn't *with* her.

"Asher? Asher?"

He blinked twice, taking a deep breath before launching back into his story. "Anyway, I found out later that it took three hours for them to take my hand off. Amputations are usually faster. It took longer because they wanted to save my elbow and the wound was filthy, covered in dirt and sand and gravel. I'm grateful they saved it."

He blinked again quickly, breathing heavily through his nose as if to keep from crying.

"Asher," said Savannah, trying to keep from crying herself, "I'm going to turn around and press up against you. I want you to hold on to me and just keep talking, okay? Just tell me everything you want to, okay?"

Without waiting for him to respond, she shifted in the bed and slid back until she pressed up against the hard, warm skin of his chest. His arm came around her firmly, pulling her against him, and he flattened his palm against her chest, under her breasts.

"Go ahead, Asher."

"They, uh, they cleaned up my face, but my head was

wrapped up. My ear was gone. Part of my cheekbone, part of my upper jawbone, … also gone. I didn't lose my eyeball or my sight. That was just luck. They put me into a medically induced coma for the pain, but I never flatlined, even on the way to San Antonio."

Savannah covered his hand with hers, squeezing lightly.

"I, uh, spent the next year at Brooke Army Medical Center in San Antonio, rehabbing. Mostly my arm. Learning how to make do with one. My lungs had sustained damage too, and I worked them back up. My leg needed work. I had over twenty surgeries on my face, too, just to get it to here. They rebuilt the cheek and jaw as best they could."

Savannah winced, whimpering lightly as tears streamed down her face, wetting the pillow beneath her head.

"You okay, baby?" he asked.

She squeezed his hand again and nodded.

"You get to a point where you have to decide whether or not you want to live," he said. "You only have one hand, and your whole body's a world of pain. And you look in the mirror and you know—" His voice hitched and halted, and he cleared his throat. "You know you're going to be alone … and that no one is ever going to … no one …"

His breathing was fraught and heavy through his nose again, and Savannah suspected he was crying as hard as she was, so she turned in his arms again, and without looking at his face, she gathered him against her body. Her legs tangled with his, her breasts pressed against his chest, and she rested her lips to the pulse in his throat. His arm tightened around her back, and his shoulders shuddered with quiet sobs.

And then she knew, she realized in startling, terrifying detail, that Asher Lee had had no one to come home to. After years away from Danvers, there was no one left to welcome him home. No loving parents. No friends. No one but an old friend of his grandmother's, who agreed to come and keep house for him. He'd been utterly alone. He'd had no one left to live for, and yet he'd decided to live.

She kept her arms around his neck as he wept into her shoulder. Her own tears kept up a steady stream as she finally understood the depths of his despair, of his crushing loneliness. It broke her heart. It dented her soul.

How in God's name had he stayed alive? With no one and nothing to return to? Unless maybe he'd known, somewhere deep and secret inside, that someday she'd come looking for him.

"Asher," she said, eyes closed, nuzzling his neck lovingly.

"Yeah," he finally managed, clearing his throat and taking a deep breath.

"You stayed alive, Asher. I think maybe you stayed alive for *me*."

The impact of her words made him quake in her arms, and he exhaled like the wind had been knocked out of him.

"Breathe," she ordered, for the second time.

***

Asher took a deep, cleansing breath, bewildered by the wave of feelings that crashed over him as she said the words: *I think maybe you stayed alive for* me. Could she possibly understand the barrenness of his life when he returned from the service? There was no one waiting. There would *never* be anyone waiting. Until this beautiful girl came knocking at his door with brownies, wearing her sister's sundress. Only then had his dormant heart started to beat again.

She was right. He didn't know it at the time, of course, but she was right. He had stayed alive for her.

"I did. I stayed alive for you. For the dream of you."

"And now I'm here."

"And I'm never letting you go," he said fiercely, his hand moving possessively to her hip, where it lay heavy and insistent.

"Are we going to have this conversation right now?" she asked, letting go of his neck to swipe at the leftover wetness on her cheeks.

He took a ragged breath and sighed. It had tired him emotionally to tell his story. He told it so infrequently, it was exhausting to relive it. But he needed to talk to her about the future. He couldn't bear not to anymore.

"I think so," he said, reaching up to trace the side of her face with his fingers.

"Asher, I ... I hate this, but ... if they offer me the job in Phoenix, I'm taking it." She said it quickly, like she'd lose her nerve if she didn't. "It's my only chance. I have to get back on my feet. I can't end my career as a failure who got sacked by the *Sentinel* because of that bastard Patrick Monroe. I can't let him win. I can't let him be the end. I have to see what the next chapter looks like. I'm sorry, Asher. I'm so sorry. I've fallen in love with you, you know that. But I'd never forgive myself if I turned my back on ... on ..." She couldn't speak anymore. Tears poured down her face all over again. "I'm n-not a crier."

"I know you're not." He wiped away her fresh tears with his thumb, loving every cell in her body, every beat of her heart beside him. She was strong and driven and brave, and if she wasn't all those things, she never would have come looking for him, and he never would have had the opportunity to know her, to love her. "Shhh, baby. Shhh. I'd never ask you to give up on your dreams. Never."

She threw her arms back around his neck and pressed her lips to his with joy and relief. He swiped his tongue across her lips, and they opened to him. When he drew back from her, panting and aroused, she wiggled her hips against him.

As much as he wanted to lose himself in her, he needed to be as clear with her as she'd been with him. *Say it, Asher. Say it.*

"But I can't go with you," he said into her ear. "When I came home, people didn't recognize me. People still cringe when they look at me. I can't be with you and look like this."

"Yes, you can. You can come to Phoenix and live there exactly like you do in Danvers. I don't care, Asher. I only—"

"No, baby. No. I can't do that to you." He licked his lips, holding her watery eyes. "I can't ask you to hide away from the world with me. It wouldn't work. I'd eventually get jealous of where you went and who you knew—this whole part of your life that couldn't include me. And you'd tire of always being at home with me. We'd kill this."

She sniffled, leaning forward to press her lips to his, and he could taste the saltiness of her tears on his tongue.

"*Please* come with me," she begged him softly, and it killed him because he'd do anything for her. And for one wild moment, he thought, *I'll do it. I'll sell my house in Danvers, and I'll buy a house in Phoenix. Screw the operations. I'll just live as I've always lived, with my books and a garden in the backyard. And at the end of every day Savannah will come home to me, and I'll be waiting. And at the end of the day, she'll tell me all about the world, and she'll go to parties and meet people and bring the world to me, and ... and ...*

Huh. *Bring the world to me.* Since when did the world matter so much to Asher Lee? It stopped his train of thought in its tracks and made his thumping heart slow down as he sorted through what he'd just been thinking. The world mattered. Damn it, it did. He missed it. He wanted to be a part of it again. This wasn't just about Savannah. This was about him too.

"I have to do this," he whispered. "Not just for you. For me too."

She leaned back to look at him. "What do you mean?"

"I'm sick of living alone. I'm sick of hiding. I want to go to restaurants. I want to go to the library. I don't want people staring at me. I think ... I mean, I thought I was done with the world, but I'm not. And I didn't know that until I met you. I want to live in the world again because of you."

He remembered the words he'd said to Miss Potts the first day Savannah came to call. *I'm not fit to rejoin the human race.* But now he was. And Savannah had made him want a second chance at living. He searched her face, looking at the slope of her cheeks, the way her lashes fanned them every time she blinked, and thought how terribly he would miss not seeing them every day.

"Do you know that I love you?" he asked.

She nodded, reaching for him, cupping his face in her hand.

"This isn't the sort of love that ends," he said softly. "It's forever. It doesn't matter if you go to Phoenix and I stay here for a while. We'll find each other again. Do you know that, Savannah Carmichael?"

She nodded again, sadly, with tears still brimming in her chestnut eyes.

"And I'll tell you something else. I'm not worried that you'll find someone else, because there isn't anyone else on the face of the earth who could ever love you as much as I do. It's impossible because no man has ever loved a woman as much as I love you. And I'm not worried about me finding someone else, because you brought me back from the dead and gave me a second chance at life. You're my miracle, Savannah, and I will *always* belong to you."

She nodded a third time, capturing his upper lip between hers and sucking on it lovingly, lazily, rubbing her breasts against his chest, as her hands cradled his face. He sensed that she had touched him to reassure him, but when she leaned away, her eyes turned luminous and dark, and his body responded to her as it always did, as it always would, hardening like stone at her command. He wanted to forget that they were leaving each other, forget that they would ever live a day apart. He wanted to get lost in her body and watch her get lost in his.

"When do you need to come back here?" she asked, her breathing quickening as she stared at him.

"A little more than a week," he said, every cell in his body begging him to take her, to taste her, to bury himself inside her until nothing existed but this moment, while they were still together. "My first procedure's on the sixth."

They were talking about something serious, something sad, and yet his heart pounded with love for her, his body straining with longing, desperate to feel the completeness he felt only in her arms.

"We have eight days," she said, reading his eyes. She pushed against his chest so that he fell back, and she swung her leg over his hips to straddle his lap.

"We'll make the most of them," he said, his fingers kneading the soft skin of her hip as she shimmied up his legs until her thighs cradled his erection. He let his hand slide forward over her hip into the tangle of curls between her thighs, stroking, seeking.

"The mo—st," she gasped softly as he pushed two fingers gently into her soft, wet heaven. Her eyes turned liquid. "Love me, Asher."

And he did.

And he would.

Forever.

***

On Monday morning, as Asher worked out in his home gym, Savannah received an e-mail from Maddox McNabb. He loved the article and told her that after some edits, it would be published on the front page of the Lifestyles section on the following Sunday, the Fourth. And while he hadn't formally offered Savannah the job yet, she assumed that was just a formality at this point. Print the article; offer the job. As much as she hated the idea of leaving Asher, she was ready with her answer. The second chapter of her professional life wouldn't be as the lead reporter at the *Sentinel* or on one of the cable news programs in New York, as she had planned, but at the *Phoenix Times*. She still didn't love it, but it was a hell of a lot better than throwing in the towel.

It was a reputable place to start over, and while she tried to feel enthusiastic about the idea of a fresh start, a part of her—the part that included her heart—bucked and wheezed at the notion of leaving Asher in Maryland for half a year while she jump-started her career across the country. Yes, he encouraged her to go. No, he'd never stand in the way of her dreams. And for heaven's sake, they'd been together only a month. But leaving him to pursue her career while he underwent six months' worth of painful surgeries? It didn't feel right, and it nagged at her, making her second-guess her life's path, making her wonder if she had her priorities right or if, as before, with Patrick Monroe, she was blinded to reality by the strength of her ambition.

She missed her mother's gentle counsel and even Scarlet's bouncy gaiety, which is why she was so grateful to hear from her sister the following afternoon.

Hey Vanna. Wondering if me and Trent can come by Asher's 2night after work?

Savannah looked up at Asher, reading in the wingback chair beside her as the summer rain pelted the windows. They'd worked all morning to pack up and box a good portion of his belongings for Maryland.

"Asher. Scarlet just texted me."

He looked up at her, his face impassive but interested. "What'd she say?"

"She and Trent want to come over tonight."

He rested his Kindle on his lap and took a deep breath. "You ready to hear what they have to say?"

"I'm not ready for more crap."

He grinned at her, tilting his head to the side. "That's my girl. Denial ain't just a river in Egypt."

"No, I mean it. I'll want to smack her lights out if she goes on about Lance being blameless."

"Won't know unless you say yes, darlin'."

Savannah took a deep breath, staring at the text.

"And I'll be with you every minute," he added quietly, reaching over the small table between them to touch her arm.

Savannah took his hand and braided her fingers through his, looking to her right to catch his eyes as they gazed at her sadly. She couldn't help the way her gut twisted at the simple sweetness of his words. *Every minute.* And then her brain tortured her by following up: *For only five more days.* And then what? The searing solitude of separation. The agony of letting go of each other for months on end.

Would like to resolve this, she typed. *See you here at 5:30.*

"I told her five thirty so they'll be gone before we have dinner."

"And if you resolve things, will you go home?"

He seemed calm, serene, looking straight ahead at the stained glass that was covered with rivulets of rain, but her eyes were drawn to his fingers, which curled quietly into a fist.

"No, Asher," she murmured, putting her book on the table and standing. She took his Kindle from his lap and placed it on top of hers, then she sat down in his lap. His arm fell around her waist, his hand resting loosely in her lap. "I want every minute I still have with you."

He twisted his head slightly to kiss her, and Savannah closed her eyes, as she often did now, cataloging the feel of Asher's skin against hers: the heat of his mouth, the strong silkiness of his tongue, the way her insides turned to lava and her panties moistened. The way his erection sprang to life beneath her bottom, pressing up through his jeans. The way his right elbow rested firmly on her hip to keep her in place as his left hand slipped under her shirt to stroke the skin of her belly. *Memorize him, Savannah. Memorize him so that when you are far away, you will remember what it felt like to be with him.* Remember the touch of his fingertips over the goose bumps on your breasts, the way his mouth sucks on your nipples, the way it feels when he slides, thick and impatient, into your waiting warmth. *Remember what it feels like to be loved.*

She sobbed into his mouth, and he swallowed it, moving his hand up her chest to slip underneath her bra. She pulled the shirt over her head and bared her breasts to him.

"I want you," she said, opening her eyes to find him staring at her. "Right now. Right here. It's the only thing that makes it bearable."

"I know," he said.

"And slowly," she added, sliding off his lap and reaching for his belt buckle. "I want to remember everything. I don't want to forget."

"Neither do I, baby."

She unbuttoned his pants and pushed them down to his thighs as he leaned up to help her. His erection sprang free, rigid and swollen, glistening slightly at the top. Raising her eyes to his, she pulled down her shorts and panties before climbing back on his lap, her knees sinking into the seat cushion on either side of his hips as she lowered herself onto him.

His arm held her around the waist, tiny sounds from his throat making her stomach jump with longing. His eyes fluttered then focused in bliss, holding her captivated as she moved as slowly as possible, trying to feel every place he touched her, inside, outside. His palm on her bare hip, the way he stretched her tight passage, the way his neck finally bent forward so he could rest his forehead on her chest.

When she'd taken all of him within her, he exhaled, his breath hot on her neck. He raised his head to find her eyes and look deeply into them as they remained motionless, joined as intimately as possible.

He throbbed within her, but didn't move, holding her eyes, regulating his breathing as a bead of sweat rolled from his forehead down his cheek.

"Have you ever tried tantric sex?" he asked in a low, gravelly voice. "I read about it."

If it was possible for her to flood wetter and hotter, she did. Her eyes widened and her lips parted in anticipation. No, she hadn't. Yes, she wanted to.

"Hold my eyes. Breathe with me," he whispered, taking a deep breath through his nose that swelled his chest and made his firm pecs rub fleetingly against her nipples, tightening them immediately. She stared at him, watching him, watching his body draw away from hers.

"Breathe in when I do."

They inhaled together, focused on each other's eyes, a shiver crawling down Savannah's back as her erect nipples came in contact with his skin again. His pelvis shifted slightly upward, and she tried to keep her eyes open as sensations assaulted her.

"Breathe again," he ordered, and she reached for his shoulders, bracing herself against him as they breathed in together and he clenched his ass to push slowly into her, then released his muscles, pulling back. These were tight movements, slow and tiny, but she felt every nerve ending as he slowly massaged her from the inside, his chest rasping against the pulsing, sensitive skin of her nipples.

"Again," he ordered, and she swallowed, clenching her internal muscles this time when he thrust up. "Hold it."

She panted, sweating against him as her nipples pushed into his pecs and his length throbbed inside her, held tight by her muscles. His breathing was becoming less controlled, shallow and ragged as he stared at her, refusing to break eye contact.

Finally he released his muscles, and she felt the slight downward movement of his sex deep inside. The pressure in her belly, in the wet, sacred place that he owned, was building to an almost unbearable intensity.

She moaned as they took another deep breath together, bracing herself for the way he slid high inside her, claiming the most secret parts of her for his own. The eye contact was blistering, searing, like he was looking into her soul, and she wanted him there, but she'd never felt so naked to anyone before. She couldn't look away, even when she felt the wetness of tears rolling slowly down her face.

"What are we doing?" she asked, locking her hands around his neck.

"I'm ruining you," he said unflinchingly, "for anyone else."

"Asher," she gasped, as he held his position high inside her again. The gathering between her hips was too sharp, too sweet, too demanding to ignore. A swirling started, making her skin hot, then cold, making it shiver, then sweat. Her neck dropped back as she released her internal muscles and felt his hardness move infinitesimally inside her, shattering her control.

Instinctively she rolled her hips forward over him, and he groaned, forgetting their breathing, his arm like iron around her back as he dipped his head, reaching for her nipple with his mouth and pounding up into her. She bowed back over his arm, offering her breasts to him, throwing her head back as the first wave of orgasm crashed over her body, splintering her thoughts until the only litany in her head was the name of her love, *Asher Asher Asher*.

His hand slid up her spine and clamped the back of her neck, pushing her head to his so he could capture her lips roughly, seeking, demanding, his tongue plunging into her mouth to stroke hers as he growled her name.

"Savannah!" he cried, raising his neck and thrusting up into her wet heat one last time. "Now!"

A scream ripped from her throat as the tip of his hardness kissed her womb and her muscles tightened fiercely around him. He came deep in long pulses as her muscles convulsed, flexing and releasing wildly around him, draining him until his head dropped, limp, onto her shoulder. The arm around her back relaxed, and she leaned forward until her forehead burrowed into the curve of his neck where, with every passing moment, she wished she could remain forever.

***

"… so you see, Vanna, you don't need to worry. Lance should be in California by tomorrow, and he's not coming back for the wedding. He's not coming back for a long time. I promise."

Asher squeezed Savannah's shoulder, and she looked up at him gratefully before turning back to her sister.

"What about what happened in Myrtle Beach?" she asked.

Scarlet nodded to Trent, reaching for his hand.

"Lance all but admitted it, Savannah … while he was under anesthesia at the hospital when they reset his nose." Trent's uneasy gaze flicked to Asher before returning to Savannah. "He said he'd been fresh with you and gotten what he deserved."

Asher felt Savannah tense beside him, and he could read her reaction like a book: *fresh* and *assault* weren't the same thing. She surprised him by taking a deep breath before correcting Trent.

"He was more than fresh, Trent."

"I'm sure he was," said Trent. "He's my brother, Savannah. That doesn't mean I don't see him for what he is."

"But, Vanna, he's gone now. He said it was too humiliating to stay here after getting beat by a—well, he just decided it was time to move on. He has a … a frat brother out in San Francisco. I think it'll be a better fit for him than here."

"I told him he's not welcome at the wedding," said Trent, "unless he comes by to apologize to you for how it all happened, but he said he didn't think he could be back in two weeks anyway." He looked down as his cheeks colored. "I'm sorry, Savannah. On behalf of my family, I'm terribly sorry that Lance frightened you and split your lip. Lance has always had a mean streak. Believe me, I know better'n anyone."

Asher had suspected as much when he caught Trent's expression on the day he paid Lance a visit. Trent gave the older man a slow, respectful nod. Asher nodded back, then turned to Savannah.

"Darlin', I'm going to leave you and your sister to some girl talk, and take Trent out to the pantry for a bourbon."

Savannah turned to him, a surprised smile on her face. He rarely turned on the full-court Southern charm for her, but it didn't mean he couldn't do it if he wanted to. He winked at her, gesturing to Trent to follow him. As they left the room, he peeked back in time to see Scarlet leap from her chair to sit beside Savannah, and watched as Savannah opened her arms to her little sister.

He put a hand on Trent's shoulder, guiding him in the right direction. "Two and a half weeks, huh? Till your weddin' day?"

"Yes, sir. Scarlet and I would sure be honored if you'd agree to attend with Vanna."

Asher led the way to the small den adjacent to the butler's pantry. He gestured to the left of two chairs. "Take a seat. I'll get us some refreshment."

He had never actually entertained another man in his parents' house, though he'd seen his parents welcome friends many times and remembered the way his father would offer bourbon in the den while the ladies strolled the gardens or visited in the parlor.

He filled two crystal tumblers with ice and poured the bourbon, swirling the amber liquid in each glass before joining Trent at one of two leather chairs set in front of a fireplace that hadn't been lit in years.

"So what do you say?" asked Trent. "Can we count you in?"

"I appreciate your invitation," said Asher, "and I'd sure be honored to attend with Savannah, but I won't be here. I'm headed to Maryland for the next few months. I leave on the sixth."

Trent took a sip of his bourbon and whistled low. "Damn, that's good."

"It was my daddy's."

"Can I ask you a question, sir?"

"Only if you stop callin' me sir," said Asher.

"Sorry, Mr.—uh, Asher. I was wonderin' … did it feel flippin' awesome to beat Lance's face in?"

Asher was surprised to see that Trent Hamilton was entirely serious. "Yes, it did. I know he's your brother, but as long as Savannah belongs to me, no one's going to lay a hand on her without a reckonin'." He shrugged. "It's our way."

Trent nodded in agreement. "I underestimated you."

Asher took a sip of bourbon. "It's my face. It throws people off. That's why I'm going away, actually. Uncle Sam's offered to work on it a little bit, fix it up."

"I'll look after Savannah while you're gone."

"I appreciate that, but I doubt she'll be here. She's headed to Phoenix."

Trent grimaced. "But you two …"

"We'll make it," said Asher with conviction, remembering the way Savannah had fallen apart in his arms a few hours ago, the way they fit together, the crazy way that he loved her more than he'd ever loved another living soul. "In fact, if I have my way … I think you and I might be brothers someday."

Trent's eyes widened, and he lifted his glass. "To the Carmichael girls."

Asher clinked his glass lightly. "To *our* Carmichael girls. To Savannah and Scarlet."

***

"So you'll come home, honey?"

"I will," said Savannah. "On Monday morning."

"Not before?"

"Asher's moving to Maryland on Monday. I'm staying with him until he leaves."

"That reminds me. Mama's having a family barbecue on Sunday for the Fourth. Family only. She wants Asher to come." Scarlet took a deep breath, grimacing at her sister. "Savannah, you're not … I mean, you're not in *love* with him, are you?"

"Totally," she answered without hesitation.

"Oh. Oh, you are? But he's … he's deformed, and he's a hermit. How do you, I mean, how do you build a future?"

"He's not deformed, Scarlet; he's disfigured, not that I give a damn. And a hermit? Well, he's been to Mama and Daddy's house how many times? And we took a trip to Maryland last weekend. And there was a rumor that he was in town just last week paying a visit on Lance Hamilton. Doesn't sound like much of a hermit to me."

"You know what I mean, Savannah. You don't have a plan. You're heading to Phoenix and he's … he's Asher Lee."

"He's mine," said Savannah, a warning infusing her tone.

"Come on now, honey, how's it goin' to work?"

"I don't have all the answers!" Savannah bit out. When she thought of the mind-blowing sex she and Asher had just shared, the intimacy of it, the love, her heart swelled painfully. She looked up at Scarlet, who was simply asking the questions Savannah would ask if the tables were turned. "Remember that article you were reading to me? The day Derby Jones called me? 'The Twelve Most Important Milestones in Any Relationship'?"

"I remember. I'm surprised *you* do. Not exactly your thing."

Savannah grinned. "You asked me that afternoon, 'Don't you want to be one of those career women who has it all? Exciting career, hot husband waiting for you at night?'"

"Yes. And you told me marriage wasn't on your radar."

Savannah sighed. "I did. I said that."

"And now? Is it on your radar now, Vanna?"

She looked up at Scarlet, her chest tight and her eyes glistening, because it was. It was bright and blaring and beeping in her ear. It was just about the only thing on her radar. No trace of New York. No glimpse of Phoenix. Just Asher, and it scared her, because being someone's sweet little wife had never been her plan. "I don't know what to do."

"Aw, honey." Scarlet put her arm around Savannah, stroking her shoulder lightly. "I think you've been sideswiped."

"I can't leave him. And I can't stay." She raised her eyes to her sister's photo-ready face. "What do I do, Scarlet?"

When she finally spoke, Scarlet's advice was delivered in a calm, clear voice, and Savannah realized that her little sister was much wiser in matters of the heart than she.

"I think you follow your heart. If your career owns your heart, you go to Phoenix. And if Asher Lee owns your heart, you go to Maryland."

"What if they both own half?"

"Can't ride two horses with one ass, honey. Try it and you'll get hurt."

Scarlet never cursed. Never. Savannah stared at her sister, dumbstruck, for a full ten seconds before bursting into giggles. Scarlet, who'd covered her mouth with her hand in shock over her outburst, joined her.

But the question remained, and long after Scarlet and Trent had left, it clung to Savannah. Her career or her heart? She was going to have to make a choice.

And whatever it was, she was going to lose.

And whatever it was, she was going to have to live with it.

CHAPTER 16
The first big blowup fight

Sunday bloomed bright, the morning sun shining on Asher's face as he turned to look at Savannah sleeping beside him. Tonight would be their last night together. Tomorrow he left for Maryland, and they started their half year apart.

A real estate agent recommended by the hospital liaison had found him a nice furnished place a stone's throw from the hospital, and Asher had signed all the necessary paperwork for a six-month lease. Ten boxes of clothes, books, and other personal items had been picked up by UPS on Friday morning, and he was almost completely packed. Two suitcases were lined up neatly by his bedroom door, while another lay open on the window seat.

Without waking up Savannah, he grabbed his boxer shorts from the floor and pulled them on, then went to go sit by the window, gazing out at the woods behind the house and the grove beyond. Despite wanting nothing more than to leave it for so long, he knew he would miss home. And it surprised him a little.

But more than home, he would miss Savannah, which didn't surprise him at all, and while he'd mostly made peace with their separation—they'd promised to send daily texts and talk frequently on the phone—a part of him still wondered if he was selfish for his choices, for prioritizing anything over her.

It's not too late, whispered a voice in his head, but he hushed it because it *was* too late. Anyway, it'd be pure weakness to follow her to Phoenix, when he had a journey of his own to make before they could be together.

He made his way back to the bed, sitting down gingerly in the curve of her body. He'd meant what he said to Trent last night. He looked at the rose on her cheek and held himself back from bending down to kiss her, knowing his morning beard would scratch a little and wake her up.

"I'm going to marry you someday," he whispered.

"Hmmm?" she murmured, her voice husky and sleep-drunk.

"Nothing, baby," he said, gently stroking her hair. "I'm going for a walk in the woods."

"I'll come," she whispered, her eyes still closed.

"You sleep."

"I can sleep when you're gone," she said, and a tear escaped through the crack of her closed eye to roll over her nose and plop soundlessly on her pillow.

His heart twisted, and he leaned down to press his lips to her temple. "Go back to sleep, darlin'. It's only eight-thirty. I'll be back in an hour."

"Okay," she said, still half asleep, and rolled over.

She woke up crying. She woke up crying when all he wanted in the world was to make her happy. He wished there was some way to reassure her that they were only at the beginning of something wonderful, that they both recognized their relationship for the special gift it was, and as long as they stayed strong and honest and true during their time apart, they'd be together at the end.

He pulled on some running shorts and a T-shirt, then fished his trainers out of the closet. Sprinting was a no-no with his bad leg, but a nice morning walk was good for him.

He found Miss Potts at the foot of the stairs. They'd been avoiding each other to some extent since Savannah's arrival on Sunday. She disapproved of Savannah staying in Asher's bed, though, to her credit, she'd kept her opinion to herself after voicing it respectfully the first day.

"Morning, Miss Potts," said Asher.

"Asher." She smiled at him, the wrinkles on her weathered face crashing together. "Don't know what I'll do in this big old house without you until Christmas. Sure you don't need me to come to Maryland?"

He shook his head, reaching out to put his arm around her shoulders and pull her against his body affectionately. For so long there had been only Miss Potts in his life. He hadn't considered much how Savannah's arrival had somewhat displaced the older woman.

"You've been good to me," he said, squeezing her shoulder.

She sniffled once. "You're like a grandson to me. You gave me something that life hadn't seen fit to bless me with."

"We'll always be family," he said, leaning back to grin at her. "No one else can give me what-for like you, Miss Potts."

"Oh, I don't know," she said, glancing upstairs. "I think that girl could keep you in line." She sniffled again before beaming at him. "Wouldn't mind a great-grandchild, you know. While I'm still young enough to enjoy 'em."

"No pressure now, Miss Potts. And here I thought you didn't like Savannah sleeping in my bed."

"I don't like your *girlfriend* sleepin' in your bed. Now, if she was your *wife* ..." Her eyes sparkled, and she touched his arm lightly. "She's good for you, Asher."

"Yeah," he said. "She is."

***

Savannah finally admitted defeat by the third buzz on her phone in a matter of minutes. She yawned, opening her eyes slowly as a fourth and fifth buzz followed in quick succession. She looked around for the damned thing. At one point, her Twitter account had been set up to alert her to scores of trends, but the only alert she'd kept after her New York debacle was her name. Buzz. Buzz, buzz.

"Damn, what's wrong with you?" she asked groggily, fishing her phone off the bedside table. She leaned back on the pillow, letting her sleepy eyes adjust to the bright light of the screen. She was greeted first by the time—9:12 a.m.—and second by the alert messages that were popping up one after the other on her newsfeed.

She sat up against the headboard and punched in her password. Her heart kicked up with a sudden burst of adrenaline at the tiny red alert dots that practically covered her home screen. Nineteen new e-mails, fifty-six new Twitter notifications, and thirty-one—no , thirty-two—no, thirty-*three*—Facebook notifications. Something was going viral, but the only alert she had programmed was her own name. What was going on? Could she have forgotten to delete another alert that had suddenly hit the news this morning?

Her neck jerked up as she heard the sound of Asher's house phone ringing. Since the day she'd arrived for their very first interview, she couldn't remember the phone ringing more than once or twice, and it was almost always in the late-afternoon when Sophia called to gossip with Miss Potts. It was ringing *now*? At a little after nine o'clock on a Sunday morning? On a *holiday* morning? No one in Danvers would bother to call someone's home during church hours, and no businesses were open to make their annoying solicitation calls. Who was calling at such an unusual hour?

Her skin prickled uncomfortably, and she turned to her phone. She clicked on the Twitter icon and swiped over Notifications. Sixty-two notifications? She hadn't had more than five during the entire month of June. The house phone rang again as she scrolled through the messages.

OMG. #GodBlessAmerica #ReadThisArticleNOW #SavannahCarmichael #PhoenixTimes Love story of the century!

#BeautyAndTheBestLoveStoryEver Twitterverse, you HAVE to read this!! #SemperFi #SavannahCarmichael

#VetReporterRomance Check out the newest Lifestyles

piece at the #PhoenixTimes and God bless
#SavannahCarmichaelAsherLee

"Wh-what? Wait!"

Her mouth dropped open as she read and reread that last tweet. Why was Asher's name showing up on Twitter? Her heart was thumping out of her chest as the house phone rang again and her phone buzzed to alert her of more messages.

She swiped at her e-mail, looking through the subjects: *Great article, Loved the new piece, Congrats* … There was no word from Maddox, so she opened an Internet session on her phone and typed in *www.phoenixtimes.net*.

"Come on, come on, come on," she muttered, swinging her legs out of the bed to slip on her panties and T-shirt. Where was Asher? Downstairs?

No. Somehow she knew he was walking in the woods. He must have kissed her good-bye before he left, though she had no solid memory of it.

"Come on, you cow," she said as the little cursor cycled, trying to load up the page. She threw the shirt on over her head, then held her phone, pacing the room, panic making her jittery and sweaty and cold.

"Breathe, Savannah," she told herself, clenching and unclenching her phone in a sweaty death grip. How in the hell had this happened? She told herself to take deep breaths, desperate to believe that despite the alerts pouring in, there was some mistake.

The front page finally came up, and she clicked on Lifestyles, waiting again as the browser cycled.

"Goddamnit, come on," she said, pacing one more time before looking down, and then … then she saw it:

"Savannah & Asher: An All-American Love Story."

"No!" she cried, swiping at the screen, as the house phone rang again. And under the story title, the name she was dreading to see: Savannah Carmichael.

She sank down onto the window seat, the wind knocked

out of her, as she stared at the small screen.

> I walked up to Asher Lee's house on a sunny May afternoon, wearing a sundress borrowed from my sister, holding a plate of fresh-baked brownies in my trembling fingers. Mr. Lee is the mythical freak of our small town. The outcast. The hermit. The bogeyman. Children egg his house on Halloween, and mothers tell their teenage daughters to be in early, lest Asher Lee find them in the darkness and have his way with them. But the truth? Asher was a man like any other man, just one who'd been hideously wounded in the service of our great country.

Savannah swallowed weakly as she read the heavily edited version of her story. The words *mythical freak*, *bogeyman*, and *hideously* had never figured in her writing, and she hadn't written that bit about mothers warning their daughters about him.

"Oh my God."

She scrolled down, barely able to stand what she was reading: her entire article had been chopped, edited and re-written for maximum sensationalism. She'd heard of newspapers doing this, but when Maddox McNabb said "edits," it never occurred to her—never, ever occurred to her—that he could possibly mean using what she'd submitted as an outline and completely re-writing her piece.

They'd used actual names and places. They'd hacked up the piece and sensationalized it. They'd given her full credit.

She stopped reading at the halfway point because her stomach was in the sort of knots that weren't going to untangle themselves. She didn't need to read further to know that the rest of it would be a shell of its original self. Meanwhile, the buzzing continued as people read "her" article and commented on it.

As shock morphed quickly to fury, she swiped her finger over the phone icon and searched for Maddox McNabb's number. It rang six times before his voice mail picked up.

"This is Maddox McNabb, editor in chief of the Phoen—"

She swiped End as a tear snaked down her cheek. She didn't have his home phone number. But she did have Derby Jones's number.

"H-hello? Whattimeisit?" asked the groggy voice on the other end of the line, and Savannah realized it was seven-thirty in Phoenix. On a Sunday. On a holiday.

"Derby? Sorry to wake you. It's Savannah Carmichael."

"Savannah. Savannah? Sure. Hi. Hey, it's early."

"I know. I'm sorry, I'll get out of your hair quick. Do you have a cell phone number for Maddox McNabb?"

"Maddox? Yeah. Somewhere. Um. Oh, on this phone that I'm holding. Can I text you?"

Savannah imagined Derby holding the phone with closed eyes, ready to roll over and go back to sleep.

"It's really important, Derby."

"No. Right. I'll text right away." Savannah heard lucidity enter her friend's voice. "As soon as we hang up."

"Thanks. Sorry for waking you up."

"S'okay. Hey … is everything okay?"

Looking out the window, Savannah saw Asher walking in from the woods, tall and proud, the sun catching the auburn highlights in his dark hair. He walked in thought, a light smile on his lips, as if pondering something pleasing. Suddenly, as if he knew she'd be watching, he looked up at the windows to his room, and finding her face in the glass, raised his hand in greeting.

Her heart clutched, and tears sprang to her eyes as she lifted her trembling hand and laid it on the glass between them.

"No," she said. "Everything's definitely not okay. Bye, Derby."

She hit the End button without taking her eyes off Asher. He grinned at her, unable to see her broken expression from that distance. He touched his finger to his lips and blew her a kiss before continuing toward the house.

Savannah's fingers lingered on the window in despair. Without meaning to, she'd betrayed the privacy of the most private man she'd ever met. How would he ever forgive her?

First things first. *Ding.* She looked down to see a text from Derby. She needed to talk to Maddox McNabb.

***

Asher stepped jauntily into the kitchen, wiping his muddy sneakers on the welcome mat that Miss Potts kept by the back door. There was hot coffee, and Savannah was awake. He hated that she'd woken up with tears in her eyes, and he knew that today would be a little sad for them, so he'd made a decision on his walk. Although he wasn't ready to ask her to marry him, he wanted her to know that that was his eventual intention. He wanted to reassure her that she was his forever; that what they had was so precious, as long as they protected it, they'd find each other at the end of their half-year separation.

When the phone on the wall rang, he jumped, surprised, then looked around for Miss Potts. When she didn't come bustling into the kitchen to answer it, he reached for the receiver himself.

"Hello?"

"Is this Asher Lee?"

"Yes."

"Mr. Lee! Hello! This is Jennifer Durant with *Fox and Friends*, and we were wondering if we could book you for—"

"Whoa!" he said. "Slow down. You're on the television show *Fox and Friends*?"

"Mm-hm. Now, do you prefer Asher or … *Harrow*?"

"*What*? What are you—"

She giggled coquettishly, then continued in a more professional voice. "We'd like for you to come on the show. Tell us all about how you two met and about how those sparks flew, from *your* point of view."

"Sparks flew? Are you talking about the article? The IED explosion?"

"Oh, no. No, we won't touch on that. What America loves is the love story."

"The love story?"

"'Savannah and Asher: An All-American Love Story.' Mr. Lee, did I catch you at a bad time?"

What? What in the world was she talking about?
"You did, Miss Durant. I need to go. Call back another time."

He put the phone back in its cradle before she could answer, trying to figure out what that was all about. He reviewed the facts. Yes, it was the Fourth of July, and Savannah's article about his time in Afghanistan and his bitter hometown reception had been printed today. He was waiting until she woke up so they could read it together. Maybe the media was trying to read into the fact that the story had been reported by a single young woman? He shook his head, filling up the two coffee cups, when something occurred to him that made him freeze.

Now, do you prefer Asher or … Harrow?

His face flushed, thinking about some unknown woman using the pet name that Savannah occasionally used. Perhaps she was a fan of the same program that had featured Richard Harrow and was making an association based on the similarity of their injuries? His heart started thumping faster. Something didn't feel right.

Ring. Ring.
Ring. Ring.
He crossed the kitchen purposefully.

"Hello?" He was terse. He was feeling confused and thrown off, and he didn't like it. He needed to get upstairs and talk to Savannah, try to figure out what this was all about.

"Asher Lee, this is Clifton Winter, vice president at Van Cleef & Arpels."

"What? Who?"

"Van Cleef & Arpels, the premier jewelry store in Manhattan. We here at VCA are big supporters of returning veterans, and we want you to know that if you're in the market for an exquisite engagement ring for Miss Carmichael, we have—"

"Mr. Winter! I think you have the wrong …"

His voice was muffled as he spoke to someone else. "Damn it, I told you to get me Asher Lee in Danvers, Virginia!"

He heard a woman's voice in the background. "That's him."

"Is this Mr. Lee?"

"Yes, but …"

The line went dead. Asher looked up to see Savannah's finger pressed over the hang-up button. She reached out without a word to take the phone from him and place it gently on the kitchen counter. Her eyes were stricken and resigned as the phone started to beep out an angry busy signal.

"Savannah," he asked, searching her eyes, "what the hell is going on?"

***

"Come sit down," she said, crossing the kitchen to pick up the coffee mugs he must have just filled.

He sat down at the table and she set a mug in front of him before taking the other cup off the counter and sitting across from him.

"Asher--"

"Why are television shows and jewelry stores calling me?"

She bit her lip. She had no idea where to start. "I used pseudonyms. I swear to God, Asher. I didn't use our real names."

"You mean, in the article?" He stared at her, confused. "I don't mind that you used my name. I gave you permission to interview me."

"I know. You did. About your, um, your in-injuries and Afghanistan and coming home."

He nodded. "Right. So …"

"That wasn't what the story was about, in the end." She searched his face, but it hadn't changed from cautious and curious. He still trusted her. He still hadn't put it together. She clenched her eyes shut, wishing she could figure out a way around this, but she couldn't. She was stuck.

"Well, what *was* it about?" he asked.

"Asher," she started, looking up at him, her eyes swimming.

"What was it about, Savannah?" he demanded.

"Us."

His eyes darkened, and his lips narrowed into a thin line. "Us."

Savannah reached out to cover his hand, praying to God he'd find a way to understand how this whole mess had happened. "*Us*. How we got to know each other. How we started spending more and more time together. How we became friends and fell in love and …"

"Jesus Christ, Savannah. *The* story is *our* story?"

She nodded sheepishly as he pulled his hand back.

"I never said you could do that."

"I never told them *they* could do it the way they did. The title I sent to them was 'Cassandra & Adam: An All-American Love Story.' I made it clear to them to use pseudonyms. The original draft never mentioned Danvers. I protected your privacy. I swear."

"It feels *really* protected right now."

"I'm sorry … I …"

"Let me read it."

Her shoulders slumped with relief. Yes. Yes, he could read

her original version, and he'd understand that she'd used their story, but she'd protected their identities and written beautiful things about how they got to know each other, how they fell for each other, how his injuries had never mattered to her once she'd gotten to know him. "I'll go get my laptop and show you my original—"

"No, I want to read what was printed this morning for the whole world to read."

"But …" She swallowed. "They changed it a lot."

His eyes challenged her. "The essence of what you wrote will still be there, won't it?"

"Please don't read it," she said.

"Why not?"

"Because it's not what I wrote." *Bogeyman. Teenage daughters.* She looked at the dignified, amazing man in front of her, and her heart bled for how he'd been portrayed. "It was hacked up. It's not what I wrote. It's not what I think of you. Of *us.*"

His eyes flashed with worry, then fury. "Get your laptop. *Now*, Savannah."

She turned and walked from the kitchen, only to find Miss Potts sitting on the stairs.

"I don't know how he'll ever forgive you," she said quietly as Savannah walked past.

"Neither do I," said Savannah. *And I don't know how I'll ever forgive myself.*

***

Asher felt her eyes on him the entire time he read the article. It was a fairly trashy piece, ramped up to be as sensational as possible. He was portrayed as a partially deranged Quasimodo, and she was painted as an all-American beauty who took pity on the beast.

Every time he read a snippet of their life together, he'd quietly conceal a gasp of surprise. The first time he reached for her hand between the two wingback chairs. Their first kiss. The first time he said he was falling in love with her. The grove.

Their car ride into the mountains. Watching *Shag*. Beating up Lance. Spending the weekend in Maryland. Telling him about Richard Harrow. It was all there. And the way it was told, she'd humanized an animal, fallen in love with his blatant imperfections. She was such a paragon of feminine virtue, she'd somehow managed to look beyond his disfigurement to see his heart. And there was a cloying happily-ever-after vibe to the whole piece that he resented: *He got his hand and face blown off, but oh, what a honey he has in his bed. Wink, wink.*

Some of it made his breath catch because it reminded him of perfect moments with her, but then his face would tighten. The best moments of his life, splashed across the Lifestyles section of a newspaper, picked up on the newswire by every paper that wanted a tearjerker of a story for the holiday.

'Beauty and the Beast' with "The Star-Spangled Banner" playing in the background.

Whoever wrote that line has talent, he thought ruefully. He finished the article, which ended with Savannah's hopes that a future was in the cards despite Asher's severe agoraphobia and a face that caused children to scream.

The confusion and anger he felt toward her were so keen, so sharp, he wondered how to speak to her without saying unforgivable things. And he was in so much pain from her betrayal, from the way she'd used their beautiful story for fodder, he wondered how his guts were still inside his body. How were they not sprawled around for the world to see? Oh, that's right. They were. He shut the laptop slowly until it latched with a quiet click.

"I didn't write that," she said softly, twisting her hands together.

"That's funny." He looked up at her. "It says you did."

"Can I show you the original?"

He shook his head. "Don't much feel like reading anymore."

"Asher, we're in this together. I swear, I'm as much a victim as you."

His eyes shot up to meet hers, and he shook his head with a slow-burning fury. His heart clutched with pain because she was so beautiful and he loved her so much despite the humiliating, emasculating, betraying exposé. He pinpointed his anger and clung to it. "No, baby. You're not. You had a choice. I didn't."

It was the first time he'd ever called her baby with anything but love, and she winced, while he remained carefully impassive.

"Asher, I can't do anything about the fact that they printed it with our names, or how they butchered it with their edits to create caricatures rather than people. But can I please explain why I did it? Why I wrote that piece?"

He nodded, desperate that she say something—anything—that would allow him to understand, to still trust her, to still love her, to still have her in his life.

"I needed this story, Asher. I needed this chance after what happened with the Patrick Monroe story. I needed to prove myself. I needed to prove that I wasn't just some talentless hack who got taken by a source. And you remember that day I came over and I told you that Maddox McNabb wanted sexy, and—"

"Stop!" Asher felt his face flush with heat. "Please be careful what you say next."

"No, it's okay. They wanted sexier, so—"

"So you screwed the cripple—the bogeyman who attacks teenage girls in the dead of night."

"Asher! Stop it!" Her face whipped back as though he'd smacked her. "No! God, no! I never wrote those words, and that's *not* how it was. Don't you *dare* use words like that about us."

"What? Words that are *true*? Yeah. I can see how that would be uncomfortable for you."

Tears brightened her eyes, and she closed her mouth, staring at him. Her breasts rose and fell quickly. She was breathing so fast, he could hear little sobs at the back of her throat, but he desperately tried to ignore them.

Something inside him was starting to hurt, and it felt

strangely like it had during those first few months in San
Antonio when he had to decide whether to live or die. And for a
moment, when he looked at the situation and realized it was
possible this entire beautiful relationship had been an act on her
part, he *wanted* to die.

He took a deep breath and collected himself. Maybe she
kept writing the IED story for weeks; maybe that *was* her story,
and she'd changed it at the eleventh hour when they refused to
print it.

"Okay," he said, attempting a level voice. "Answer me one
thing. How long have you known?"

"Known?"

"That this was your angle? That *we* were your angle and
not the IED explosion and my unwelcome reception back to
society?"

She must have known what he was getting at because her
face fell. He wanted to know if their relationship began before or
after the new angle. And yes, she was about to tell him that it
had started after. He closed his eyes.

"Please, Asher," she whispered.

"How long?" he demanded, his eyes flashing open.

Her voice broke when she answered. "Since the grove."

"Wow," he gasped, looking away from her. "The first night
we kissed. The first night we made out." He breathed out, and it
was a harsh and labored sound. "What a vixen. You really threw
yourself into the role of seductress."

"No, it's *not* like that. There was no role. Maddox *knew* I
was falling for you. He knew it, and that's the story he wanted.
And I just …"

"… screwed the cripple. For a story. To save your career."

"Stop it! No!" she said, with surprising conviction. She
swiped at her eyes. "How I feel about you is real. None of it was
an act, and I was uncomfortable writing our story for a
newspaper, so I thought if I used pseudonyms it would protect us
but still deliver the story. But they must have wanted it to feel
more genuine. If I'd known … Asher, I never would have sent

the story if I'd known they'd use our real names."

"Do you think that's what matters to me? *The use of my name*? Savannah, what happened to me in Afghanistan? That was terrible, but it wasn't a secret, and it wasn't sacred. *You* were sacred to me. *We* were sacred. What we were building. What we had." He swallowed the massive lump in his throat, running his hand through his hair. He looked into the face of the woman he loved, the woman he'd started today wanting to marry, and his stomach turned as he realized that they were in such different places. "What bothers me is that you took the most meaningful, most amazing moments of my life and splashed them across the Lifestyles section of a newspaper for anyone to read. You took words that we said to each other, our feelings, our most personal, intimate moments, and you *used* them. For entertainment. To get your precious career back.

"Whether you started off meaning to or not, you ended up using us. You didn't just tell some sweet, anonymous story. You told *our* story, and without my permission. You used specific details that defined who we were to each other. How I told you I was falling in love with you in bed? That was personal. Really personal. It is *not* okay that you shared that. And it makes me wonder what value you put on us. Because for me, what we had was everything. It was paradise. It was forever. And for you ... it was just a scoop." He paused, his chest heaving. He was exhausted and dizzy, and he wanted to curl up on his bed and cry like a baby. "Did *any* of it matter to you? *Really* matter?"

She reached for him, but he pulled his arm off the table and leaned back in his chair.

"It *all* mattered to me. *You* matter to me more than anything, Asher."

"No. No, you don't get to say that." He stood up from the table and looked away from her because the sight of her was almost unbearable. "That's a lie. Clearly I *don't* matter to you more than anything because you turned in a story about us even though you just said it made you uncomfortable. You knew what you were risking, but your career trumps all."

"It doesn't, Asher. It did, but it doesn't now."

"Even if I believed that, it's a little late now, don't you think? For an attack of conscience?"

"Don't say that. Please don't say it's too late. I already told Maddox I don't want the damned job. I told him I could *never* work for him after what he did."

"That's a shame. You worked hard for it."

He heard the icy tone in his voice, but he couldn't help it. He didn't know what to believe. He wanted to believe her, but it didn't look good from where he was standing. She'd used them to put her career back together, not to mention the scorching embarrassment of the article itself. There were parts of the love story that had touched him, or would have, if it hadn't been about him. But it *was* about him, and the way he was portrayed was beyond humiliating.

"Asher," she sobbed, standing up to reach for him, then lowering her hands when he backed away.

"Savannah, I have no idea what's true and what's not. Things between us happened really fast, but I believed that it was because we felt so much and we just opened and followed our hearts. But I have to wonder now if you were motivated by delivering the article they wanted. I have to wonder if your feelings were fabricated for the sake of a good story. The beautiful things we said to each other are all out of context and cheapened in that article, splayed out like a whore who tripped on the pavement."

Tears covered her face as she stepped forward and pressed her palms flat against his chest. "I'm so sorry for how this happened. I'm so sorry I ever wrote it. I'm so sorry I trusted them not to betray us."

He gulped, his body jolted by the touch of her hands, combined with the inaccuracy of her words. "*You* betrayed us when you sent that story to them, Savannah, when you exposed us to that sort of public inspection."

"I didn't mean to."

"But you did, baby. You did."

"Asher, please tell me you still love me. Please tell me you're just angry and it's not too late for us."

His breath hitched, and he groaned from the pain her words caused him. He took two deep breaths and clenched his jaw as he peeled her hands away before they could make him weak. His voice shook and rasped from the effort it took to put distance between them because he was steel to her magnet, and all he wanted was to be with her, even if it was wrong.

"This is killing me right now, Savannah. I barely had the strength to say good-bye before this happened. I can't handle this right now. I have to leave for Maryland in the morning. I have an operation on Tuesday. I can't do this anymore right now."

"Please tell me this isn't over." Tears fell down her face in streams. "I made a mistake. Such a big mistake. I love you so much."

"I think you love yourself more." The words were out before he could stop them, before he could evaluate if they were even true. But he was so angry, he leaned into them and felt surrender course through his body like a balm against his anger and shock and sadness. His voice was bitter and soft. "You got your story. You're back in the game."

"Ash—"

"But now I think you should leave."

He turned his back to her, heading toward the kitchen door.

She wept in heart-wrenching sobs behind him. "Oh my God, Asher, *please* don't do this."

"*I* didn't do anything," he said in a broken voice. When he turned to look at her, the morning sun filtering through the kitchen window made her so beautiful he couldn't bear it, so he looked away from her. "Except make the mistake of actually falling in love with you while you were"—he shrugged— "giving an Academy Award–winning performance to save your career."

She gasped, holding her breath for a moment like it hurt to breathe. He ordered every cell in his body not to reach for her, and they obeyed, but it cost him, and he ached from the deprivation. He turned to walk through the door, and her voice stopped him.

"I know you're angry, Asher, but it wasn't an act. None of it was an act," she said, her voice thick with tears and regret as she spoke to his back. "I made a mistake. I just made a mistake."

Tears burned his eyes as he walked through the door, letting it slam shut behind him.

CHAPTER 17

The first time you realize he's your home

Over the next week Savannah learned something terrible.

She learned that when your heart is broken, the rest of your body stops working too.

Her eyes, which started every day watering, looked fruitlessly for the one face that could relieve her pain and soothe her swollen, burning eyes. Her ears tuned out every sound around her, recalling only the timbre of his beloved voice. Her fingers reached into the void beside her in the dark of night, seeking the warm skin of his body. And no matter the depth or volume of the air she breathed, she couldn't assuage the terrible tightness in her lungs that was a constant reminder of her loss.

Her regret was unyielding.

And her heart, which had never been broken before, felt empty, as though something beautiful had once made its home there, but vacated without notice or permission. And the beauty left behind only an essence, sharp and elusive, like a deeply imbedded splinter that ached constantly as it reminded her:

I lost him.

Scarlet picked her up from his house after their fight, and Savannah had called and texted Asher several times since, but his house phone was off the hook indefinitely and he didn't pick up his cell phone or return her messages. By Tuesday she stopped trying, as she didn't want to distract him from his surgery, but by Wednesday her resistance dissolved, and she called again to tell him how much she loved him and that she was thinking of him. She developed a compulsion for checking her phone, which invariably led to unceasing tears because, while her phone was inundated with messages from various news shows looking for interviews and editors looking for scoops to further exploit her relationship with Asher, there were never any messages from *him*. By the weekend, she had had enough. She threw the phone in the toilet and hadn't seen it since.

Killing her phone had the benefit of *mostly* cutting her off from the world, but when the house phone rang, her heart still leaped with hope that it was Asher … and then bled some more when it wasn't.

Twice she got into her car to drive to Maryland and demand that he listen to her and give her another chance to explain. Though she wanted badly to be with him, for him to have her love and support as he underwent painful procedures, she stopped herself both times, knowing she was probably the last person he'd want to see, the last person from whom he could find comfort. He didn't even believe that what they'd had was real.

Sometimes she would feel angry at him. Hadn't he said he loved her? Hadn't he promised that he belonged to her just as certainly as she belonged to him? How could something like a newspaper article make him turn his back on his feelings for her so completely? But then she'd review the article in her head—the way it read, the way it looked—and she understood why he'd asked her to leave. She could blame Maddox McNabb and the *Times* until she was blue in the face, but if she hadn't written and sent the article, if she'd placed a higher value on Asher than on her career, none of this would have happened. It was her fault her life was now separate from his.

Though Asher hadn't actually said the words "It's over," the anger and betrayal in his eyes as he asked her to leave his house made it feel like he was also asking her to leave his *life* too. And without him, it was as though the anchor of her life had been pulled up and she'd been set adrift on a cold and dark ocean. With regret as huge and sweeping as that cold sea, she knew that she'd made the biggest mistake of her life. In trying to even the score with Patrick Monroe and the *Sentinel*, she'd risked Asher, the love of her life. And she'd lost. She'd catastrophically lost. And it was unbearable.

Ironically, the career for which she'd risked everything meant nothing to her. In the days after the article was printed, she turned down the job at the *Phoenix Times* two or three times, and if she still had her phone, she'd be turning down offers from other newspapers every day as well. She never wanted to write another newspaper article for as long as she lived.

Ha. If you could even call her life *living*.

Savannah felt the world moving around her—Scarlet leaving for work in the morning, her mother baking goodies for the local tea shop, her father occasionally peeking into her room to remind her of the other fish in the sea—but her deep regret set her apart from the rest of humanity. She lost interest in everything around her except for one thing on which she worked obsessively: recording every detail of her time with Asher.

After the dinner she didn't eat each evening, she climbed the stairs back to the bed she'd left just hours before, closed her eyes, and remembered the details of each specific day she'd spent with Asher, starting from the very beginning, when she saw the flash of his eyes in the mirror. She remembered every touch, every look, every word spoken between them, and then she'd re-create the days on the page, painstakingly recording every detail as accurately as possible until her eyes burned and dawn lit the skies outside her window. Because for Savannah, reliving the days they'd spent together was the only bearable way to live through the days that they were now apart.

The future was too bleak without him, so she tried desperately to hang on to the past, to ignore the eventuality that she would run out of precious days to remember and drift into the dark void of a long life without Asher Lee.

***

"Wake up, Vanna."

"Go away, Scarlet," she mumbled into her pillow.

"It's four o'clock in the afternoon. On a Monday. You have to get up. We're going for a walk."

"No. Not gonna."

"This whole poor-me pity party is getting a little tired, Vanna. I know you're hurtin', but you need to pull up your big-girl panties and get ahold of yourself. For Lord's sake, I'm getting married in six days."

That jolted her out of sleep, which, Savannah suspected, was its intention. "Oh, I'm so sorry my broken heart is interfering with your wedding."

"No, you're not. You're wallowing. And we're still going for a walk." Scarlet threw some sweats and a T-shirt at her sister's head.

Savannah sat up groggily. "You're the devil."

"I know you don't mean that, my sweet sister."

"The hell I don't." She pulled the T-shirt on over a sports bra she'd been wearing for two days straight.

"You don't. I know how much you miss Asher," added Scarlet softly, and Savannah froze for a moment, suppressing the sob that threatened to break from her throat just from the mention of his name.

Scarlet held out a pair of sneakers. "Come on now. Put these on. I want to talk to you."

Scarlet led the way downstairs, and Savannah stopped at the bottom step to find her mother looking up at her worriedly.

"Off for a walk, button?"

"Scarlet's insisting."

"It's good for her, Mama."

Judy nodded at Scarlet before turning her glance back to Savannah. "It's been over a week, honey. Haven't you—"

"Haven't I *what*? Let go? Gotten over it?" Savannah's voice was full of misery and fury. "I love him, Mama. He's *everything* to me. I'm not letting go of him. I'm not going to just get over it."

"That's not what I was going to say, although now that you've mentioned it, this looks a heap more like givin' up than holdin' on." Her mother palmed her hot cheek gently. "I was going to say, 'Haven't you felt sorry for yourself long enough? Don't you think it's time to figure out how to get him back?'"

Savannah sucked in a breath. *Get him back.* The words were hopeful and tantalizing, and her mother had used them as if they were possible. As if Savannah hadn't betrayed him, exposed him, humiliated him, lied to him by omission, and devalued their relationship so much that she'd exploited it to save her drowning career. Get him back? He'd have to forgive her first, and that didn't seem very likely.

Still, she couldn't lie to her mother. A tear trickled down her cheek, over her mother's hand.

"Go with Scarlet, button. Listen to what she has to say."

Judy turned and headed back to the kitchen, the smell of something lemony and sweet wafting into the hallway, and for the first time in more than a week, Savannah's mouth watered.

Scarlet took her arm, leading her sister through the front door, down the porch steps, between the once-crimson azaleas that flanked the picket gate, and out to the sidewalk.

Get him back. Savannah's heart leaped hopefully, repeating the words in a loop, wondering if it was possible. How could she fix everything she'd done wrong? How could she convince him that despite the mess she'd made of everything, she loved him more than her career, more than anything else in the world? She thought of the flinty anger in his eyes as he'd asked her to leave, and her heart clutched.

"I did something," blurted Scarlet, tightening her grip on Savannah's arm as they neared the end of the block.

"What? What did you do?"

"I found your phone in the toilet, and, well, I read that if you put a wet phone in a bowl of rice for a while sometimes it will fix itself."

"Did it work?"

"It did."

Savannah's heart sped up, and she stopped walking, one question crowding out every other thought in her head. "Has Asher—"

"No. No, honey," said Scarlet, shaking her head with sympathy. "No. I didn't mean to get your hopes up. There wasn't any message waiting from him." She waited a beat, then started again with a brighter tone. "But a whole bunch of other folks want to talk to you."

"I don't want to talk to anyone else, Scarlet! That's how I got into this whole mess! There is only *one* person I want to talk to!"

"Well, he doesn't much want to talk to you, now, does he?"

"Screw you!"

Scarlet clasped Savannah's arm and marched her down the hill to their elementary school playground. "Don't you *dare* speak to me like that, Savannah Calhoun Carmichael. I don't care how much your heart's been broken." She took a seat on one of the swings and looked up at her older sister, brooking no argument. "Sit. Swing. Listen."

Savannah was taken so off guard by the command that she complied, sitting down, then pushing off gingerly to set her swing in motion.

"Have you gotten me a wedding gift yet?" Scarlet asked.

Savannah's shoulders slumped. No, she hadn't, and she hated that she'd allowed herself to become so selfish, so consumed with guilt and sadness and regret that it hadn't even crossed her mind.

"I'm sorry, Scarlet. I'm a mess."

"I'll take that as a no," said Scarlet primly. "For the record? You are, hands down, the *worst* maid of honor I have ever seen, heard about, read about, or encountered in my entire life. I know my wedding isn't at the top of your list, but you're my sister, and I know you're sad about Asher, but you did this to yourself, and you're not doing a danged thing to make it right or get him back." She huffed once, angrily, then she seemed to center herself, pulling back from her rant. "Listen, there's only one thing I want from you. So don't bother with a gift. Just give me what I ask for."

"What is it?"

"Say you'll *do* it first."

"Fine. Whatever you want."

"I want you to call Todd Severington at True Love Publishing. He's an editor. He's expecting your call, and I want you to listen to what he has to say. That'll be your wedding gift to me. Making that call."

"A romance editor?" She tried to keep her voice calm. "Have you lost your mind?"

"It's possible Trent thinks so when I'm going off on bouquets and boutonnieres, but in general? No, I'm quite sane."

"No, you're not. You have lost your ever-lovin' mind if you think I'm going to call some romance editor, Katie Scarlet Carmichael."

"Oh, good Lord, you are trying!" Scarlet took hold of the chain on Savannah's swing and yanked it hard until it stopped. "You are depressed and despondent. You barely eat. You barely bathe. You don't do anything but tap on your keyboard all night long keeping me and Mama and Daddy awake. You've made a *royal mess* of your life, and I am trying to *help* you, you mule of a big sister. I told you that you couldn't ride two horses with one ass, but did you listen to me? No, you did not. Now you will. You *will* talk to Todd Severington, and you *will* listen to what he has to say. Do you hear me?"

Savannah wondered if it was possible for someone's face to actually get any redder. She was afraid Scarlet was about to burst something if she didn't agree. "O-Okay. Fine. I'll listen to what he has to say."

With that, Scarlet smiled and fished Savannah's phone out of the back pocket of her floral capris. "Right here, right now." She tapped the keyboard and handed it over.

Savannah looked down at the screen, blanching as she realized that her sister had dialed the number.

"Hello? Hello?" She could faintly hear a man speaking.

She shook her head at Scarlet wordlessly, but Scarlet lifted her sister's arm and pressed the phone up to her ear, mouthing, "Say hello."

"He-Hello?" said Savannah.

"Miss Carmichael? Savannah Carmichael?"

"Yes."

"Well, terrific. Scarlet said you'd be calling this afternoon."

"My sister's very persuasive," she said tightly, narrowing her eyes at Scarlet.

"That she is. And completely charming."

Savannah glanced at Scarlet. "*Some* might think so."

"She says you've been writing every night. Real good stuff too."

Savannah covered the phone and whispered. "Have you been reading my stuff?"

Scarlet shrugged, looking slightly guilty, then looked at the sand at their feet like it was utterly fascinating.

Savannah swallowed. "Sir, I have to be frank. I'm not interested in anything you have to say. I promised Scarlet that I'd hear you out, so why don't you make your pitch so I can tell you no, say good-bye, and stop wasting your time and mine."

"I see. Well, Ms. Carmichael, I appreciate your honesty. I'll cut to the chase here just in case you're interested. Like everyone else in the publishing world, we'd like to option your story. The *real* story of how you fell in love with Asher Lee."

"I'm sorry, sir," she said dully, feeling sad and tired and extremely annoyed with Scarlet. "That story's not for sale. Thank you for the offer, but I—"

"Well, I am thrilled to hear that because I don't want to buy it."

At first she didn't think she'd heard him correctly. "Wh-what?"

"I *do not* want to buy your story," he said again in a clear voice. "I want to auction it. For charity. Specifically, for a charity associated with UCLA called Operation Mend. Have you heard of it? It's a favorite charity of mine since my brother had thirty-two percent of his body covered in burns after an IED exploded near his Humvee in Iraq. Operation Mend reconstructs the faces of wounded veterans. They're having a big benefit in Washington, D.C., on Labor Day, and if you'd be willing to write your story, we could auction the first copy, then print more copies for sale, with one hundred percent of the profits benefitting Operation Mend after we've covered our expenses. You and Mr. Lee are very popular right now, and I bet your story would be a big money maker for Operation Mend, and, well, I thought maybe ..."

Savannah shook her head back and forth as tears streamed down her face. Somehow she managed to look up at Scarlet, who had stopped swinging and was smiling at her through tears of her own.

"Is this something you'd be interested in talking about, Ms. Carmichael?"

Savannah cradled the phone between her shoulder and ear, using the back of one hand to swipe at her eyes, and the other to reach for the hand of her compassionate, smart, amazing little sister.

"Yes, Mr. Severington," she answered in a shaking voice, tentative hope making her heart lighter for the first time in a week. "That's definitely something I'd be interested in talking about."

***

Savannah looked up at Asher's house and then back down at the manuscript on the passenger seat beside her. She took a deep breath, wondering, for the hundredth time, if this was all a big mistake.

It had been four weeks since she first spoke to Todd Severington, and other than attending Scarlet's wedding, Savannah had spent all day, every day, writing the story of how she and Asher fell in love. Her way. She had shared the book only with her mother, Scarlet, and Todd, and they all agreed it was a beautifully told story of two misfit people who found each other and fell in love. It was the story Savannah wished had been told in the *Phoenix Times*. It was the truth, and its beauty shone through.

The novella had already undergone one edit and would need one more before the auction in three weeks. But before they could take another step forward, Savannah insisted that she needed Asher's permission.

She swallowed the lump in her throat and opened her car door, taking the red binder off the seat and carrying it under her arm to the front door. Miss Potts answered after two rings.

When the door swung open, Savannah was assaulted with memories of her time with Asher, and she sucked in a ragged breath. Coming to his house the first day … his eyes in the mirror … the way he looked on the stairs with the sunlight bright behind him … pulling her up the stairs to his bedroom. She whimpered, then forced herself to focus on the reason she was here. Miss Potts's face wasn't especially welcome, but at least she didn't slam the door.

"Hello, Savannah Carmichael."

"Hello, Miss Potts. It's good to see you."

"Hmm," she said, glancing at the manuscript, then back at Savannah. "You know Asher's not here."

"I know." She took a deep breath. "How is he?"

"Coming along."

Savannah was desperate to ask more questions, but she could see Miss Potts mentally closing ranks around Asher to protect him.

Since Scarlet had returned her phone, Savannah had written one text to Asher every afternoon at four o'clock, and the sentiment was always the same: *I made a mistake. I'm sorry. I miss you. I love you more than anything. I hope that someday you'll give us another chance.*

She had yet to receive a response, but as she wrote their story, she relived the tenderness and richness of their relationship. The words that circled in her mind the most were the ones he'd said to her after their weekend in Maryland together. While discussing her impending move to Phoenix and his move to Maryland he had said, *This isn't the sort of love that ends. It's forever. It doesn't matter if you go to Phoenix and I stay here. We'll find each other again.*

She knew that anger and hurt took time to heal, especially when someone was already undergoing the trauma of medical procedures. But she had faith that they still had the sort of love that didn't end, and she still had faith that they would find each other again.

"Has he been home at all?"

Miss Potts's lips tightened into a thin line. "Can I help you, dear?"

"I was asked to write a book."

Miss Potts's face pinched with disapproval, and her eyes flicked to the binder like it was covered in mud. "I think it's best we say our good-byes, dear."

As the door started to close, Savannah stuck out her sneakered foot to stop it. "Please!"

Miss Potts cracked the door open, giving Savannah a death stare.

Savannah spoke quietly, her voice trembling with nerves. "It's Asher's and my story, the way it should have been told. The way I wish it had been told. The way I see it. It's beautiful and tender and shows everything good about him, about us. I promise you, I did it right this time."

Miss Potts' face softened ... barely. "Good for you. But making money off that poor man's story would be—"

"I'm not!" Savannah said. "I promise you. I haven't made a dime on Asher's and my story. I tore up the check from the *Phoenix Times* and told them I wouldn't work for them if my life depended on it."

"And this?" Miss Potts gestured to the book like it was a pile of poo, one ancient nostril flexing with disgust.

"It's for a good cause."

"Would that cause be your career, dear?"

"N-no. I wrote it for an auction … to benefit Operation Mend."

Miss Potts couldn't conceal her surprise. She looked at the red binder again like maybe it didn't actually stink to high heaven. "Operation Mend?"

"Yes, ma'am. It's Asher's and my story, yes, but all the proceeds will go to Operation Mend."

"Hmm." Her eyes were considerably less frosty. "What do you want *me* to do?"

"I was hoping you would give me his address. I need his permiss—"

"Absolutely not." She looked down at the ground, blinking several times. Her voice was sharp when she spoke again. "You have no idea how much you hurt that boy."

"I do," whispered Savannah, a tear snaking down her face. "I promise you, I know. There isn't enough regret in the whole world to express mine."

Miss Potts's eyes were glistening when she looked back up. "I can't give you his address, Savannah."

"Can *you* mail it to him? I'll pay for overnight delivery. But will you ask him to read it? Ask him for permission to print it?"

"*I* have to read it first."

Savannah's mouth dropped open in amazement and gratitude and she nodded vigorously. "Of course! Of course you can read it. Please read it."

"And I'll decide whether or not I send it. You don't have to pay me."

More tears joined the first as Savannah handed the manuscript over to her second-grade teacher.

"That newspaper piece was terrible, Savannah. Lots of room for improvement."

"Yes, ma'am, but I didn't write that. I know he didn't believe me. But I swear to you, what I submitted and what they printed were completely different. This," she gestured to the manuscript, "is *our* story."

"Well, then, we'll see. Good-bye, I guess."

Miss Potts started to close the door, but Savannah felt a sudden burning in her belly to say more, to be sure that the person closest to Asher knew how she still felt about him.

"Miss Potts?"

Miss Potts stuck her head back out the door. Savannah spoke in a rush. "I love him. I love him so much. I love him more than anything else. It's killing me not to be with him."

Miss Potts stared at her for a moment. Finally she sighed loudly, shaking her head at Savannah with disapproval.

"Despite everything," she finally said, "he still loves you too. And he wishes he didn't, but he can't help it." She shrugged. "People wait a lifetime for what you two found with each other. It doesn't just go away no matter how much you hurt one another."

Savannah's shoulders trembled with silent sobs as Miss Potts spoke.

"Thank you," Savannah managed, overwhelmed by Miss Potts's generosity. She closed her eyes momentarily to let the miracle of the words sink in. "Thank you so much."

"You should know something else, dear." Miss Potts anchored the binder under her arm and reached into her pocket, pulling out Asher's phone and showing it to Savannah. "He knew he needed to concentrate on the medical procedures once he got to Maryland, so he left this with me. Truth be told, I don't think he could bear to take it with him. Not when all those awful calls were coming in nonstop as he left for Maryland. Anyway. You probably don't deserve to know this, but I'll feel guilty every day at four o'clock if I don't tell you. He's not ignoring your messages every day, Savannah. He's just not getting them."

Miss Potts closed the door after promising she would be in touch.

He still loved her. Despite everything, he still loved her.

For the first time in weeks, Savannah took a deep, full breath that filled her lungs without aching. And her heart, which

had felt so orphaned and adrift without him, remembered—
without the piercing pain of loss—that Asher's heart was still
her home.

CHAPTER 18

"Damn it!"

Army Specialist Fred Knott sat across the table from Asher, trying without success to pick up the first playing card on top of a neat deck.

"Try again," said Asher, using his new hand to pick up the pile of cards in front of him and fashion them into a fan with a little help from his left hand.

"That's easy for you to say."

"Hey, I had to learn everything just like you. I've got only five weeks on you, soldier. Five weeks from now, you'll be as fast as me." Asher reached over and neatened the deck. "Go ahead. Try again."

Fred reached forward, his severely burned face a mask of concentration as he used the bionic index finger to slide the first card off the deck and pick it up between his index finger and thumb. He held it up and beamed. "Look at that!"

Asher grinned back. "See? Told you you'd get there."

Fred stared at the card and his face fell a little. Asher knew the signs. His friend was about to get a little sad.

"I took it for granted, you know?" said Fred, blinking rapidly at Asher before staring back down at the card. "The stupidest, littlest things I could do before. I wasn't even thankful."

"Having hands was something we *all* took for granted. You're *supposed* to take them for granted. Does no good to dwell on it, Freddy. Try the toothpicks now." He slid a box of toothpicks across the table and watched Fred's concentration return as he tried to pick up only one.

Over the past five weeks, not only had Asher nearly mastered the use of his bionic hand, which he wore almost constantly unless he was sleeping, but he'd already had two procedures on his face. He'd had the magnets fitted into the skin where his ear used to be, and a prosthetic ear had been fitted. The first time he looked in the mirror at his new ear, he had to look twice, it was so shocking to see a matching ear on either side of his head. The first thing he did was make an appointment with a nearby barber recommended by one of the nurses and had his hair cut short and preppy like he used to wear it in high school.

They'd done two straightforward operations to remove areas of deformed scar tissue on his face and to raise his eyelid and replace the heavily scarred areas with healthy skin grafts. In two weeks, they'd take a small graft of skin from the right side of his forehead, near the hairline, and use it to rebuild the corner of his nose and establish the normal contour of his eyes. And he still needed to have his jaw and cheekbones evened out with silicone implants in September. Asher was really starting to feel different, like he recognized himself a little more, like he was coming into focus.

But while his face was undergoing such successful improvements, there was nothing in the world that could be done to mend his broken heart.

When Asher lost his parents, he'd learned, with the help of an excellent therapist, how to compartmentalize his grief so that it didn't take over his whole life. He'd allow himself about an hour every day to remember his mother and father, pore over photos, and recall favorite moments, but when the allotted time was over, he'd force himself to think about other things, force himself to call a friend or get some exercise, or somehow reengage with his life.

He employed the same strategy now. In quiet moments, he

allowed himself to think of Savannah for a set amount of time, but the mix of emotions he felt were so brutal, even fifteen minutes would leave him physically breathless. Anger, betrayal, love, longing, and aching sadness. Mostly he just prayed for the aching to end. To not feel so lonely and adrift. To find a way to let go of her, or get her back, because he couldn't live in this bleak place indefinitely.

He'd reread the article twice once he got to Maryland, and quietly wept after the second reading, overwhelmed by the pain he felt. *Bogeyman? Beast?* He'd purposely hidden himself away from the world to avoid those types of scathing comments, and hearing them from her hand—from Savannah, whom he loved more than anything—was ripping him to shreds. He'd broken his own rules by inviting her into his life, and this was the result: humiliation, embarrassment, betrayal, total and complete heartbreak. A roundhouse kick to the gut couldn't possibly make him physically hurt more sharply than the dark memories of that terrible morning in his kitchen.

When he recalled that morning in all of its heart-wrenching detail, he waffled between believing that she was an ambitious, soulless fraud who should win an award for her acting skills, and a young woman who'd been betrayed by a slick editor all because she'd been blinded by the opportunity to revive the career she'd worked so hard for and lost.

He still would have been angry with her if the story had been printed with pseudonyms, but it would have been easier to believe that she'd just tried to have her cake and eat it too: delivering the story she'd been commissioned to write while protecting their anonymity. He still wouldn't have liked her using their story without his permission, but without his intense humiliation layered into the situation, he might have been able to forgive her the mistake of letting her ambition overrule her judgment.

More than anything else in the world, he missed her. He wanted to know that their time together was real, and that, yes, she'd made a pretty bad mistake, but that her intention had never been his humiliation and betrayal. He just didn't know how to figure it all out.

In his dreams, he'd see her face as she wept in his kitchen. He'd hear her voice in his head, begging him to tell her it wasn't too late, that she loved him more than anything. He would wake up in the same cold sweats he used to get when he returned home from his tour, because—*oh my God*—he wanted to believe her. He'd never experienced the sort of love he had for Savannah and he believed she'd had for him. After knowing what life looked like with a Savannah who loved him, a life without her was almost unbearable.

Like most amputees, Asher knew what it was like to feel a phantom limb. He often felt his hand, as though it were still attached to his body, and still reached for it in the middle of the night, only to realize all over again that it had been taken away on an operating table in Kandahar.

Like a phantom limb, Savannah's presence haunted him. Where she used to lie beside him. Where she used to live in his heart. When he thought of her smiling face, or her body rising up to meet his, or her voice speaking the words *I'm falling in love with you*, or the way her eyes softened with love as she looked at him, he couldn't convince himself that it had all been an act. His heart wouldn't let his mind believe it, despite the overwhelming evidence against her. He missed her in the same way he missed his hand, as something that had belonged to him, and had been, in one terrible, brutal moment, ripped away from him.

Despite everything, Asher was still deeply, irrevocably in love with her, but he hated himself for it because until he understood what had really happened, loving Savannah wasn't smart or safe. And because he no longer trusted her, no matter how much he wanted to believe her, no matter how much he wanted to forgive her, and despite how deeply he still loved her, finding out the truth seemed the most elusive thing of all.

***

"You're doing well, Asher," said Colonel McCaffrey as he inspected Asher's face. "I like how quickly the swelling's gone down. I think we can start on the next procedure a few days sooner. I'm going to check the OR for tomorrow, see if we can fit you in for the nose graft."

Asher nodded.

"I also hear you've been very encouraging to some of the recent amputees who are trying to learn how to cope."

"I know how it feels, sir, to come home to nothing. Looking like this."

"From what I hear, you've got a way with the kids coming in. You ever considered getting more involved?"

"How do you mean, sir?"

"Paid position or volunteer. Sharing your story, offering support, even studying up on the therapeutic side of care. Maybe getting that degree you never got at Johns Hopkins."

Asher had to admit, he liked working with the new guys. They were young, and many of them seemed so hopeless. He was in the unique position of being able to understand.

"I'll give it some thought, sir."

"If you don't mind my saying so, Asher, you seem a little down, though. When you were here in June, we talked very briefly about a young lady."

Asher looked away. "It's complicated, sir."

"You sure look miserable about it." The doctor took a deep breath. "I read the article, Asher."

Asher winced, embarrassment making his cheeks hot.

"I could see how you'd be angry about it."

Asher nodded, still looking away.

"She's not a very good writer, but the story?" He made a clicking sound. "Aw, I don't know. Sure seemed like you kids loved each other a lot."

Asher swallowed the lump in his throat and finally looked up at his doctor. "I love her. I want to kill her most days, but I love her. I just don't know what to do with her."

"Women. Can't live with them. Bad idea to kill them,

though. Have you tried talking to her? Now that the hubbub has died down?"

"I've been trying to concentrate on being here."

McCaffrey nodded. "I understand that. Especially if you don't want to be with her anymore. She did call you the bogeyman."

"She didn't write that, sir."

"Oh, no?"

Asher blinked, realizing what he'd said, how he'd just defended her without thinking about it. It confused him, but he didn't want to think about it. "Well, she claims she didn't."

"Huh. I guess you have a few things to figure out, Asher."

"I guess so, sir."

"Can I just say one thing?"

Asher nodded.

"You'd been coming here for years for checkups, and we couldn't get you to try a new hand or let us put you under again after what you'd been through at Brooke. Then suddenly you're here. You want the new hand; you want to work on the face. That article? It was a mixed bag: part love story and, yes, part humiliation. But, see, she changed you Asher. For the good. She helped you move forward. And we only let certain people change us. We only want to change for certain people. If she was worth changing for, she's probably worth talking to."

"Thank you, sir."

Doc McCaffrey stood up, and Asher followed suit, offering his right hand, and feeling proud when his doctor was able to shake it firmly. He turned to leave.

"Oh, and Asher?"

"Yes, sir?"

"I looked her up. She's a mighty pretty thing. If she's not the girl for you, I guess she won't be single for too long, huh?" Then he grinned and sat back down at his desk, immediately turning his attention to the files waiting there.

Asher closed the door, standing in the small waiting room with his good hand curled into a fist. The idea of Savannah with someone else, anyone else but him, made him so desperate and so furious he wanted to hit something. He still wasn't sure what to do, but he missed her fiercely, and while he wasn't ready to talk to her, he at least needed to find out if she'd started moving on.

***

"Asher!" Trent Hamilton's voice was surprised but delighted. "How you doing? My daddy and me been suckin' down that bourbon I had at your house that day. Can't barely keep it in stock over at Jingles Liquor."

"Good for you. Glad I could introduce you to a classic." Asher was strangely comforted by the familiar hometown lilt of Trent's accent. "I guess congratulations are in order."

"Yes, sir. I am now a married man."

"Happy for you, Trent. How's Scarlet?"

"She's just fine. We spent a week in Maui and had quite a time."

"Glad to hear it."

Asher paused. He felt a bead of sweat trickle down the side of his face.

"Um, Asher, don't you want to know about Savannah?"

Another long pause. His voice was husky in his ears when he spoke again. "How's she doing?"

"Well, sir, she was not good for a while after you left. Stayed in bed all day. Wouldn't eat. Slept weird hours. Scarlet could barely get her to go for a walk for fresh air. She lost some weight, and her face was always puffy."

Asher's heart twisted to think of her so unhappy. "You said 'a while.' And now?"

"She's a whole lot better. Once she started writing that book, she seemed—"

"Savannah's writing a book?"

"Yep. You know those reporters and publishers bothered her for weeks. She finally settled on one."

Fury rose up in him like acid. She'd spent a week feeling

sad, then she'd caved—probably regretting her rash decision to turn down the job in Phoenix—and accepted a contract to write a book. Damn it, she was just as soulless as he'd feared.

"Well, I hope she got a good advance. I have to get going, Trent."

"Oh, well, I … Okay. It was good to hear from you, Asher."

"Yeah. You take care, now."

Asher hung up the phone, took a tumbler out of his kitchen cabinet, and filled it half full with the same bourbon that Trent liked so well.

He paced his kitchen, adrenaline making his whole body tremble with anger. She'd mourned him and the death of their relationship for one week before accepting a contract to write a book about them, and then, suddenly, she was a whole lot better. He picked up the glass, downed the contents, and was about to throw it against a wall when the doorbell rang. Putting the glass down on the counter, he went to open the door.

A delivery person held out a parcel. "FedEx. Signature, please."

Asher signed the delivery slip, then took the box back inside. He placed it on the counter and filled the glass again. His heart had been bleeding all over the state of Maryland while she'd gotten over him and started writing a book. It wasn't bad enough that she'd eviscerated him in the *Phoenix Times* article. She needed to do it in book format too.

Well, this time he'd sue her. He'd sue the pants off her for libel and slander and anything else he could think of. He sucked down the bourbon and ignored the burning in his eyes.

"God damn it!" he yelled, finally throwing the glass at the wall with a sob. It shattered into pieces all over the kitchen floor. He was *not* going to cry about her, no matter how hurt he was.

He turned to the box on the counter. He could use a distraction, even if it was just his weekly mail delivery from Miss Potts. He ripped open the pull tab and sat down in the living room, still seething over Trent's news.

Turning the box over, he shook it lightly, and a red binder spilled into his hands with a yellow sticky note on top. It read, simply, "Dear Asher. Read this. I wouldn't ask if it wasn't important. Miss Potts."

He stared at the nondescript binder, wondering what it was.

Nothing prepared him for the shock of the cover page when he opened it.

Once Upon a Time
By Savannah Calhoun Carmichael

He ran his good hand over the words, touching them, wondering if Savannah's fingers had touched them too, and somehow he knew that they had. His eyes, already burning, watered painfully now as he stared at her name.

"Once upon a time," he breathed.

He flipped the binder closed and read Miss Potts's note again, then opened the binder and stared at the title for a few more seconds. Dare he read? Miss Potts, who loved him like a grandson, was asking him to, telling him it was important. He took a deep breath, turning the page.

Once upon a time, I walked up to Asher Lee's house on a sunny May afternoon, wearing a sundress borrowed from my sister, holding a plate of fresh-baked brownies as a Southern-style peace offering. Honestly, I had no idea what to expect.

Here is what I knew about Asher Lee: he was a soldier who'd been disfigured in Afghanistan, after which he'd moved back to our small town of Danvers, Virginia, and barely anyone had seen him since.

I had no idea that I was starting the most important journey of my life that day—that I would, quite literally, meet the man of my dreams. That I would fall in love so deeply, so fully and completely, that I'd be almost unrecognizable by the time I lost him. I had no idea that my greatest love would become my greatest regret and that I would be trapped in a half-life of loving someone who could barely look at me anymore. And yet, knowing everything that I know now, I still would have borrowed that sundress and baked those brownies, because loving Asher Lee was the greatest gift I was ever given, and being loved by him for the short time we were together taught me everything I will ever need to know about true love. Even if I can't ever have it again, I knew what it was to be someone's everything … once upon a time.

"Oh my God," he said as the words on the page swam before him. "Savannah."

He leaned back in the chair and kept reading, not moving except to turn the pages for the next three and a half hours. He laughed and cried, closed his eyes in anguish, and stopped for moments at a time when he was too overwhelmed to continue.

It was the most beautiful love story he'd ever read. Ever. In his entire life. In his entire library there wasn't a story to match it. And as he read he recalled every word, every moment, every glance and touch. He smelled her lemon shampoo and tasted the French toast casserole. He remembered the smooth heat of her belly under his fingertips, the way she sighed into his mouth as they made love.

It ripped his heart to shreds and mended it at once. What he'd never known was how desperately she'd struggled with her decision to write the story, fearful of his reaction, always hoping he'd understand, wishing there was another way, finally betting everything on the trust she'd established with her editor, only to have it completely betrayed. He didn't question her truthfulness; he could feel it. And he finally understood how it had happened, how she had fallen in love with him and how she had believed that even if the story upset him, their love would be able to handle one small article in one small paper so many states away. She'd certainly never expected it to be hacked and edited. She never expected it to be picked up by a major newswire. She never expected it to go viral.

She had turned down the job at the *Phoenix Times* and every other newspaper, including the *New York Sentinel*, which had offered her a job in their Human Interest section. How it must have hurt—or felt great? —telling them to shove it. He almost grinned.

The one thing he didn't understand is why she'd finally caved and decided to make money off the story. He had to admit, this book was beautifully written and portrayed them both accurately, if not slightly romanticized. It was a story to be proud of, though he still objected to her capitalizing from the *Phoenix Times* fiasco. It still felt wrong.

Then he reached the final page.

I thought that getting my career back was more important than anything, but I was wrong. The most important thing was Asher, and losing him has been the most difficult thing I have ever experienced in my life, though I force myself to survive.

The worst thing about surviving sometimes, though, is what waits for you on the other side. Asher knew this when he returned home from Afghanistan to an empty house in a town that couldn't accept him, but he chose to survive and keep on living. At one time, I believed that he'd survived for me;
now I'm not sure whether or not that's true, since I have surely hurt him more than anyone ever has or ever will.

Like I said, I thought that getting my career back was more important than anything, but I was wrong. Now I know what I lost, and my regret is epic and endless because I will always love Asher Lee, and all I can do is attempt to be the person he loved so much once upon a time.

THE END

Asher took a deep, shaky breath, tears coursing down his face. They slipped from his chin to plop quietly on the page, and as they spread, he realized that there were words on the next page too.

He turned the page, and if he'd already been doubled over by the impact of their story, what he read next leveled him to rubble:

100% of the proceeds from
Once Upon a Time will
benefit Operation Mend, a
UCLA-based nonprofit
organization that provides
medical experts necessary to
make wounded warriors
whole again.

He clenched his eyes shut, closing the binder but holding it against his chest tightly. He sat still for a long time, letting their story sink in, coming to terms with the fact that she'd been telling the truth, and aching to be with her, to touch her, to talk to her, and tell her it wasn't too late, that it would never be too late, because he would never love anyone as much as he loved her.

When he couldn't stand it anymore, he turned to page one and started reading it all over again. He read long into the night, over and over and over again, until his eyes burned and it was time to leave for the hospital for his next surgery.

CHAPTER 19

The first time you realize that he loves you as much as you love him

"Savannah Calhoun Carmichael, are you even listening to me?"

Scarlet, who held a thick parenting magazine suspended between her elegantly manicured fingers, was giving Savannah a familiar pinched look. Savannah adjusted her seat on the porch railing to look squarely at her little sister, who'd found out just that morning that she was expecting.

"Yes. I am. 'Twelve recommendations for getting your little one into the best-possible preschool.'" Savannah sighed. "Isn't it a little early to be thinking about that?"

"It is *not*." Scarlet shut the magazine and rested it on her lap. "A May baby. Isn't it wonderful? Happy you're going to be an aunt?"

"Very wonderful. And very happy my niece or nephew is going to have the best mama in town."

Scarlet smiled and looked over the porch railing as the sprinkler started its lazy rotation. "Hard to believe that the summer's almost over. Just two weeks until Labor Day."

Savannah nodded, thinking of Asher. The familiar heaviness was not as heavy as it had been before writing *Once Upon a Time*, but ever present nonetheless.

Miss Potts had sent a note last week: *Asher says you may publish. —Miss Potts*

Savannah had been cheered, at first, by the note, because it meant that Asher had read her book, which she had painstakingly written as a love letter to him, baring her heart to him on every page and hoping that by reading the truth of their story, he would understand the decisions she'd made. But as the days moved on and there wasn't any follow-up from Asher, her spirits had dipped again. Lately, especially as the evenings got cooler, she turned her thoughts toward Christmas, wondering if she and Asher could start all over once he was home again. It was the one fantasy that really kept her going.

"Glad you're still writing," said Scarlet. "I think it's wonderful that Todd offered you an advance on your next book."

"Mmm," murmured Savannah. "I think I'll get a little apartment in town. Get out of Mama and Daddy's hair. A sunny room where I can write."

"Baby and I will come and visit famous Aunt Vanna, the romance writer. Who knew that's what you would end up doin'?"

Savannah grinned at her sister. Lately she'd been able to grin again. It's not that she was happy, but life kept moving, kept demanding to be lived, and Savannah was a survivor, just like Asher.

"Certainly not me. It's a long way from investigative reporting, but it feels right. More right than I could have expected. And no one will ever hack up something that I write ever again. I made sure of it. Final approval on all edits was the first thing I insisted on in my new contract."

"Your book was wonderful, Vanna. No way Asher could have read it and thought any different."

Savannah shrugged. "By my best guess, he read it at least five or six days ago. I was sort of hoping to hear from him. But …"

"Give him a little time," said Scarlet. "Maybe he had a surgery planned for the day it arrived, or the day after. Maybe he needed to get his head around it. I know it's hard, but be patient."

Savannah nodded, but inside she was losing hope. "There's

no other way I could tell him, you know? That I'd made a mistake and how terribly sorry I was. That he was and is and will always be the love of my life."

Scarlet stood up, putting her arm around Savannah's waist. "I just know it's all going to work out."

Savannah wished she shared her sister's optimism. Instead she changed the subject. "Thank you, Scarlet."

"For what?"

"For forcing me back to the land of the living. For loving me when I was so hateful. I called you the devil, you know."

"Oh, I know. I was there."

"I was the worst maid of honor who ever lived."

"That's right," Scarlet said. "You'll have to make it up to me by being the best godmother who ever lived, you hear?"

Savannah laughed. "Why do you keep giving me chances?"

"Because that's what you do when you love someone. Which is how I know Asher will be back someday, Vanna. Because he loves you. More than I ever saw a man love a woman. That doesn't just go away."

Tears sprang into Savannah's eyes. "Thank you, Scarlet," she mouthed, not trusting her voice.

Scarlet looked at her watch. "Have to get going. I like to have dinner waitin'. And I have big news to share tonight. Poor Trent. I hope he's ready to be a daddy."

"If he's not," said Savannah, pulling her sister back into her arms, "I know you'll get him up to speed."

Scarlet walked down the porch stairs to her car, turning back once to smile at Savannah. "I meant it. I know he'll be back someday."

Scarlet seemed so sure, it was almost like she knew something, but that couldn't be. She'd know if Asher had ever been in touch with Trent or Scarlet. No. She was just trying to be reassuring. Savannah's eyes burned, but she grinned and nodded, waving good-bye.

After Scarlet was out of sight, Savannah sat on the swing

and watched the evening settle in. The bright-red geraniums were looking a little tired now as summer came to a close, and the azaleas wouldn't bloom again until next year. Children rode their bikes back and forth down the street, and a couple of young mothers walked by with matching carriages. Life buzzed on around her, and though Savannah did her best to force herself to stay engaged, it took effort. She closed her eyes, leaning back in the swing.

She missed Asher.

She missed him every second of every day.

And while the pain was bearable now, it was no less constant.

It had been almost six weeks since the Fourth of July, six weeks without a word from Asher. She wondered what he had thought as he read her book, their story. She wondered if he laughed and cried as much as she had, clutching the words to his heart, remembering the very best moments they'd shared. Or had he read her words with cool indifference, only agreeing to let her publish because of the cause it would benefit? Did he think of her at all anymore? Did he still love her?

"I'm sure he doesn't," she whispered softly as the cool evening breeze kissed her cheeks.

"You're sure he doesn't what, darlin'?"

She gasped, then calmed herself. Asher's voice. Of course. Rarely an hour went by without having an imaginary conversation with him, her head re-creating his voice so effortlessly she could almost be tricked into believing he was beside her.

She inhaled deeply, keeping her eyes closed, determined to enjoy the fantasy for as long as it lasted. "I'm sure he doesn't love me anymore."

"Then you'd be wrong."

"Then I'd be …" Her heart started thumping and she took a deep, gasping breath. It couldn't be. It couldn't actually be him. She froze, afraid that breathing would steal him away. "Asher?"

"Keep your eyes closed, Savannah."

She heard him walk up the steps of the porch and fought to obey his instruction, her fingers lifting from her lap, dangling over her legs and trembling fiercely with her longing to reach out for him. She heard him step onto the porch and move around the table until he settled himself on the swing beside her.

"You're here," she sobbed. "You're finally here."

"I'm here," he said softly, and she heard the emotion in his gravelly voice. His hand reached for hers, effortlessly lacing through her fingers.

"I want to open my eyes."

"I need you to listen to me first, darlin', okay?"

She nodded her head with a jerk, her fingers tightening around his. It was Asher. It was Asher come home to her, just as Scarlet had predicted. She'd do anything he asked. Anything to know they weren't over, that they'd never been over, that their future still included each other.

"That article."

Her head fell forward in sorrow. "Asher—"

He spoke in a rush, but softly, tenderly. "I know you didn't write it that way. I know you wouldn't have," he paused, swallowing, "used those words about me. I know you meant to protect our identities, and I know that you were shocked by how much attention it got. I believe you."

"I swear to you—"

"Shhh. You don't stop interrupting me, Savannah, I'm going to have to kiss that mouth to keep it quiet."

Her heart fluttered wildly, and she seriously considered interrupting him again as soon as possible, but she knew it was important for them to talk first.

"That morning, I didn't know what to believe. But I'm sorry that I didn't believe you. I should have believed you. I should have—"

"No," she said in a broken voice, her fingers kneading his. "You don't have to say you're sorry to me. I did this to us. I—"

She gasped as she felt the warmth of his lips press against hers, and she couldn't hold back the tears anymore, crying as she reached for his face with her free hand, which was stopped by the firm grip of something hand-like. Her brain worked hard to process what was stopping her, but then his tongue touched hers, and every thought in her head vacated as she sank into the heaven that was his mouth on hers once again. Whatever had held her hand back moved away and suddenly he was encircling her with two complete arms, pulling her against his chest as two hands settled on her back. She tasted the salt of her tears, and maybe his tears too, as he delved into her mouth, slanting his lips over hers to kiss her silly, to kiss her senseless, to kiss her like he still loved her just as much as he ever did before.

He drew back from her but quickly adjusted their position so her chin rested on his shoulder and her breasts were flush against his chest. She opened her eyes and looked down at her hands clasped around his back, resting her cheek on his shoulder.

"You're holding me with two arms."

"Yes, I am."

She laughed, tears still streaming down her face.

"You stopped me from touching your face with your … your hand."

"That's right."

"I want to see your face, Asher."

"Not yet," he said softly. "We have to finish talking about the past first. When we talk about the future, then you can see."

Savannah took a deep breath and sighed, closing her eyes and thanking God that she was back in his arms, and that talking about the future was part of his plan. "Okay."

"I got your book last Monday, baby. I read it. And then I read it again. And then I read it twice more, until the sun came up and I had to go to the hospital in the morning for my third surgery."

"Oh," she breathed. Scarlet had been right. He hadn't been avoiding her. He was unable to contact her.

"Savannah, I wanted more than anything to call you or come to you, but I had to show up for that surgery, and I had to heal a little before I could drive here."

"Of course."

"That book—" His breath hitched with emotion, vibrated against her chest, and she savored the feeling of him so close. "That book was the most beautiful thing I've ever read. It told me everything I needed to know. I ... I understand, Savannah. I understand how it all happened."

Tears welled in her eyes again as she clutched him more tightly.

"I won't lie to you. When Trent told me you were writing a book, I just about lost it, but then Miss Potts sent it to me, and, aw, Savannah, I'm so sorry I doubted you."

"You had every right to doubt me," she sobbed, shuddering against him. "E-every right."

"And you did it for Operation Mend, which means our story will raise money to help other wounded guys. And I'm ... Well, I'm just so proud of that, and though there's still a private part of me that wishes our story had never been anyone's business but ours—that's selfish when publishing it can do so much good. Somehow it makes it okay. Makes it more than okay. Means that I'm able to serve one more time, do some good, give something back. All because of you."

"All because of *us*," she said. "I need to see you."

"Okay. One more minute. I have a couple more things to say before you look at me, okay?"

"Why can't I see you?"

"Because I look different, darlin', and I want to say these things while I'm still the Asher you fell in love with—I mean, assuming that you, that is ... if you still ..."

"You can't possibly wonder."

"I didn't believe you. I turned my back on you."

"I hurt you. I hurt you so much. I'm so sorry, Asher."

"Shhh. I know, baby. I know." He rubbed her back gently.

"I never stopped loving you, Asher. Not for a second. Not once. I was stupid enough to think my career could possibly matter more to me than you. Because what I quickly found out was that nothing matters more to me than you. Nothing. And I'll survive without you … but I can't really *live* unless I'm with you."

She felt the shudder rip through his body at her words, the old swing creaking under them as he pulled her as tightly to him as possible. Her bare legs wedged between his, and his fingers curled against her back, and how she wished they were naked in his bed, limbs entwined, skin to skin.

"I love you too," he finally rasped into her ear. "I love you so much it felt like slowly dying to be away from you for so long."

"For me too."

"I don't ever want to be apart from you again," he breathed against her skin, and it made shivers sail down her back. "Not from this moment on."

"Me neither," she gasped, feeling overwhelmed and breathless, and happier than she'd ever been in her entire life.

She felt his jaw clench against her cheek, like he was gathering his courage. "Okay," he breathed. "You ready to see?"

"I was always ready, Harrow."

***

"Harrow," he repeated quietly, with wonder. The broken man of her dreams.

During some of their darkest moments apart, he'd worried about never hearing her call him that again. It felt so wonderful to hear the word that he laughed into her ear, and it broke the tension just enough for her to relax as he loosened his grip, and she pulled back, keeping her eyes open as she looked at him.

She gasped, holding her breath, then gasped again, as her face contorted and she started sobbing again. "Oh … my … God," she whimpered, reaching up tentatively to touch his face with trembling fingers. "Oh, Asher."

He quickly cataloged the changes she was looking at: a new ear, a smoother cheek, a normal-looking eye socket, and, most recently, a completely reconstructed nose. He still needed the implants in his jaw and cheek, but he already looked very different from the last time she'd seen him, and, for a moment, as she stared at him with her hands covering her mouth, he felt nervous. What if she didn't like the changes? What if she wanted the man she'd fallen in love with?

So she shocked him, as she always did, when she said through tears, "Your hair's so short."

He laughed, and she started laughing too, her beautiful smile taking over her whole face as tears wet her cheeks and her shoulders shook with sobs and laughter mingling.

"I have all this work done, and she notices my hair." He reached out with his i-Limb forefinger, barely hearing the light whirring of the motor as he wiped a tear from her cheek.

She reached up, grinning, and grabbed hold of the finger gently, lowering it to look at it. "My partially bionic man," she said, holding the silicon-covered skeleton in her hands and staring at it.

She finally raised her eyes to him and smiled a little sadly. "You look good. But so different. You don't look like the Asher Lee I met four months ago."

"Maybe not, but I'm still him. And you're still the girl who loves him, aren't you?"

"Yes," she said, nodding. "I am."

He reached up with his real hand and palmed her cheek, watching as she closed her eyes and leaned into him, reaching up to cover his hand with hers.

"Savannah."

"Hmm?"

"I have to go back to Maryland tonight. I wasn't actually supposed to leave at all, but after my all-okay this morning, I said I couldn't wait anymore to see you, and Doc McCaffrey said he couldn't stop me if I was hell-bent on being a fool for a woman." He grinned, remembering the doctor's sly smile. "I still have a few procedures left. And I've been working with some of the guys there. Encouraging them and reminding them that there's a big world out there and they need to figure out a way to be a part of it."

She winced, nodding, trying to be brave. He knew her so well, it clutched at his heart, and he leaned forward to press his lips against hers in reassurance.

"But I don't want to go back without you."

He searched her eyes, feeling it in his heart, in his soul, that he was ready to take a big step toward forever.

He reached into his jacket pocket with his i-Limb thumb and forefinger, taking out the shiny gold band he'd asked Miss Potts to find in his mother's jewelry box and have cleaned for him. He'd stopped by for it on the way to see Savannah, and gotten a huge tearful hug from his housekeeper/surrogate grandmother, who wished him luck and told him, "Savannah Carmichael isn't a danged fool, so don't be nervous."

He held the ring carefully, reaching with his real thumb and forefinger to adjust it so that the diamond shined brightly at the top.

She whimpered and started crying again as he held it out to her, taking her hand in his real one.

"Savannah Calhoun Carmichael, the day you walked up to my door in a borrowed sundress holding a plate of brownies was the first day of my life. Knowing you, loving you, being loved by you—it's been like being reborn. An angel giving me a second chance to live.

"You once told me that you thought I stayed alive for you, even though I didn't know you yet. And I told you that not only had I stayed alive for you, but I'd never let you go.

"I never did. Not when I was so hurt and angry, not while we were apart. You were with me every minute—your smile, your laughter, the way you look at me, the way you touch me, the way you tell me that you love me. Every minute, you were with me. So deeply bound to my heart, so fiercely bound to my soul, I realized that me without you is impossible."

He searched her face, which was soft and tender, gazing back at him with enough love to last a lifetime and beyond.

"Savannah, will you be my wife? Please, darlin', please say you'll marry me."

He held his breath, watching her eyes. It had occurred to him during his ride home that she could say no. She could say that he hadn't trusted her, hadn't believed in her enough. She could tell him they needed a break or more time to be sure that they were right for each other. And if she said that? Well, he wouldn't give up until she said yes. He'd come home as often as he could, and after Christmas he'd camp out on her porch. Eventually she'd see that he wasn't ever going to give up on them, that the love he had for her was deathless. If he had to wait, he'd wait, but oh God, how he hoped as he stared back into her deep-brown eyes. How he hoped that the girl of his dreams would say …

"Yes! Of course, yes!"

She lifted her trembling hand and lowered her fourth finger so he could slide his mother's ring onto it, and his whole body shuddered with relief.

She reached up to cradle his cheeks, pulling his face to hers, then tilted her head so that their lips met as he pulled her into his arms, determined never, ever to let her go again. When they drew back from each other, panting and breathless, he rested his forehead against hers.

"Just so you know, your daddy said yes first."

"Wouldn't have mattered if he said no."

He kissed her, then, because she was his. Because he was so relieved and grateful that he'd never have to endure another day of his life without her. Because she was his best friend and his lover and his fiancé and the someday mother of his children. Because she was his second-chance and his happily ever after when all hope seemed gone.

"I'll love you every day for the rest of my life, Asher Lee," she whispered, her breath warm on his lips, making him wonder if there was time to stop by his bedroom for an hour or two before heading back down to Maryland together. "I promise that nothing will ever be more important to me than you. I love you more than anything else in the world, and I promise I always will."

There was definitely time for a quick stop, he thought, grinning at his bride-to-be.

"I promise the same," he vowed, his voice low with emotion, with love and requited longing and the relief of knowing Savannah belonged to him forever. "I'll love you more than anything else. Every day for the rest of my life."

***

Savannah heard Scarlet's voice from that May evening so long ago, clear as day—*number twelve, the first time you realize that he loves you as much as you love him*—and she drew back to look into the eyes that had first captured hers in a mirror so many months ago.

"What did you say?" she asked, her voice soft and breathless.

"I promise the same," he repeated. "I'll love you for the rest of my life."

"Number twelve," she murmured, shaking her head with wonder. "Scarlet was right."

"Number twelve? Scarlet?" He grinned at her, his face a mix of love and light confusion. "What does it mean?"

Her heart surged with tenderness as she smiled back at her handsome man, leaning forward again to whisper the words against his lips, before kissing him with all the love in her heart, every bit of which belonged to him:

"It means we're ready for forever."

THE END

Thank you so much for reading Asher and Savannah's story!
I hope you loved it.

--*Katy*
xoxoxo

*****

Operation Mend is a real-life organization that has made a difference in the lives of over one hundred wounded veterans.

I was proud to donate fifty percent of my profits from the sale of *The Vixen & the Vet* to Operation Mend in June and July 2014, an amount of almost $1400. I humbly thank my wonderful readers for sharing this book with their friends and family and raising awareness for this amazing cause.

Learn more here: **operationmend.ucla.edu/**

*****

Katy Regnery loves to hear from her fans!
Connect with her on **www.facebook.com/KatyRegnery**
For news on upcoming romances, sign up for Katy Regnery's newsletter at **www.katyregnery.com**

KATY REGNERY'S
a modern fairytale
COLLECTION
beloved fairy tales ♥ *modern love stories*

The Vixen and the Vet
2015 RITA[R] Finalist
2015 Kindle Book Review Winner
(inspired by *Beauty and the Beast*)

Never Let You Go
(inspired by *Hansel and Gretel*)

Ginger's Heart
(inspired by *Little Red Riding Hood*)

Dark Sexy Knight
(inspired by *Camelot*)

Don't Speak
(inspired by *The Little Mermaid*)
Coming in 2017

Swan Song
(inspired by *The Ugly Duckling*)
Coming in 2017

ACKNOWLEDGMENTS

To all of my friends on Twitter and Facebook. I am so excited to share *The Vixen & the Vet* with you! Thanks for your daily support and encouragement. I have the best fans ever!

A special shout out to Katy's Ladies, the kindest, most amazing street team an author could ask for. I am so grateful for all of you.

To Kayla, Marijke, Cheer, Veronica, Summer, and Winnie. Thank you so much for the naming help! I hope you all enjoy seeing your terrific suggestions in print!

To Marianne Nowicki. Thank you for your stunning cover design. You are my beloved partner in this journey.

To Jami Davenport and Allie K. Adams. Your invitation set the wheels in motion.

To Jennifer Bloechle, who sent me an article about the "10 Most Important Firsts" in any relationship, which got my motor revving.

To my beta readers, who rock my world: Pam, Peggy, Summer and Tricia. Thank you, thank you, thank you for reading my story in record time and giving me feedback. Your comments and feedback shaped this story into the book it is today.

To Chris Belden and Melissa DeMeo, my editors, who don't let me get away with anything. That's the way I want it. That's the way I need it. Your insight, notes and advice make my writing the best it can be. I am so thankful to work with a team like you.

To my parents, who never fail to encourage and inspire. You are what true love is all about.

And finally, to George, Henry, and Callie, my dearly beloved. The *most* important thing is kindness, and I love you all the much.

ABOUT THE AUTHOR

New York Times **and** *USA Today* **bestselling author Katy Regnery** started her writing career by enrolling in a short story class in January 2012. One year later, she signed her first contract and Katy's first novel was published in September 2013.

Now exclusively self-published, Katy claims authorship of the multi-titled Blueberry Lane Series, which follows the English, Winslow, Rousseau, Story, and Ambler families of Philadelphia; the six-book, bestselling ~a modern fairytale~ series; the Enchanted Places Series; and a stand-alone novella, *Frosted.*

Katy's first modern fairytale romance, *The Vixen and the Vet*, was nominated for a RITA® in 2015 and won the 2015 Kindle Book Award for romance. Katy's boxed set, The English Brothers Boxed Set, Books #1–4, hit the *USA Today* bestseller list in 2015, and her Christmas story, *Marrying Mr. English*, appeared on the list a week later. In May 2016, Katy's boxed set, The Winslow Brothers Boxed Set, Books #1-4, became a *New York Times* bestseller.

Katy lives in the relative wilds of northern Fairfield County, Connecticut, where her writing room looks out at the woods, and her husband, two young children, two dogs, and one Blue Tonkinese kitten create just enough cheerful chaos to remind her that the very best love stories begin at home.